John Dickson Carr and The Murder Room

>>> This title is part of The Murder Room, our series dedicated to making available out-of-print or hard-to-find titles by classic crime writers.

Crime fiction has always held up a mirror to society. The Victorians were fascinated by sensational murder and the emerging science of detection; now we are obsessed with the forensic detail of violent death. And no other genre has so captivated and enthralled readers.

Vast troves of classic crime writing have for a long time been unavailable to all but the most dedicated frequenters of second-hand bookshops. The advent of digital publishing means that we are now able to bring you the backlists of a huge range of titles by classic and contemporary crime writers, some of which have been out of print for decades.

From the genteel amateur private eyes of the Golden Age and the femmes fatales of pulp fiction, to the morally ambiguous hard-boiled detectives of mid twentieth-century America and their descendants who walk our twenty-first century streets, The Murder Room has it all. **>>>**

The Murder Room
Where Criminal Minds Meet

themurderroom.com

T0352014

John Dickson Carr (1906–1977)

John Dickson Carr, the master of the locked-room mystery, was born in Uniontown, Pennsylvania, the son of a US Congressman. He studied law in Paris before settling in England where he married an Englishwoman, and he spent most of his writing career living in Great Britain. Widely regarded as one of the greatest Golden Age mystery writers, his work featured apparently impossible crimes often with seemingly supernatural elements. He modelled his affable and eccentric series detective Gideon Fell on G. K. Chesterton, and wrote a number of novels and short stories, including his series featuring Henry Merrivale, under the pseudonym Carter Dickson. He was one of only two Americans admitted to the British Detection club, and was highly praised by other mystery writers. Dorothy L. Sayers said of him that 'he can create atmosphere with an adjective, alarm with allusion, or delight with a rollicking absurdity'. In 1950 he was awarded the first of two prestigious Edgar Awards by the Mystery Writers of America, and was presented with their Grand Master Award in 1963. He died in Greenville, South Carolina in 1977.

(Titles in bold are published in The Murder Room)

Poison in Jest (1932)
The Burning Court (1937)
The Emperor's Snuff Box (1942)
The Nine Wrong Answers (1952)
Patrick Butler for the Defense (1956)
Most Secret (1964)

Henri Bencolin

It Walks by Night (1930)
Castle Skull (1931)
The Lost Gallows (1931)
The Waxworks Murder (1932) *aka* The Corpse in the
    Waxworks
The Four False Weapons, Being the Return of Bencolin (1938)

Dr Gideon Fell

Hag's Nook (1933)
The Mad Hatter Mystery (1933)
The Blind Barber (1934)
The Eight of Swords (1934)
Death-Watch (1934)
The Hollow Man (1935) *aka* The Three Coffins
The Arabian Nights Murder (1936)
To Wake the Dead (1938)
The Crooked Hinge (1938)
The Problem of the Green Capsule (1939) *aka* The Black
    Spectacles
The Problem of the Wire Cage (1939)
The Man Who Could Not Shudder (1940)
The Case of the Constant Suicides (1941)
Death Turns the Tables (1941) *aka* The Seat of the
    Scornful (1942)
Till Death Do Us Part (1944)
He Who Whispers (1946)

The Sleeping Sphinx (1947)
Below Suspicion (1949)
The Dead Man's Knock (1958)
In Spite of Thunder (1960)
The House at Satan's Elbow (1965)
Panic in Box C (1966)
Dark of the Moon (1968)

Historical mysteries

The Bride of Newgate (1950)
The Devil in Velvet (1951)
Captain Cut-Throat (1955)
Fire, Burn! (1957)
Scandal at High Chimneys: A Victorian Melodrama (1959)
The Witch of the Low Tide: An Edwardian Melodrama (1961)
The Demoniacs (1962)
Papa La-Bas (1968)
The Ghosts' High Noon (1970)
Deadly Hall (1971)
The Hungry Goblin: A Victorian Detective Novel (1972)

Short story collections

Dr Fell, Detective, and Other Stories (1947)
The Third Bullet and Other Stories of Detection (1954)
The Exploits of Sherlock Holmes (with Adrian Conan
    Doyle) (1954)
The Men Who Explained Miracles (1963)

The Door to Doom and Other Detections (1980) (includes
    radio plays)
The Dead Sleep Lightly (1983) (radio plays)
Fell and Foul Play (1991)
Merrivale, March and Murder (1991)

Writing as Carter Dickson

The Bowstring Murders (1934)
Drop to His Death (with John Rhode) (1939) *aka* Fatal
    Descent

Sir Henry Merrivale

The Plague Court Murders (1934)
The White Priory Murders (1934)
The Red Widow Murders (1935)
The Unicorn Murders (1935)
The Punch and Judy Murders (1936) *aka* The Magic
    Lantern Murders
The Ten Teacups (1937) *aka* The Peacock Feather Murders
The Judas Window (1938) *aka* The Crossbow Murder
Death in Five Boxes (1938)
The Reader is Warned (1939)
And So To Murder (1940)
Murder in the Submarine Zone (1940) *aka* Nine – and Death
    Makes Ten, also published as Murder in the Atlantic
Seeing is Believing (1941) *aka* Cross of Murder
The Gilded Man (1942) *aka* Death and the Gilded Man

She Died a Lady (1943)

He Wouldn't Kill Patience (1944)

The Curse of the Bronze Lamp (1945) *aka* Lord of the
    Sorcerers (1946)

My Late Wives (1946)

The Skeleton in the Clock (1948)

A Graveyard to Let (1949)

Night at the Mocking Window (1950)

Behind the Crimson Blind (1952)

The Cavalier's Cup (1953)

Historical mystery

Fear is the Same (1956)

Short story collections

The Department of Queer Complaints (1940)

In Spite of Thunder

John Dickson Carr

An Orion book

Copyright © John Dickson Carr 1960

The right of John Dickson Carr to be identified as the author of this
work has been asserted in accordance with the Copyright, Designs and
Patents Act 1988.

This edition published by
The Orion Publishing Group Ltd
Orion House
5 Upper St Martin's Lane
London WC2H 9EA

An Hachette UK company
A CIP catalogue record for this book is available from the British Library

ISBN 978 1 4719 0523 0

All characters and events in this publication are fictitious and any
resemblance to real people, living or dead, is purely coincidental.

No part of this publication may be reproduced, stored in a retrieval system
or transmitted in any form or by any means without the prior permission
in writing of the publisher, nor be otherwise circulated in any form of
binding or cover other than that in which it is published without a similar
condition, including this condition, being imposed on the subsequent
purchaser.

www.orionbooks.co.uk

ACT ONE

"*That man can't be trusted. I tell you, I've played too many criminals! I* KNOW *that man can't be trusted.*"

—SIR HENRY IRVING

I

Understand, Brian, I have no proof against this woman. Even the Foreign Office have no proof. But I don't want my daughter to associate with her.

Yes, he thought wryly, that was fair enough. Brian Innes had no need to re-read the letter in his pocket; he knew it almost by heart.

Audrey will fly BEA from London on the same day you return to Geneva from Paris. She will spend one night at the Hotel Metropole, Geneva, before going on to this woman's villa. For old friendship's sake, then, I rely on you to see Audrey and stop her from going there.

Old friendship's sake, eh?

Load me with the dirty work. That could be called characteristic too.

It was past seven in the evening when Brian Innes left the airport at Geneva. The customs-examination did not detain him; they knew him there and waved him on. Then, after hailing a taxi, he hesitated.

3

There could be no great hurry. He could at least drop his suitcase at his own flat before he went on to see Audrey.

"Monsieur?" prompted the taxi-driver.

"Number three, Quai Turrettini," said Brian, and pitched his suitcase inside. "No, wait!" he added in his excellent French.

"Monsieur?"

"I'll change that. Hotel Metropole, Grand Quai."

The taxi-driver gave a massive shrug like a diplomat at the United Nations. The door slammed, the metal flag snapped down.

On clear days, when you drove away from this airport, you could see the peaks of the nearer Alps outlined ghostly white against a pale sky. They were invisible this evening. Thick overcast air, a hollow of thundery heat, pressed down on the mind and spirits in early August. It was more than twenty minutes, growing darker, before he watched suburbs thicken into a grey-white city round its lake.

Tram-cars clanged through the more modern section of Geneva, always bustling. But no breeze stirred from the lake; the *jet d'eau*, lonely out there against a vast sweep of water, seemed to fling up motionless spray. And over on the south bank, beyond all those bridges, the quais below the Old Town looked half-deserted and even a little sinister.

Brian Innes sat back in the cab, his black Homburg hat across his knees.

Damn this conscientiousness! But there it was. Possibly he had more interest in Audrey Page than he would ever have confessed.

He was forty-six years old, though not much grey showed in his wiry red hair. Long and lean, easy-going, with much imagination and a sardonic sense of humour, he himself looked like the popular notion of a diplomat.

The sense of humour didn't help much. He was, in fact, a successful painter of what they called the conventional school, though Brian himself much disliked those terms. Northern Irish, he belonged to that international group who maintain residence abroad while still keeping up British nationality.

Restless and uneasy, most of them! Geneva was their point and their focus. Without Geneva, he supposed, this situation might not have arisen at all.

De Forrest Page, compelled to remain in London and with various tricks to nurse what was left of a once-great fortune, usually managed to keep his daughter in London too. De Forrest seldom lost his temper and never lost his head. And yet his worry rang through every line of that last letter.

The point is, Brian, that you know the real story about Eve Eden and her late boy-friend in Germany just before the war. I don't know it. However unsavoury that story is—

Unsavoury? Well, yes.

—I rely on you to tell Audrey. She's not a child any longer; she is nearly thirty; and it's time she developed a sense of responsibility. You seem to be the only one who's got any influence with her.

"Kindly forgive me," thought the recipient of this, "if I utter a loud ha-ha."

Then Brian woke up.

His taxi had been speeding along the Grand Quai, hushed and dusky before street-lamps were kindled, with the formal stretch of the English Garden on the left. On the right ran tall formal houses, after the French fashion in this French part of Switzerland. An even sedater-looking building of the eighteen-nineties, all massive stone outside and red plush inside, loomed up near the intersection of the rue d'Italie.

"Hotel Metropole," the driver said rather grandly. "Is one required to wait?"

"No, one is not," said Brian, climbing out. "Good God!" he added under his breath.

The unexpectedness of what happened, when he had scarcely put on his hat and paid the driver, took him aback. A small cool whirlwind, high heels rapping, marched out of the hotel and hurried towards him.

"What on earth do you mean by this?" cried a familiar voice, soft and breathless. "You're too early! You'll spoil everything! And worst of all—"

"Good evening, Audrey," he observed with much politeness. "Were you expecting somebody else?"

"Well, really!" said Audrey Page, and stopped short.

She was rather elaborately dressed for dinner, in a low-cut white

5

gown that set off the firm sleekness of her shoulders. Though her face remained in shadow, a dim light from the hotel-foyer touched her heavy, glossy dark-brown hair. As usual, breathing out emotion, she seemed all contradictory qualities: stolidness and yet fragility, poise and yet indecision.

Audrey moved a little sideways. Long blue eyes, black-lashed and a little slanted up at the outer corners, regarded him with an innocence which did not hide either anger or uneasiness. She carried a handbag and a short wrap, at which her fingers were beginning to pluck.

"Well, really!" she breathed. "I shouldn't have expected this honour. Brian Innes, of all people! May I ask what *you're* doing here?"

"You may. I live here."

"Here?" Her eyes flashed towards the suitcase. "At this hotel?"

"Not at the hotel, no. Here in Geneva. You hadn't forgotten that, I *hope*?"

"Whether I forgot it or not," answered Audrey in a shaky voice, "I think this is a bit much and I'm getting fed up with it. I came here for a few days, just a few days, to visit a friend of mine who's got a villa just this side of the French border on the road to Chambéry."

"Yes; so I've heard."

"Oh. I see. Then he did send you here."

"Who?"

"De Forrest. My father. He sent you here to spy on me."

Brian began to laugh.

"Hardly that, young lady. I seldom carry a suitcase when I go spying. And please don't make all those gestures as though this were high tragedy." His tone changed. "But I do want to talk to you about your friend Eve Eden, the former film-star with the improbable name."

"Her real name," cried Audrey, "is Eve Ferrier. Mrs. Eve Ferrier. All the same, she's got a right to the other name too. She used it on the screen. Lots of people call her that." Then Audrey stamped both feet. "Ugh, you red haired goblin! I could cut your wretched heart out!"

"That would be a pity."

"I'm not so sure it would be. If ever once in the past you'd been willing to take me seriously, just once and for a change, so many things might have been different between us. But, oh, no! You think I'm stupid; you want to treat me as a child whatever I say or do; you make me so cross I want to kill you."

"*Audrey. Listen to me.*"

Both their voices rang louder in the shadowed street. Thick heat pressed down. Distantly, through the quiet of the pre-dinner hour, motor-horns hooted above a clanging of trams.

"In the first place, Audrey, I don't think you're stupid."

"No?"

"Definitely no. In the second place, since your father wants me to prevent you from going to this woman's house—"

"He's got rather a nerve, hasn't he?"

"Maybe I think so too. Don't imagine I enjoy being here; it's none of my business. However, since I seem to have been saddled with the responsibility, I'll tell you what he wants me to tell you and then you can please yourself. Suppose we sit down and have a drink for just five minutes?"

"Even if I wanted to sit down and have a drink, Mr. Brian Innes, you're too late. There's someone coming to take me out to dinner, and he'll be here at any moment."

"You won't miss him. We can wait in the bar."

"Oh, no, we can't! This hotel hasn't got a bar."

"Damn it, woman, surely there's a lounge of some kind?"

"Even if there is, what have we got to talk about? Eve, of all people! I've heard all those old rumours, thanks very much."

"What particular rumours?"

Audrey made a gesture with her handbag.

"Just before the war, when Eve was a great star, she kept saying she favoured Hitler and the Nazis. All right; so did a lot of people. But that was seventeen years ago; they were wrong and they've admitted they were wrong, just as Eve has. Isn't that what you want to tell me?"

"No. That's only a part of it."

"Is it her love-affairs?"

"No. Except indirectly."

"Then what on earth are you accusing her of?"

"I'm not accusing her of anything. The woman may be entirely innocent. On the other hand"—and doubt, brooding indecision swept over him like his attraction towards Audrey Page—"on the other hand, if that business in '39 didn't happen to be an accident, she was guilty of a neat little murder."

"*Murder?*"

"That's what I said. She killed Hector Matthews for his money; she's the only one who could have done it; and this blonde charmer is about as safe a bed-mate as a king cobra."

"I don't believe it. You're joking!"

"It's anything but a joke, I can assure you. Come with me."

That was the moment when the street-lamps flashed on.

They glowed out white against the trees of the English Garden; they made a necklace westwards along the great length of the Grand Quai to a traffic-mutter round the Place du Rhône.

Audrey, gripping her handbag, had thrown back the heavy, glossy brown hair which curled almost to her shoulders. Her expression as she looked up at him, mouth partly open, carried behind its incredulity some emotion which he ought to have studied more closely.

"Brian, you're not to be silly! I never heard. . . ."

"You wouldn't have heard. Come along."

The Hotel Metropole was a luxury establishment, though not the most luxurious and far from the most modern. To the left of the front door, past a tiny foyer and a lift like a rosewood coffin, Brian impelled his companion towards a lounge with a high ceiling and high windows overlooking the quai and the lake.

Its massive oppressiveness lay unbroken. Dim lights from corners shone on arsenic-green furniture, on much gilding, and on naked goddesses carved and painted in plaster. Audrey, throwing handbag and wrap on a table, faced him with a mood in which curiosity struggled against defiance.

"Audrey, when and where did you meet this woman?"

"Oh, good heavens, does it *matter?*"

"Probably not, but we'd better have the record straight. When and where did you meet her?"

"I met her in London last winter. She was there with her husband, going to all the theatres. And her husband is Desmond Ferrier, if you know who *he* is?"

"Yes. I know who he is, and I know those two were married during the war."

"Well, I can't say *I* did at first. In the old days, it seems, Mr. Ferrier was as famous a star of the legitimate stage as Eve was on the screen. Though I'm afraid I'd never even heard of him except in a vague sort of way."

"That's not surprising. Desmond Ferrier was a great actor; there's never been a better Othello or Macbeth. You're too young to remember him."

"Young! Young! Young!"

(And yet it's true, my dear. You are twenty-seven and look much younger; I am forty-six and look older. It's damnably and undeniably true.)

A car whushed past in the street outside, making dim lights vibrate. Audrey hurried to one window and glanced out; the car did not stop, and she returned to the table.

"I don't think Eve and Mr. Ferrier get on very well. They're both retired, and they don't like it. Anyway," Audrey lifted one shoulder, "I was telling you about meeting her. Eve took a tremendous fancy to me. She invited me to visit her at any time I liked. Later she began writing to me, and three weeks ago she set a definite date. That's all there is to it."

"She invited you to the villa, and yet you're putting up here at this hotel?"

"Of course! Naturally!"

"I don't quite follow you."

"It's a sort of party, with other guests too; it doesn't begin until tomorrow. Well! Considering how my father spies on me, naturally I—I sneaked the chance to have twenty-four hours on my own. But Phil 'phoned and asked me to dinner, so of course I said yes."

"Phil?"

"Philip Ferrier." The soft voice rose up. "He's Desmond Ferrier's son by a previous marriage. I met him in London too, if you insist on knowing. *He's* serious-minded, and *he* doesn't laugh at me; and he's nice and rather thrilling too."

"Good for Phil." (Another car whushed past outside; Audrey turned her head.) "You're anxiously awaiting him, I take it?"

"Yes, I am! Really, Brian, what are all these questions in aid of?"

"Nothing at all. I was trying to find some connection, where admittedly none exists, between a villa in the hills towards Chambéry and something that happened above Berchtesgaden in July of '39."

"Berchtesgaden?" Audrey cried.

"Yes. At the famous *Kehlsteinhaus*, Hitler's 'Eagle's Nest' high up at the southeastern end of the Bavarian Alps. That's where somebody's brain turned. That's where Hector Matthews died."

Neither he nor Audrey had sat down. Though he pressed the bell to summon a waiter, it was not answered; only the naked goddesses yearned down from the ceiling as though regretting they were immured there.

And Brian made a baffled gesture.

"I can tell you very briefly what happened," he said. "But it won't mean much unless you understand the mood, the background, the atmosphere: as many microphones as there were flags and banners, and mobs roaring, 'Sig heil!' like the delirium of that whole summer.

"Even then it won't help without some knowledge of the human motives behind this woman's behaviour. What prompted her? What did she think she was doing? And that's where I bog down.

"Your friend Eve couldn't have been any older then than you are now. She was at the peak of a fairly successful Hollywood career. Early in June she visited Germany. Immediately she began praising the New Order right and left.

"The New Order loved it. In addition to being a well-built blonde, she spoke very good German for an Englishwoman. They'd never dreamed of such propaganda and they couldn't do enough for her. She was all over the newspapers, the newsreels, the magazines. She seldom took a step without being photographed on the arm of a Nazi V.I.P.

"A publicity stunt? Possibly. But some people doubted it.

"First, it wasn't doing her career any good outside Germany. Second, I understand that in private life she tries hard to be the sort of character she usually played on stage and screen: voluptuous, world-weary, all that. Except for some reason far stronger than a publicity stunt, she'd never have gone about saying that woman's place is in the home and that man ought to grab all the limelight from her."

Brian hesitated, glancing sideways.

"You've met her, Audrey. Does that strike you as being a fair estimate?"

"No, it's not fair! It's making her sound like a bundle of affectations."

"And isn't she a bundle of affectations?"

"Well . . . maybe. Why ever is it so important?"

Here Audrey's gaze slid away from him.

"The clue, if it is a clue, must lie with Hector Matthews. In the middle of all this turmoil and heiling, while Eve made a tour of the Fatherland, Matthews went with her.

"I can't give you much information about him except what's in the official record. A self-made man, a Yorkshireman, a hard-headed man. Bachelor, aged fifty-eight: a food-faddist who never ate breakfast and wanted to tell you all about it.

"His hosts laughed at him and slapped him on the back and welcomed him. You'll see his bowler hat at the edge of every photograph. When they presented her with a bouquet of flowers or a consecrated flag, he carried it for her. When a brown-shirt or a black-shirt got too attentive towards her, his jaw was there too.

"He was the most devoted of her worshippers. He was also the richest. It was known he had followed her to Germany because she begged him to. However, few people knew that before leaving England he had made a will in her favour."

Audrey took a step back beside the table.

"A will? Are you insinuating . . . ?"

"No. I'm telling you what happened. At Munich, where she ended her tour, Miss Eden said that she and Mr. Matthews were engaged to be married.

"Though the hosts may not have been too pleased, they slapped *her* on the back and shouted congratulations. Were they to announce this? Not yet, she said: she and Mr. Matthews were being reticent for the moment. Well, then! She had done great service for the New Order: couldn't they give her an engagement-present or show their gratitude in some way?

"Oh, yes, please! She said there was the very best of presents. Could she and Mr. Matthews pay their respects to the Führer himself? They were at Munich, no great distance away. Might they visit Hitler himself in his mountain-eyrie at Berchtesgaden?

"That did it. The Führer, much flattered, invited them to lunch.

11

"Fourteen guests, escorted by Scharführer Hans Johst, made up a party for that visit. With the exception of the engaged couple and of two additional guests (both reluctant guests, both British too), the names of the other ten visitors don't matter. All were Nazi security-police who later died by violence. You need picture them only as gaudy uniforms and would-be jovial smiles.

"But we can follow every detail of what happened.

"A fleet of cars carried them to the *Gasthof zum Türken*, Hitler's guest-house partway up the mountain. They spent one night there. Next morning they drove on up a winding road to the Wendeplatte. When they got up inside the Eagle's Nest, taking the famous lift built smack through a mountain, they found it wasn't cold at that season. Clear sunlight, exhilarating air, rolling ridges of trees spread out below: you picture it, don't you?

"Everybody was in excellent spirits except Hector Matthews, who seemed to be distressed by the thinner air at that altitude. The camera (eternally the camera!) shows a very tall man with scanty hair blowing, and an unhappy look on his face.

"No matter! It was all in fun.

"While the guests waited for Inimitable Adolf in a big room overlooking a part of the terrace, Miss Eden seized her fiancé by the hand and dragged him out on the terrace to admire the view. They were all alone there, some say out of sight and some say not, beside a rather low parapet above a sheer drop.

"Then somebody screamed. It may have been the woman, or it may have been Matthews himself when he went over.

"Anyway, he pitched over head-first and was smashed to death in a pine-tree some hundred-odd feet below. They could see what remained of him when they ran out on the terrace and looked down.

"Scharführer Hans Johst supported Miss Eden, who was leaning against the parapet in a state of near-collapse. One witness, not a Nazi sympathizer and not precisely a strong admirer of the lady herself, is inclined to think her shock and horror were quite genuine. At that moment she hadn't any affectations, or seemed to have none.

" 'I did not know,' she kept saying. 'Dear God, I did not know. It was the altitude. He turned white and dizzy. I could not help him. Dear God, it was the altitude!'

"Scharführer Johst, portentously solemn and tender, spoke out and said of course it was the altitude. He said this was a most regrettable accident; he said he had seen it happen. Two other voices chorused out and said *they* had seen it happen. Eve Eden fainted in Scharführer Johst's arms. Then nothing moved on the terrace except a big flag, a black swastika on a red-and-white ground, curling out above them and throwing shadows.

"I think that's all."

II

"All?" echoed Audrey, in a whispery kind of voice. "*All?*"

"Officially, yes."

"But that's what happened, isn't it? I mean, that's what really happened?"

"Please explain your definition of the event that really happened."

"Brian Innes, stop being cynical and tormenting me. You know perfectly well what I'm talking about. Those three officials did see the poor man fall?"

"No. They lied. Not one of them was even looking in that direction."

"But—!"

In his mind, as he shook his head to clear it, the vivid picture faded.

He was back in a thick-carpeted lounge, airless despite full-length windows open behind curtains of lace and dusty green velvet. He was back in the present of 1956, troubled by the fleshly presence of Audrey Page as once Hector Matthews had been troubled by the presence of a younger Eve.

Audrey stood behind the table, her fingers touching a china ashtray. Even now she had that look of innocence, of too-great innocence, which in some fashion suggested wantonness instead. She saw him look straight at her, and dropped her gaze.

"Listen!" Brian insisted. "I don't say it wasn't an accident. I only say they didn't see it happen. Nobody saw it."

"Then why should *they* say . . . ?"

"I can't tell you. Medically speaking, it's not very likely a man blacked out so as to tumble over a waist-high parapet. Not likely, and yet it's possible. On the other hand, if he did feel faint and she gave him only a sharp push . . ."

The china ashtray rattled across the table.

"In any case," he continued, "you'd better hear the end of it."

"They didn't arrest her, or anything?"

"No; how could they? The press published an official story: Mr. Hector Matthews, an English tourist, had met with an accident while rock-climbing in Bavaria. No mention of Eve Eden; or, naturally, of the Eagle's Nest either. However, since he was well known as a 'friend' of hers and he didn't have any living relatives, she was permitted to ship his body home. It's the least she could do. After all, she was his heir."

Audrey opened her mouth, and shut it again. Her companion began to pace up and down the lounge.

"Afterwards," he said, "the war caught everybody. All interest in Hector Matthews was washed out, which may have been just as well. She never returned to Hollywood; her contract with Radiant Pictures wasn't renewed, as she must have known before she went to Germany. Financially it didn't matter. When Matthews's will was admitted to probate, she inherited everything except some bequests to charity."

Audrey spoke in a sudden forlorn voice.

"You know, this is rather awful. I wouldn't admit it before, but it *is* rather awful."

"A striking coincidence, at any rate."

"It doesn't mean anything, of course—!"

"No. Still, young lady, I can understand why your father doesn't want you to visit her."

"Wouldn't *you* visit her?"

"Certainly. With pleasure. But then virtuous people never interest me, and the other kind always do."

15

Audrey turned her head to watch him. A strange look flashed through her strangely shaped eyes and was gone in an instant; it may only have been a trick of the light above one bare shoulder.

"Brian, how much does De Forrest know? And, if it comes to that, how can you repeat every word that was said? Were you there? Did you see it happen?"

"Hardly. In '39 I was a struggling young painter, of even less importance to the world than I am now. In a sense I'm betraying a confidence in telling you this, but I felt I had to tell you. I wasn't there, no; but a great friend of mine was. Gerald Hathaway."

Audrey uttered an exclamation.

"What's the matter?"

"Sir Gerald Hathaway? The Director of the Something-or-Other Gallery?"

"He's that, yes. He's also a remarkably fine painter. I've known him for a good many years, though I haven't seen him in quite some time."

"Well, you may see him sooner than you think. He's here."

"*Here?*"

"Oh, not here at the hotel or even in Geneva! But he'll be here tomorrow. Eve's invited him too."

Brian, with something of a shock at his heart, paused beside one long window and swung round towards her.

"Audrey, that can't be. —No; wait; listen to me!" It was a tone of desperate reasonableness. "Hathaway's curiosity got the better of him when he was asked to have lunch with Hitler at Berchtesgaden. He's ashamed of having gone there; he's concealed it ever since. He only talked about it to me because we talk so much about crime and detective stories. Even if your friend Eve had the nerve to invite him here, he'd never have agreed to come. You must have made some mistake."

"All I can t-tell you," cried Audrey, who in moments of great earnestness had a tendency to stammer, "is what Eve wrote in her last letter. Sir Gerald Hathaway said he'd be delighted to accept. Do you imagine she'd have written one name and really meant somebody else?"

"No, I suppose not."

"There can't be any such great mystery about it, you know.

16

Couldn't he be just as curious about Eve as he once was about Hitler?"

"You take grisly suggestions in your stride, don't you?"

"Well, couldn't that be it?"

"Yes, it could be. Probably it is. All the same, I wish I knew more about the lady's motivation." Brian, staring out of the window, hardly saw the street-lamps or the ordered quiet of the Grand Quai. "Audrey, hold on! How many people are coming to this house-party of hers?"

"It's not a house-party, really. There's only one other person."

"Only one, eh? Who is it?"

"I don't know. Eve didn't say."

"No; I'm wool-gathering. It can't possibly be what occurred to me. But I don't like this situation one little bit. Why not obey your father and take the next plane back to London?"

"Obey! Obey! Will you try to stop me if I do go to Eve's?"

"No, I will not." He spoke formally, but with anger kindling. "You're over twenty-one; you must please yourself."

"Thanks *so* much for making it clear. In that case, I'd better tell you—"

Audrey never finished what she meant to say, if in fact she meant to say it at all.

The head-lights of a car, driven fast, brushed their dazzle outside curtains of velvet and lace just before a Bentley two-seater pulled up outside the hotel. Audrey drew a deep breath and ran across to stand in the window beside Brian. But she did not look at her companion; it was plain that she had forgotten him.

Out of the car climbed a hatless, dark-haired young man in a white dinner-jacket. Audrey flung the lace curtains wide open.

"Phil! Phil, dear!"

The young man, who could be nobody but the son of Desmond Ferrier, stopped short.

"I'm here," Audrey said rather unnecessarily. "I'm waiting for you! I'm here!"

"Yes. I see you are. Who's that with you?"

The voice, though pleasant enough, held sudden hostility and suspicion. Audrey tried to laugh. Still she did not look at her companion, but Brian could almost feel the lift of her eyebrows.

17

"Oh, Phil, don't go on like that again. It's nobody! It's nobody at all!"

Brian said nothing.

"I mean," cried Audrey, turning out her wrist, "I mean, Phil, it's nobody you need think about. It's only an old friend of mine from home, Brian Innes, and I don't know why—"

Again she stopped. The pronouncing of Brian's name had a curious effect in that quiet street.

The name meant nothing to Philip Ferrier; Philip merely nodded and entered the hotel. But it had a very definite meaning for someone else. On the opposite side of the street, in the shadow of the English Garden, a shortish and tubby man with an intent manner had been stumping along the pavement as though talking to himself. Here he stopped, peered round, and instantly crossed the road towards the Hotel Metropole.

"Ha!" breathed the tubby man.

He was the more striking a figure in that he wore a close-cut greyish beard and the sort of steeple-crowned hat which used to appear on figures of Guy Fawkes. This disreputable dark hat contrasted with full and formal evening-clothes.

A flicker of heat-lightning paled and pulsed in the sky towards the lake. Audrey, for all her preoccupation, could not help staring at this newcomer.

"Brian, look! The odd-looking man with the hat. He seems to be coming straight over here!"

"So he does. Your odd-looking man, though, isn't in the least odd; and he's got a good reason for everything he does. That's Gerald Hathaway."

"*Sir Gerald Hathaway?*"

"In person."

"But what does he want here? What's he doing in Geneva so soon?"

"I haven't any idea. All the same . . . you remember I said there were two English guests at Berchtesgaden on the famous occasion? Two guests, that is, besides Eve Eden and Hector Matthews?"

"Well?"

"One was Hathaway. The other was some newspaperwoman named Paula Catford. Ever since you mentioned Hathaway, I've been wondering if history would repeat itself and Paula Catford would turn up too."

Another flicker of heat-lightning lifted beyond motionless trees. But they had no time to consider this. A voice called out from the door. Into the lounge, conspicuous in white dinner-jacket, strode Philip Ferrier.

He did not resemble his father, Brian noted. The Desmond Ferrier of legend had been as long and lean as Brian himself, with a booming voice and deplorably frivolous ways. The son, at twenty-four, was stern and earnest to the verge of pompousness. He was also a trifle chunky. But Philip's striking good-looks, from dark curling hair to classic profile and wide nostrils, carried an intense vitality.

Audrey almost yearned at him.

"Mr. F-ferrier, may I present Mr. Innes?"

One glance, raking Brian with powerful scrutiny, had shown Philip he need fear no rival here. His hostility vanished.

"How do you do?" he said. "Er—Aud and I are having dinner at the Richemond and then going on to a night-club. You won't mind if we push off now?"

"No, not at all."

"Thanks. We're very late." Relief whistled through the wide nostrils. "I'm late, Aud, and I apologize. Our two geniuses have been throwing fits of temperament again."

"Phil, I wish you wouldn't talk like that. It's not fair!"

Philip bit his lip.

"Maybe it's not. I dunno. I'm fond of the old man and of Eve too. But you don't have to nurse 'em."

Whereupon something new, something intensely human and very likeable, peered out from an apparent stuffed-shirt. Worry surrounded Philip Ferrier like an aura.

"The trouble is," he said, "that you can't tell what's real and what isn't real. They can't tell either; they don't know. Stage-people! Screen-people! *You're* not connected with the stage or the screen, sir?"

"Not in any way." Brian laughed. "Do I look as though I were?"

"Well, no," Philip said seriously. "But there's something about you: what is it? Anyway," and he made a gesture and turned back to Audrey, "now that they're both writing their reminiscences, and trying to beat each other to a publisher, and getting out their books of press-cuttings at every other word, it's quite a wing-ding."

"I—I daresay it is," Audrey agreed.

"You bet it is. See what James Agate wrote about me in '34? And I forget: wasn't it Old So-and-So who played Lord Porteus in Binky Beaumont's production of *The Circle* in '36? And Old So-and-So is a grand person and a wonderful person and we love him very dearly, but just between ourselves he's the world's lousiest actor. Stage-people!"

Brian, listening hard for the approach of Sir Gerald Hathaway through the foyer, turned his attention back. Audrey moistened her lips.

"Phil, do you mean to say you don't like it?"

"I've never been sure whether I like it. I do know it's getting me down."

"Why are you telling me this? There isn't anything wrong, is there?"

"My poor girl, there's never anything actually *wrong!*"

"Well, then?"

"But you're coming to visit us, Aud. When the old man tells you Eve is trying to poison him, try not to take it too seriously. Now come along and let's get some food."

Footsteps echoed in the marble foyer; the lift hummed. But one set of footfalls had stopped short.

"Mr. Ferrier! Just a moment!" Brian said sharply.

"What is it?"

Philip had picked up Audrey's wrap from the table and was holding it out for her. Audrey, her sex-appeal never more vivid than with heightened colour, lifted her arm as though to ward off a blow.

"Your father says Miss Eden is trying to poison him in the literal sense? With arsenic, strychnine, something of that sort?"

"No. *No.* That's not it at all. That's why I say: deliver me from people with temperament! That's why I'm here." Philip struggled for words. "I wanted to warn Aud—"

"Of what?"

"It's the old man's idea of being funny; and Eve's too, recently. He'll explain how she would like to poison him or creep up and stab him, and describe this in all apparent seriousness. Once or twice

Eve's got back at him in the same way. Unless you know they're both playing the fool, it can be hair-raising. A reporter from *Woman's Life* was so shocked I had to talk to her for an hour afterwards at the airport. And it isn't funny in the least. Or it isn't funny to me. Can't you understand all this?"

"*I* can understand it, Mr. Ferrier. I wonder if they do."

"Meaning what?"

The conjectures that floated in Brian's mind . . .

From the corner of his eye he could see the door of the lounge, opening on a little passage that ran to the foyer. Though no light burned in the passage, it was floored with marble and lined with mirrors. He could see reflected outlines in a cuff, a shoulder, the edge of a hat. Gerald Hathaway, that distinguished man, was frankly if grotesquely listening.

A car hooted in the street.

"Mr. Ferrier, will you answer me just one question?"

"Yes, if I can."

"There are to be two guests in your home besides Audrey. One is Sir Gerald Hathaway. Do you know who the other is?"

"Yes, of course. I've never met her—"

" 'Her?' "

"Yes; what's so peculiar about that? She's another journalist, a very big wheel. Writes books about the celebrities she's met, and she's promised to help Eve with the memoirs."

"Is her name Paula Catford?"

"Yes. Now forget Paula Catford. We were talking about Eve and the old man. They're artists; I don't understand artists. But they're human beings, for God's sake. Whatever they say or however they show off, they don't really do the things people keep doing in plays."

"Are you sure? Has Miss Eden, for instance, never been involved in a case of violent death under suspicious circumstances?"

"No. Of course not. Never."

"Suppose she has been? Suppose I brought a witness to prove the fact here and now? What would you say then?"

"I wouldn't believe a word of it." Philip let out his breath with a gasp. "You're talking about my father and a decent woman he's been married to for years."

"Nobody is saying anything against your father. On the contrary! It may be very unpleasant for him if the same sort of 'accident' should occur again. And what about Audrey?"

"Audrey?"

"You haven't thought about that side of it, and neither has she. I ask you to think of it now."

Brian spoke steadily, his eyes on the younger man's.

"A former fiancé of Eve Eden fell to his death from a balcony-terrace in the Alps when she was alone with him. Miss Catford and Gerald Hathaway were in an adjoining room at the time this happened. Years later, many years later, she invites both of them to a villa in the hills south-west of Geneva. We don't know why she issued that invitation; probably they don't know either.

"The point is that Audrey, who was only a child when Hector Matthews died, *Audrey* has been carefully brought here as well. Why? These may only be suspicious circumstances, like all the other facts, and yet they yell to high heaven for some kind of explanation. How does Audrey fit into the pattern? Are you so very happy to see her here?"

"Look—!" Philip began.

"Just a moment!"

It was so quiet that they could hear Philip's wrist-watch ticking.

"Eve Eden inherited a fortune. If that wasn't sheer accident, it was part of a campaign in murder. Hathaway and Miss Catford *can't* be here by accident. Neither can Audrey. If I convinced you of all this, would you keep her present to see what happens? What would you do?"

"May *I* say something?" cried Audrey.

"No, you may not. Mr. Ferrier, what would you do?"

"I'd send her home," Philip said, "and I'd send her home damn quick."

"Then you'd better begin preparing her mind. The witness I can produce is just outside that door. —Hathaway!"

Philip, in a bursting kind of pause, threw down Audrey's wrap on the table. This too-solemn, over-dignified young man, as Brian quite correctly felt, was deeply and sincerely in love with Audrey Page. And Audrey (this part, at least, he believed at the time) would throw herself into agreement with the least request of Philip Ferrier.

And yet even as he thought this, even as he called for his witness,

22

an enigmatic expression in her blue eyes baffled him again as it had made him wonder once before.

"Hathaway!"

There was no answer. Brian went to the door of the lounge, confronting only his own image in the mirrors that lined the passage outside. A marble floor stretched away to the foyer on the right. His witness wasn't there.

III

Nearly two hours later, in the modernistic bar of a very different hotel on the north bank instead of the south bank, two men sat facing each other across a table beside the French windows to the *terrasse*.

They had dined here at the Hotel du Rhône, and adjourned to the bar. Their brandy-glasses were long empty; dregs of cold coffee congealed in the little cups. But a good dinner had not brought peace or stopped a violent argument.

"You say you were hiding in a telephone-box?" Brian Innes demanded.

"In effect," confessed Gerald Hathaway, taking the cigar out of his mouth, "in effect, yes."

"Well, well! For how long?"

"Until those two young people had cursed you and departed. Then, you may recall, I stood up and pushed the door open and said good evening?"

"Curiously enough," Brian told him with powerful restraint, "I do recall it."

"Tut, now! There is no need—"

"There is every need. A sense of the picturesque," said Brian, "is an excellent thing. But I don't feel this was carried far enough. If you wanted to avoid being my witness, couldn't you have adopted some even subtler course? Couldn't you have slipped out of the Metropole mysteriously disguised in a false nose and a crêpe-paper wig?"

Hathaway, short and tubby, appeared to bounce in his chair.

"Oblige me," he said testily, "by refraining from this childish sarcasm. We are not amused."

"Neither are we."

"More and more," said Hathaway, pointing the cigar at him, "you begin to sound like your friend Gideon Fell. Fell? Bah! The man is no such great hand at solving murder mysteries. I will beat him yet."

"What's Dr. Fell got to do with it? Would you mind explaining any of this hocus-pocus?"

A distant church-clock sounded the quarter-hour past ten. The Hotel du Rhône, raising a vast elegance of chromium and glass on the Quai Turrettini above the Pont de la Tour de l'Ile, seemed as somnolent as its austere bar.

"My dear fellow—!" began Hathaway.

He took out a large watch and consulted it. He peered round the room, deserted except for these two and for a white-coated young barman drowsing against a wall of bright-labelled bottles.

Indirect lighting lent a spectral air to Hathaway's bald head and his close-cropped beard and moustache. His Guy-Fawkes hat, together with an old leather brief-case, lay beside him. Frowning, he stubbed out the cigar in an ashtray. Then Sir Gerald Hathaway—fashionable portrait-painter, ladies' man, amateur criminologist—regarded Brian with an air in which amiable cynicism blended in a frantic preoccupation with his hobby.

"My dear fellow, I apologize if I caused you embarrassment. Especially," he added with a faintly malicious twinkle, "in the presence of Miss Audrey Page. But it's your own fault."

"It is, eh?"

"Yes, it is. You wouldn't tell her not to visit this damned villa of Mrs. Ferrier's. You were too proud to forbid her in so many words; you wouldn't admit you were interested. If anything happens to her within the next week, it will be your responsibility."

Brian struck the table with his fist. The barman opened drowsy eyes but did not stir.

"Listen to me!" said Hathaway, also striking the table. "We are dealing with a murder mystery far more curious than it appears to be. And with a woman far more clever than *she* appears to be."

"Eve Eden?"

"I prefer to call her Mrs. Ferrier."

"Call her what you like. Have you made up your mind whether she did or didn't kill Hector Matthews at Berchtesgaden?"

"Oh, she killed him. But not in the way we thought."

"Not in the way we thought? If it was deliberate murder, she must have given him a shove or toppled him over in some way when he turned faint?"

"No. She chucked him over, and yet she didn't touch him."

"What the hell is all this about? And who's talking like Gideon Fell now?"

"Ah!" murmured Hathaway. "You'll see. As for the reasons why I am here a day early, and staying at this particular hotel, and constructing (if you will pardon me?) a scheme on which I rather flatter myself . . . !"

Once more Hathaway consulted his watch. Once more he looked towards the door leading to a foyer so large and lofty that voices were toned to murmurs there.

"By the way," he added abruptly. "You once told me you never met Mrs. Ferrier, or saw her except in films. Did you ever see her on the stage before she took up film-work?"

"No. Was she good on the stage?"

"Oh, the lady was competent. Especially in emotional parts. That means nothing: every young hopeful at Rada wants a stab at Ibsen or Chekhov. If you go still further and cast any actress as a glamourous trollop with a hundred lovers and a misunderstood heart: cripes, how they all love it! And every woman in the audience, even the most respectable, sees herself as potentially the same character."

"Well, what's wrong with that?"

"I don't say there's anything wrong with it. I do say that Mrs. Ferrier, at heart, is a thoroughly respectable woman who nevertheless wouldn't stick at murder to get what she wanted. And that's the most dangerous kind of all."

"Look here, isn't this a change of view since we talked about it last?"

"Agreed. It is." Hathaway brooded. "Just four weeks ago, out of the blue, she wrote me a letter care of the Savage Club. I didn't bring the letter with me; one day it may be needed. But I can give you the exact terms of it.

"The whole thing was a cry of horror. Recently in Geneva, she said, she had heard a rumour so appalling that she couldn't believe her ears. Certain people appeared to be whispering that the death of poor Mr. Matthews, at Berchtesgaden in '39, hadn't been an accident and *she*, she of all people, was suspected of dirty work. Not once in seventeen years had she ever dreamed of this possibility."

Brian stared at him. "She said . . . ?"

"Yes!"

"But she couldn't have believed that!"

"Couldn't she? I wonder. Now oblige me," and the pudgy hands made a fussed gesture, "by letting me repeat her story in the letter. On that dreadful day at Berchtesgaden (I quote her own words) she had been standing at least a dozen feet away from Mr. Matthews when he cried out and fell. Scharführer Johst and two other men immediately said they saw it happen. How could she anticipate suspicion? It *did* happen.

"This was all past and gone; it might be very laughable. But it troubled her. She was writing to 'that nice girl,' Miss Paula Catford, in care of Miss Catford's publisher. Meanwhile, couldn't I (strictly between ourselves), couldn't I reassure her and say *I* saw it happen? And she was, mine sincerely and with a passionate flourish of the pen, Eve Ferrier."

There was a pause.

Hathaway made a face and spread out his hands.

"Well, I couldn't say that. I rather doubted Miss Catford could say it. So I wrote to Mrs. Ferrier and told her so."

"And then?"

"Her reply, by air-mail return, was more passionate still. Why, she asked, hadn't I said as much at the time? She was in a frightful position; her good name might be at stake. Could I possibly arrange to visit her for the week beginning Friday, tenth August, so that we might talk the matter over? She would try to get Miss Catford too.

"In my letter of acceptance (and who wouldn't have accepted?), I refrained from pointing out a few obvious things. When you are the guest of a roaring Nazi amid his hatchet-men, and he declares somebody fell over a parapet by accident, you're apt to remain discreetly silent. You don't say, 'My dear Scharführer, draw it mild; that's only another of your thumping lies.' Or I don't say it, anyway. I also refrained from asking Mrs. Fe· ·er what there was to talk over. But I did make one obvious move."

"Oh? What was that?"

"Why, curse it," retorted Hathaway, "I tried to get in touch with *you*. I tried it as soon as I received her first letter. And you weren't in Geneva."

"I was in Paris."

"Yes; so I eventually discovered. The point is, who started that rumour about a suspicion of murder? I'm not proud of visiting Berchtesgaden; I told the story to nobody except you. And—and one other person. How many people have you told?"

"Only Audrey Page. Tonight, and at her father's insistence."

"You're sure of that?"

"Absolutely. Even then—"

"Even then, am I to assume, you told her only because you have fallen for the young lady?"

Brian smiled, though he was smiling against his feelings and arguing against his convictions.

"That doesn't matter."

"Indeed? What spirit you have!"

"I mean the question doesn't arise even if it were true. Audrey has fallen very hard for someone else."

"For young Philip? H'm." Hathaway struck one finger on the table. "Then you're not at all alarmed about her safety?"

"There's no actual reason to be. Mrs. Ferrier's letters to you may be those of an innocent woman trying to protect herself from slander. She invited Audrey as long ago as last winter, a casual invitation to a casual friend; and she made it definite about a month ago, at the same time—" Brian stopped abruptly.

"A casual invitation, eh? And Mrs. Ferrier made it definite a month ago, when she couldn't think about anything except a rumour of murder? And there's nothing suspicious in that circumstance either? Don't make me laugh!"

Hathaway, a humped interrogation-point with a bald head, had bounced to his feet. Brian also jumped up. And then, in a heavy silence while the minute-hand clicked on a big electric clock, they looked at each other unmirthfully. Hathaway seized hat and brief-case.

"Come along," he said. "Come along, now!"

"Where are we going?"

"Don't ask questions. If you are not interested in protecting Miss Page, I am. I have some information still to get. And we will beat Gideon Fell at his own game."

Restraint was abandoned.

"Will you tell me," Brian demanded, "why you keep dragging Dr. Fell into this? He isn't concerned in the matter, is he? Eve Ferrier hasn't invited *him* for a pleasant week at the villa?"

"No," Hathaway said curtly, "but Desmond Ferrier has."

Chairs scraped on a hard-rubber floor.

"Yes!" continued Hathaway, jamming the Guy-Fawkes hat on his head and immediately snatching it off again. "That was what I said: Desmond Ferrier. He whistled to your elephantine friend; Fell has been at the Villa Rosalind since noon today. Now pay our bill and follow me."

Brian put a bank-note on the table. He acted slowly, to gain time for thought. Past open French windows, past the *terrasse* and the Quai Turrettini, he could hear the River Rhône foaming at its narrowest round the island bridge. Its sound, unnoticed by day, grew loud in the quieter hours. Brian stalked after Hathaway into the foyer.

Few of the hotel's guests had yet returned from theatre or res-taurant or night-club. The dining-room was still open. Chromium clock-hands above the reception-desk, in a foyer resplendent with colours of cream and orange and black, pointed to nearly half-past ten. Hathaway dragged his companion over towards the lifts.

"We are shortly to discover," he announced, "whether my careful planning is better than Gideon Fell's scatterbrain. By the way! Did you ever meet Miss Paula Catford?"

"No."

"But you've seen a photograph of her, perhaps?"

"Not to my knowledge."

"Ah! Then if you will glance where I am pointing—so!—you may get something of a surprise."

One of the lifts had swooped down and rolled open its green metal door. Brian stopped short. Hathaway was right: he had half-expected any globe-trotting woman journalist to be a tough and strident egomaniac with elaborate gestures and too much make-up. Astonishment, when he saw Paula Catford, took him in more ways than one.

Out of the lift stepped a gentle, modest, well-rounded girl, tall and slender, with black hair and a sympathetic manner. You thought 'girl' rather than 'woman,' though she must have been in her middle or later thirties. Though she was not exactly pretty, a clear complexion and large eyes made her seem so. And, except for her very fashionable clothes, she might have been the vicar's daughter on holiday.

She hurried up to Hathaway, putting away a room-key in her handbag.

"Am I late, Sir Gerald?"

"On the contrary, dear lady, you are five minutes early. And here and now I apologize for all."

"Well, I do wish you wouldn't. You're rather an overpowering person, and I'm not all that used to so much attention."

Hathaway's beard vibrated with gallantry.

"Dear lady, it was bad enough to drag you here from Stockholm without one proper word of explanation. But to offer you dinner, and then 'phone and put you off because of this miscreant Innes . . . !"

Paula, smiling, extended a warm and friendly hand.

"Mr. Innes? It's a great pleasure. Sir Gerald couldn't seem to find you."

"At his flat," and Hathaway pursued a grievance, "they said he was due back by a plane arriving at seven o'clock. By eight o'clock, when he still hadn't turned up, I was unfit for human company until I had tramped the streets to work off steam. Even then, when by sheer accident I met him at the Hotel Metropole, he delayed me another half hour by going home to change his clothes."

Brian bowed.

"Sir Gerald is quite right, Miss Catford. You must never put your faith in temperamental people."

"I—I beg your pardon?"

"Beware of these painters, as Hathaway says. They insist on changing their clothes; they hide in telephone-boxes; you can't trust 'em an inch."

"Oh, you're all guilty of great enormities. I'm sure of that. I . . ."

Suddenly Paula woke up. So did Brian.

All this time he had been holding her hand. Her eyes, large and luminous hazel, looked straight into his as though rapt at every word he said. And yet she had not heard him, Brian thought; behind that gentle barrier lurked some emotion he sensed rather than defined. Hathaway sensed it too; a spark flicked the group; all gallantry dropped away.

"Yes, my dear?" the older man demanded. He was like a sharp if indulgent uncle. "What is it? What's the matter?"

"Nothing at all. I was thinking—well! Of Berchtesgaden. Can that be seventeen years ago?"

"Just over seventeen years. In those days they called you the Infant Prodigy of Fleet Street, didn't they?"

"Yes; that's what I was thinking. My God!"

Paula made a wry mouth and shivered and retreated.

"In '39," she went on, "I had just published my first travel-book. I wrote the most horribly inaccurate descriptions, I fired off silly-clever political views, in a way that turns me hot and cold when I think of it today. And yet I wonder if any of us, really, is a bit more grown up now?"

"I wonder too," Hathaway said sharply. "You know why I'm here?"

"Of course I know."

"Well, then! It's about Mrs. Ferrier. Didn't she ask you to give her an alibi in the murder of Hector Matthews?"

"We can't talk here," Paula said after a hard-breathing pause. "Come with me, please."

"If we go into the bår . . . ?"

"No! Not in the bar, or I shall have too many. This way."

At the front of the foyer, facing the quai, glass doors in a glass façade glittered open as a party of guests laughed their way back to the hotel. To the right of the front doors, down two steps and past a newspaper-kiosk, the marble floor had been set out with easy-chairs for a lounge. Paula led them there.

"You see, Sir Gerald, I'm afraid it wasn't only your distinguished name that brought me from Stockholm. I had to see you before you saw Eve."

"Yes, dear lady?"

"The Infant Prodigy of Fleet Street was a very silly person. But I was very lucky in one way. I must have had a guardian angel, or an innate sense of decency, or something else I haven't got now." Paula straightened up. "When that man Matthews went head-first over the parapet, and Eve screamed as she saw him fall, I didn't use it as a news-story. I didn't do what I'm afraid you're trying to do now. I couldn't hurt her that much. Don't you understand? *I saw it happen.*"

"You saw her push him?"

"She didn't push him. She wasn't anywhere near him."

"Ah!"

They stood amid leather chairs, with a sofa on which Hathaway softly put down hat and brief-case. Echoes struck and rattled back.

"I saw it through a window. The others, those fat officers who were ogling her so much I was jealous: maybe they saw it, maybe they didn't. I don't know. But I was looking out of a window towards the terrace. —Don't you understand what I'm telling you? I saw it happen!"

"What did happen?"

"Eve *didn't*, that's all. She wasn't within twelve or fifteen feet of where he was standing. She called to him, I think. There was a little wind. All she did was bend forward at the parapet, and turn slightly to the left, and point at something on a hill below."

"Ah!" said Hathaway.

That one syllable, so often repeated, might have been comic without its sudden note of enlightenment. Paula Catford stood motionless. Glass cases for luxury-goods, set round the walls with little lights inside them, silhouetted her soft slender figure and threw a glow on the dark hair.

"The Infant Prodigy of Fleet Street, Sir Gerald, is telling you the truth and the whole truth and nothing but the truth. Don't you believe it?"

"Dear lady! Of course I believe it. As far as it goes."

"As far as it goes?"

"Dear lady! If I do our friend an injustice—"

"Oh, stop this!"

"Mrs. Ferrier had no need to touch her victim. She was used to being stared at; she expected to be stared at; she would never have dared touch him. He did turn faint, I grant you; but not from the altitude. I am now quite convinced she had drugged or poisoned him. And I think I see how she did it."

IV

Hathaway, peering round the side of his beard and moustache as though half triumphant and half defiant, bent forward to unfasten the clasp of the brief-case.

"I've got an album of photographs here," he continued, "which may convince both of you. Hector Matthews was a very tall man: six feet three inches, to be exact. A fairly low parapet, to him, could be a death-trap. Once you've drugged or poisoned him (eh?), you make him lean forward by pointing out and down. —Stop!"

Brian, with bursting lungs, had been about to comment.

The other man wouldn't hear of it. Out of the brief-case on the sofa he took a large cardboard album, much thumbed and time-battered.

"You have seen this before, I think?" And he held it up. "To keep any sort of photograph album is a loathsome and provincial habit. I don't recommend it, except for a scientific (a purely scientific!) study of crime."

"Did you say scientific?"

"I did."

"What else?"

"Every photograph pasted in here, with the exception of the first one, was taken by the official Ministry of Propaganda in Germany. Pay no attention to the first one. That doesn't concern us."

But it did concern them.

"Hathaway, shall I tell you something about yourself?"

The other man, as though struck in the face, opened the album so violently that he all but tore it apart. When it opened at the first page, a large full-face photograph of Eve Ferrier looked out with a glossy vividness as though alive in black and white.

"Look at that!" Brian said. "Look at *her*. Then listen to yourself speak."

"Well?"

"To anyone who didn't know you, you'd sound like an obnoxious bounder with a personal spite against Mrs. Ferrier. But you're not that. You're a thoroughly good fellow."

Hathaway's voice went high.

" 'Obnoxious bounder.' Confound your pompousness." Breathing thinly, he flung the album on the sofa. "And don't stand there and boom at me; this is insufferable; I won't have it."

"Very well. I am as pompous and stuffy as you think I am. But somebody has got to be. We're not the police, and Mrs. Ferrier is no case-history in a prison-record. You're forgetting that; I was in danger of forgetting it myself until Miss Catford said what she did say."

"Thanks!" whispered Paula, who had taken a step forward. "Thanks!"

Hathaway ran round behind the sofa, facing them over the back of it as though he were being physically attacked.

"There's no case against Mrs. Ferrier? Is that what you say, Innes?"

"That's it exactly. This talk of drugs or—"

"Oh, no! I'll remind you of what you yourself heard at the Hotel Metropole tonight. Desmond Ferrier says his wife is trying to poison him."

Back they swung in the old, ugly circle.

"*Poison:* that's the operative word. I overheard it at the door, so don't deny it. That's why I didn't intrude. I 'hid,' as you so sneeringly put it, because I wanted time to think. And in a telephone-box, just remember, because I had to put off a dinner-engagement with this lady here. That's a part of the case; don't think it's not. And I shall be very happy to take it to Mrs. Ferrier herself."

"Yes, Sir Gerald, I'm quite sure you will," said Paula. "So I think you ought to hear there's not a word of truth in it."

"Madam, the value of your opinion . . . !"

"It's not my opinion. Please! I can show you proof, but I don't even ask you to accept my word or anybody else's."

"Indeed? Whose testimony is being offered?"

"Your own. You were with us. You were one of the party that spent one night at the guest-house; and then, next morning, we all drove on up to Hitler's lodge for a lunch we never had. If Eve drugged or poisoned Mr. Matthews in some way, how did she do it?"

"Madam, we're here to *determine* that point!"

"I couldn't agree more. How did she do it? And when? And where?"

Here Paula lifted a trembling hand as though to shade her eyes.

"I don't understand that part about Mr. Ferrier," she cried. "I don't even think it matters. Whatever he said, you can put it down as a joke. How stupid people are! They're always associating Mr. Ferrier with Shakespeare. And yet, if they've ever seen him as Shaw's Caesar in *Caesar and Cleopatra*, or as Higgins in *Pygmalion*, they should know he's best in satiric comedy. He's like that in real life. No, no, I can see what you're going to ask. I don't know him well, though I've met him often. Eve says he's like that; so does everyone else."

"Go on, dear lady," Hathaway cried in sudden suavity. "Continue my interesting conversation with yourself."

"Wait, please! I was thinking. . . ."

Paula's eyes, of that luminous and disturbing quality, looked past Brian as though she had observed something in the foyer. But she did not even see the marble-floored foyer, or the colours of cream and orange and black, or the glittering glass doors to the street.

"The *Gasthof züm Türken!* That was the name of the guest-house, or hostel, or whatever it was, where our party spent the night. Do you remember?"

"All too well. I have a photograph here—"

"Never mind the photograph! Next morning the four of our particular group, you and Eve and Mr. Matthews and I, all had breakfast at the same table. There was nobody else at the table. It was just eight o'clock. Is that true?"

"Granted, granted!"

"Mr. Matthews wouldn't have a mouthful to eat or drink. He said he never did at breakfast. You called him a food-faddist; you urged him to have a cup of coffee at least, because you said we shouldn't get lunch until half-past one. Is *that* true?"

"I don't deny. . . ."

"From that moment onward the four of us stayed together in a very close little group. That's natural; people do; Eve was the only one of us who spoke German. We sat on the terrace together. We waited for the cars together. We drove up to the Eagle's Nest in the same car. Between eight o'clock and at least a quarter past one, we were closer together than I am to you now. Do you agree?"

Hathaway stood motionless, his eyes searching.

"Sir Gerald, do you agree?"

"In candour and honesty: very well. Yes!"

"At a quarter past one, as soon as we had reached the Eagle's Nest, Eve and Mr. Matthews went straight out on the balcony-terrace? And it was only a matter of seconds, thirty or forty for all I remember, that Eve screamed? You're nodding, aren't you? Then when and where and how was the poor man poisoned?"

"I might remind you, dear lady! The victim was showing signs of this 'altitude' giddiness by one o'clock. If the dosage occurred before eight in the morning . . ."

"Five hours?" Paula breathed. "Honestly; five hours? I've known a lot of amateur detectives, believe me; every paper has one. Can you name any poison or drug, even the slowest on earth or one in capsule form, that would hold off for five hours?"

"No. There is none. I concede it."

Hathaway strode round from behind the sofa.

"Stop!" he added. "I further allow that the victim took nothing to eat or drink between eight o'clock and one-fifteen. What is more, with all of us so close at all times, the murderer could not have used a hypodermic needle or any form of subcutaneous injection. By the same token we may rule out a chloroform sponge or its equivalent. The whole thing, I grant you, seems flatly impossible. And yet—!"

"And yet?"

The photograph album, where it had been thrown down on the sofa, still lay open at a full face of Eve Ferrier yearning upwards. Hathaway pointed.

"A minute ago," he said, with malevolent eyes on Brian, "you told me to look at that. All right, my fine friend. *You* look at it."

"I'm looking! What about it?"

"Between eight o'clock and one-fifteen," announced Hathaway, "she killed Hector Matthews."

"How? Do you mind telling me how?"

"By God," said Hathaway from deep in his throat, "I do indeed mind telling you how."

"Do you intend to tell anybody?"

"At the proper time, yes."

He was still pointing at the photograph. By this time neither Brian nor Paula could look at anything else.

Brian had almost forgotten this woman's striking beauty. The picture suggested colour without showing it. Eve Ferrier's heavy fair hair, done in a style of the nineteen-thirties, surrounded a face redeemed from classic regularity by heavy-lidded eyes and a full mouth. The eyes were wide-spaced, the nose short. You might fancy a hint of mockery or cruelty round that mouth; but it was only your own imagination. Whether or not Eve Ferrier had a sensual nature, few women knew better how to express it with a look. She was not quite smiling.

"You see?" inquired Hathaway.

"See what?" Brian was beginning. Then he caught himself up, and wouldn't be drawn.

For Gerald Hathaway was really triumphant. Nor was this all.

At the other side of the foyer, towards the east, the orchestra in the dining-room began to play a popular air. These three scarcely heard it.

During a space of perhaps ten seconds, while certain forces were locked and fighting above the photograph, Brian became aware with heightened senses of all visual shapes and colours: of Hathaway in full formal evening clothes with a crumpled shirt-front, whereas neither he nor Paula had troubled to dress formally; of the big windows to the Quai Turrettini, and the night-porter hailing a taxi outside; but, in an impressionistic sense beyond these, of the change in Paula Catford.

Paula, who had been standing close enough to brush his shoulder, suddenly drew back. She was no longer quite the 'gentle' figure of the vicar's daughter.

"I can't force you to talk, Sir Gerald. I'm only a humble member of the press."

"It is wise of you, dear lady, to accept that fact."

The voices flew out and clashed.

"But you can't mind telling me," retorted Paula, "what anybody can find from the record. Wasn't there a post-mortem examination of Mr. Matthews's body?"

"If they held one, Miss Catford—"

" 'If?' By German law, even under the Nazis, wasn't it necessary to have a full post-mortem in all cases of violent death? And, if Mr. Matthews was poisoned, wouldn't they have discovered it?"

"That's exactly what I mean. They never published the results. You may draw your own conclusions."

"Then what was the poison? Or have you made all this up? And why do you hate Eve as much as you do?"

Hathaway went rather white behind beard and moustache.

"I have not made it up," he answered clearly. "You may call me a busybody, as Innes does. But I am neither a knave nor a liar, and I don't make dupes of people. If this is a journalistic trick to make me speak . . ."

"It's not. I swear it's not!"

"Hate Mrs. Ferrier? I don't hate her. You seem to think this extraordinary character, who conveniently inherited a great fortune when Matthews died, somehow needs to be treated with kid gloves or at least the greatest kindliness."

"I do think so. And she hasn't any 'great fortune' now; she and—and Mr. Ferrier are flat broke. But that isn't the point. How well do you know Eve? How long has it been since you last talked to her?"

"Talked to her?"

"Yes! Please tell me!"

"My dear young lady, I have not set eyes on Mrs. Ferrier in seventeen years. The last time I talked to her was at Berchtesgaden on the day we've been discussing just now."

Paula whispered a curse.

But she did not speak. She was looking past Hathaway towards the entrance of the hotel. Hathaway swung round to follow her glance, and so did Brian.

The night-porter outside, first saluting, pushed open one big glass door. Into the foyer, amid a backwash of perfume, swept a woman wearing a shimmering blue-and-silver evening gown curved to make the most of a magnificent figure.

The woman halted just inside, head raised, every gesture of an unconscious graceful fluency larger than life. If she had turned her head to the left, she would have seen Paula and Hathaway and Brian. But she did not turn. Instead she looked towards the dining-room at the opposite side. You would have guessed her suppressed rage or fear even without a glimpse of her face.

Gerald Hathaway, incredulous, suddenly cast a glance at the open photograph album—and back again.

"That's not . . . ?"

"Shut up!" Brian said under his breath.

The woman in blue and silver, shoulders moving and fingers with red-varnished nails gripping round a handbag, hurried towards the dining-room. There, at the doorway, she seemed to be asking questions of a head-waiter. Then, with the same unconscious if exaggerated grace, she swept back across the foyer in the direction of the three who waited. What warned her to look up they never learned. But again she stopped.

The hands of the clock stood at twenty minutes to eleven.

"Well?" asked Paula Catford in a ventriloquial tone. "She can't avoid meeting us now. What about it, Sir Gerald. Are you going to accuse her of murder?"

Hathaway did not reply.

"Are you?" whispered Paula, tugging at his sleeve. "Or, as Mr. Innes says, is it the business of the police and not yours?"

Still he did not reply.

Eve Ferrier, caught off guard, regarded them with a dismay she could not hide. But they were not now concerned with her mission here. The light lay too clearly on her features.

It is hardly a tragedy that the face of a once-famous beauty is no longer its smiling image of twenty years ago. Only the too-romantic could expect it to be. On the other hand, the face that looked at them should not have been as nerve-ravaged and sagging as this one. The shock was there; Eve had seen it.

Charm remained to her, or would remain when she recovered her poise; and a still-handsome if somewhat overblown body; and a personality better than pretty looks. Something else, Brian was thinking, something indefinable, something beyond beauty-parlours, had blurred the image and muddled its edges. The tragedy might be in Eve Ferrier's mind if she were not emotionally mature enough to accept facts.

Only a flash; it was gone. She laughed, nearly herself again, and moved forward in an almost-convincing lightness.

"Paula, my dear! It's good to see you, and it's extremely kind of you when I was so foolish as to write that letter."

"It's not foolish at all." Paula hurried up the two little marble steps. "Who wants people screaming a lot of ridiculous nonsense and making it unpleasant for everybody?"

"For me, certainly. Yes; there I must agree. I can't help it. It may be foolish," the fine voice rang out, "but there it is. How good to see you, or did I say that? And isn't that Mr. Hathaway? I do so beg your pardon! I mean Sir Gerald now, don't I?"

Hathaway looked up.

"What you like, madam," he said.

He was still pale. Eve, making an entrance of the two steps, poised there an instant more.

"I *can* rely on you, I hope?" she suddenly asked Paula.

"Of course! You know it!"

"Yes. To be sure. Dear Sir Gerald." Glitter and brightness surrounded the too-yellow hair; then sincerity coloured her voice as she extended her hand. "It was a most unhappy occasion when we met last. I loathed troubling you. And let's not talk about those old days, shall we? But I do hope you're not going to say I poisoned anyone, are you?"

Again Hathaway looked up.

"Madam, why should I say that?"

("Steady!" thought Brian.)

"Well, everyone else does." Eve laughed. It was as though a wheel went round behind her eyes. "I—I came here tonight to find Desmond. It's absurd, isn't it, to be so fond of my own husband after all these years? It seems so horribly uncivilized. But there it is. Can you understand that, Paula?"

"Yes, I think so."

"That's what I mean. And I do intend to be serious, Sir Gerald," declared Eve, "as you will see very shortly. It's only that I don't want to interrupt any sort of conference, and I don't seem to have met that gentleman there."

As she looked at Brian, her gaze slid over the sofa where the album had lain open. He saw with a shock that it was closed now; Paula must have closed it, though he could not remember seeing her do so. And Brian introduced himself.

"I'm a friend of Audrey Page's father, Mrs. Ferrier."

"Audrey? Ah, yes. I'd heard *she* was here. That doesn't surprise me. But the rest of you . . ." Eve had a really magnetic smile. Everything else was subtly wrong: the colours of her clothes and make-up, the series of wrong contrasts, in a woman once noted for good taste. "Now I'll be serious. I won't ask you what you're doing at this hotel. But I will ask you: are you ignoring me? Is everybody ignoring me? Have you decided you won't come to the Villa Rosalind after all?"

"Are you speaking to me, madam?" asked Hathaway.

"If you please, yes."

"The question, Mrs. Ferrier, is whether you still want us there. Miss Catford is trying to help you. I am not."

"And why should you help me? I can't expect it. But we want something from each other, don't we?"

"If you put it like that . . . !" And Hathaway lifted his shoulders.

"I do. You want to play detective. I want these old rumours killed and killed forever. Killed!" said Eve, seeming to stare at the past. "I have had much trouble, you know. A new life can open for me, even a return to the stage and a triumphant one, once I've finished the book I'm writing now. It's inexpressibly sweet to think of that. But I can't do it if they still say I'm a murderess and half mad as well. *Are* the three of you staying at the Hotel du Rhône?"

"Miss Catford and I are staying here, yes."

"Is there any reason why you should? Can't you occupy the rooms ready and waiting for you at my villa? Now? This very night? That is, unless you're afraid?"

"Hardly afraid, dear Mrs. Ferrier."

Eve nodded. Lithely, with the flash of an ugly look, she sat down in the leather sofa beside the brief-case and the album.

"This is yours, I imagine." She picked up the brief-case, stamped

42

with the letters G. H. "And this too." She picked up the album and riffled through its pages. "For God's sweet sake, my dear man," she added in a startlingly different tone, "do you really think I drugged or poisoned Hector Matthews?"

The words, though not loudly spoken, had a rasp which startled Eve herself. She sat up straight.

"Sir Gerald, I beg your pardon. That was unforgivably crude of me. I am desperate, you see; this means my happiness. *Do* you think that?"

"Yes. I do. But what makes you say I do?"

"That's obvious, isn't it?"

"Not at all obvious. No, no, no! Most people think you deliberately pushed him when he turned dizzy. Since you ask me the direct question, I give you the direct answer."

Eve closed her eyes.

"You must have known that, Mrs. Ferrier. Your letters indicated you did. Where did *you* get this notion of drugging or poisoning? It only occurred to me after you wrote to me a month ago."

"Only then?"

"Only then. When and where did *you* get the notion?"

"Seventeen years ago," Eve answered clearly. She put down the album, and rose to her feet. "From the German surgeon who did a post-mortem examination of poor Hector's body."

Paula Catford turned away, but turned back again.

"I never dreamed at the time," said Eve, "those Nazi officials could be suspicious of me. Never! But they were suspicious of everyone; they were guarding their precious Führer; they had the security-police there. When they told me privately there would be a post-mortem, and in my naïve way I asked why, Dr. Richter laughed and said it was only a formality. 'We must look for poisons, you know.'"

Whereupon, in a flash-brief but vivid piece of mimicry, they saw the doctor's face and heard his voice as Eve imitated it.

"Seventeen years! I never even remembered it until people began whispering. Did I throw poor Hector over the parapet? Or was it something else? God! Why are they all so vicious? Why won't they let you be happy?"

"Eve," cried Paula, "you have got to stop this. You'll kill yourself with worry. You can't go on."

43

"I greatly fear, Mrs. Ferrier," snapped Hathaway, "you will have to go on. You are not saying there *was* a post-mortem?"

"Oh, but I am saying just that!"

"Hardly a post-mortem by a reputable surgeon?"

"Oh, but it was by a very reputable surgeon. Dr. Walter Richter. He's a friend of yours, I think? Or he says so?"

"He is a friend of mine, and a sound man. How do you know all this?"

"I wrote to him. There was no drug or poison in poor Hector's body."

Outside, in the hot night beyond the goldfish-bowl windows, a breeze stirred for the first time. A faint rumble of thunder came prowling in from the direction of the lake. Brian, the only one who glanced up, saw the glitter of the opening glass door; that, for the moment, was all he observed beyond their group.

"Madam," Hathaway was crying, "that's impossible!"

"I have here," said Eve, opening her handbag, "a letter from Dr. Richter. Here is his address at Koenigstrasse 15, Stuttgart; also his telephone-number."

"And what of that?"

"Please read what Dr. Richter says. It's written in English. If you still think this is a game of some kind, I want you to telephone him at my expense."

In taking a letter out of the handbag, Eve discovered something else which seemed to startle her. It was, apparently, a two-ounce perfume-bottle of clouded glass and glass-stoppered, across which curled a gilt label with the raised red name of *Spectre de la Rose*. Eve turned it over in a rather shaky hand.

"Come, now!" she added. "I never carry this in a handbag. Why should anybody? I really must be losing my mind. Anyway, though!—"

And she gestured.

Behind her back, up the two marble steps, appeared a tall man who had entered by the front doors a moment before. In a black soft hat and a careless dark lounge-suit, his figure stood out rakishly against light-coloured walls. He was well into middle age. But you would have noticed him anywhere by an air, a presence, an unpredictable aliveness like the steel and coil of a taut spring.

"Anyway, though," Eve continued, "that post-mortem examina-

tion was done so soon after death that even a drug to make him un-
steady would have left traces. And there wasn't anything at all. Will
you read this, Sir Gerald?"

"As you like, madam."

She extended the letter in the same hand that held the perfume-
bottle, and Hathaway took it.

"I want to be friends with everybody," said Eve. "I do! I want
you to come out to our house tonight, this very night, and talk it
all over. There isn't any poison! There never was!"

Behind her back, up the two steps, the tall man stopped.

Again Brian glanced up. So did Paula, who was standing so close
to Brian that her shoulder brushed the upper part of his left arm.

Brian saw the hat, the shoulders, the bearing of the man in front
of him; and an explanation of one part of the problem suddenly fell
into place. But he had no time to consider this, or to think of its
implications.

"Madam, this letter—!"

"You *must* believe it! I've often played a murderess. It's rather
amusing and exciting. This isn't. Paula and I aren't liars. We can't
make a man die by accident. That's what happened to poor Hector.
Let's all be friends, can't we?"

And then, behind her back, Desmond Ferrier spoke.

" '*How now, ye secret, black, and midnight hags?*' "

Eve did not scream.

But her face turned a muddy colour under the make-up. The
little perfume bottle flew out of her extended hand and smashed in
three pieces on the marble floor at Hathaway's feet. Hathaway
jumped back with a bouncing curse. The contents of the bottle,
with a sizzling noise and an acrid odour, burnt in spattered little
puffs growing black against the floor. Catching up Paula under
knees and arms, Brian swung her off her feet just before the living
burns touched her shoe.

"Throw some magazines down there," he said, "before anybody
else sees. That's oil of vitriol. Or you can call it sulphuric acid."

V

Audrey Page's white gown, no less than her arms and shoulders, could be seen even in smoke-blurred gloom. She was at a table just beyond the spotlight. Tango-music, though it had a beat of South American drums, to Brian always suggested Paris because he associated Paris with that particular tune.

Brian was still swearing.

He shouldn't have been so enraged with Audrey for what she had said that night. Unless he did happen to be in love with a girl nearly twenty years younger than himself, he had no right to be enraged.

But the impulse to wring her neck . . .

This night-club called *La Boule Noire*, which is not far from the *Ba-Ta-Clan* and very much like it, can be found one floor up in one of those steep, narrow streets rising through the Old Town towards the Cathedral.

Clocks rang the quarter-hour to midnight, startling him with the realization that oil of vitriol had splashed a danger-warning only an hour ago, as Brian went upstairs at *La Boule Noire*. Afterwards he could have heard no clock in Geneva.

Music smote out at him above the blur of voices. Spectators' faces, spirit-photographs built up in a pyramid above the long bar-counter, looked out and down towards the stage across a waxed floor-space between.

"Monsieur, there is no room! The second sitting will begin—"

Brian produced a Swiss fifty-franc note. There was room.

On the waxed floor, beneath and in front of a gaudy stage, the spotlight followed two dancers amid roars of mirth. Heat and a dampness of alcohol flowed over a mob through which waiters with trays wormed like rabbits into burrows.

"If you please! If you please!"

Only a hundred-franc note halted one of these waiters with the if-you-please shouts.

"You see that dark-haired young man there? With the young lady in the white dress? Sitting at the table midway across on the edge of the dance-floor?"

"There?"

"Just there. Tell him he is summoned to the telephone. Tell him it's here, by the bar. Tell him it's very important. Tell him it's from his home."

The waiter shouted assent and dived again.

On the floor, wearing only her body-powder and a G-string, a tall and supple blonde was engaged in a mock Apache-dance with an undersized man wearing sinister underworld clothes from cap and muffler to chequered suit. Only, instead of the Apache hurling his girl all over the floor as the drums whacked on the down-beat, she was hurling him.

Again the Apache struck wood with a crash that jarred cham-pagne-coolers and sifted up dust. The crowd whooped. The girl, icy-faced, caught him as he danced back. Next time he landed almost on the table of a stout, elderly couple in evening-clothes.

Philip Ferrier, white dinner-jacket somewhat rumpled, pushed through the crowd.

"There isn't any 'phone-call," said Brian, seizing his arm. "I've got to talk to you alone."

"Listen! Audrey's there by herself!"

"Suppose she is? This is quite a fashionable haunt."

"Maybe it is," retorted Philip, straightening his tie, "but it's no place to take your girl unless she insists. If somebody thinks she's one of the entertainers and asks her to go home with him—"

"Let's not worry about that, shall we?"

"Look, what's up? What's the situation?"

"The situation," said Brian, "is just about as bad as it can be."

"Why?"

"Murder."

He had to yell this word. The Apache went face down and managed to upset half a dozen glasses. Heat, doubt, uncertainty all wove like the beat of music.

"No, nobody has been killed just yet," said Brian. "But it's being arranged and I don't know for whom. Paula Catford and Gerald Hathaway have both been persuaded, or challenged, to leave their hotel and go out to the Villa Rosalind tonight. I want you to do me a great favour. I want you to make the excuse that you've been called away. I want you to leave here now, and let me take Audrey back to her hotel."

"That's asking a hell of a lot, isn't it?"

"Yes, it is. All the same, if you think as much of that damned fool girl as I believe you do, you'll agree to it."

"Look, I couldn't leave her here even if I wanted to! If this is important, I can go with you!"

"No. You can't do that either. I must talk to *her* alone."

Philip swayed to keep his feet in the crush.

"So help me," he began, "if I didn't know you were old enough to be Aud's father . . . !"

"I'm not quite as old as all that, you know." Brian found himself talking more loudly than was necessary. "This way; do you mind?"

It might be quieter away from the centre of noise. Brian impelled his companion down past the length of the bar, where spectators stood on the rungs of bar-stools to peer over the heads of others. At the end of it, between the angle of the bar and a heavily curtained window overlooking the street, he spoke again.

"At any other time, I might feel inclined to give you some competition. Not now. I have no more interest in Audrey than I have in—in Paula Catford."

(Now why had he said those last words?)

"You want me to say good-night to Aud here and now?"

"I don't even want you to say good-night. Let me take the message for you; that's even more important. When you understand the reason for all this, which may be quite soon, you'll see it's just

48

as vital to you as it is to Audrey. If you care for her, you'll go."

Brian paused. He looked once, and looked again.

In the dim corner beyond the bar sat his friend Dr. Gideon Fell.

A mountain in the corner, his bandit's moustache drawn down above several chins, his eyeglasses askew on the broad black ribbon, Dr. Fell cleared his throat with a rumbling noise that could be heard even here. He had an intent expression on his face and a large glass of Carlsberg lager in his hand.

"Sir," he said courteously to Philip Ferrier, "may I urge you to do as Innes asks?"

"So-and-so!" breathed Philip, and tugged at his collar. "Can I depend on this?"

"You can," said Brian, "and you know it. How soon is this first show over?"

"At any minute. We were going after that. The bill—"

"I'll pay the bill. Try to believe Audrey's future may depend on your going home now and asking no questions. You can 'phone her later, or she'll 'phone you. Well?"

A slight hysteria had infected the night-club. Philip, a dazed young man who liked to feel he was being heroic, tried to take a last look in Audrey's direction. Then he elbowed round and stalked away. Dr. Fell, glooming down over the mountainous ridges of himself, held up the glass of beer like a powerfully impressive television commercial.

"Sir," Dr. Fell intoned with stately thunder, "I myself can refrain from asking questions in the event of necessity. However! In one word, what explains all this?"

"In one word: vitriol."

"Oh, ah?"

"That's not the only word, but it will do. You don't put vitriol into a perfume-bottle as a joke."

Dr. Fell's eyes slid sideways.

"Not customarily, I agree. But I find the word vitriol less interesting than . . . harrumph! No matter! Go and see to the young lady."

From the dance-floor, which was now invisible, a thump and angry cries rocked the house as the Apache shot feet-first into another party. Brian, butting his way through the crowd, emerged at the edge of the dance-floor.

49

Momentarily he was blinded by a second spotlight wheeling into his eyes from the gold and crimson stage. He stood there, shielding his eyes, amid a haze of cosmetic-dust and tobacco-smoke. With several conflicting feelings he watched Audrey at her ring-side table.

There could be no doubt she was enjoying herself hugely.

Though perhaps a little nervous in addition to being rapt and gleeful, she bent forward as the dancers stamped back for their final gyrations. Brian stared at her. Circling round the edge, he stopped at the table, moved in front of it, and towered above her.

"Oh!" said Audrey, almost as though she had seen a ghost.

"Good evening again," said Brian, and sat down in the chair opposite.

"Really! What are *you* doing here?"

"Looking for you."

"How on earth did you find us?"

"Philip said you were having dinner at the Richemond, and then going on to a night-club. There aren't all that many places to choose from."

"I mean," and two spots of colour burned in Audrey's cheeks, "*what* are you doing here? What do you want with me?"

"I'm here to tell you something."

"Oh?"

"Yes. You are not going to visit Eve Ferrier, either now or at any other time. Tomorrow morning I am putting you on a plane for London."

"Now, really!" said Audrey. Her mouth fell open. "And what if I won't do it, Mr. Brian Innes? What if I don't choose to obey you? What will you do then?"

In the background, where the Apache groped towards his fellow-dancer, the tall blonde caught him a ringing wallop across the face and sent him sprawling as the music soared to its end. Brian pointed.

"*That*," he answered. "Which is a great deal less than you deserve."

The dancers, panting, bowed at the end of their number. A torrent of applause burst over the tables, drowning out what Audrey might have been saying. But she said nothing; she sat bolt upright and stared back at him. As the dancers scampered back up on the stage, bowing, the curtains swirled together and hid them. Every light in the room went out to mark the end of the first show. By this time Audrey was speaking, but he couldn't hear her.

A long drum-roll was followed by the noise of shifting chairs, shifting people, a babble of talk. Ten seconds later the house-lights glowed out softly against a painted ceiling. Audrey had stood up, facing him across a silvered bucket with a champagne-bottle.

"As soon as Phil comes back from answering a 'phone-call," Audrey cried, "we're leaving here."

"You think so?"

"Really, now!—"

"He isn't coming back."

"I don't know what you think you're talking about, but it doesn't matter in the least. I'll go alone."

"Oh, no, you won't. Sit down."

Audrey sat down.

"You and I," Brian went on, taking the champagne-bottle out of its cooler and inspecting it, "are going to get a few things quite clear. Here." Comparatively little was gone from the bottle; he filled Audrey's glass. "People in love don't drink much, do they?"

"What do you mean by that?"

"Don't you know?"

"No, of course I don't! You—you say Philip's not coming back? Why ever not?"

"Because I persuaded him not to see you for the moment. I said your future might depend on it. That happens to be true. He's in love with you."

"Whereas you're not, are you?"

"Certainly I'm not. What makes you think I should be fool enough for that?"

"*Oh!*" said Audrey, and clenched her fists. But she had never been more attractive or desirable than as she said it. "You wouldn't forbid me to go to Eve's, would you, when we talked about it earlier tonight? Why are you doing it now?"

"I'll give you just one of the reasons first."

"Just one?"

"Just one?"

"Yes. Sit still."

Briefly but vividly, he sketched out the meeting with Hathaway, the meeting with Paula Catford, the aching reasons why a man couldn't have been poisoned at Berchtesgaden, the entrance of Eve

51

Ferrier, the appearance of a perfume-bottle and a letter from a German surgeon.

"Oil of vitriol?" echoed Audrey. "The stuff they throw in people's faces?"

"It's been known to happen."

"But Mr. Matthews couldn't have been killed with it, could he?"

"Oh, no. Think of what I've been saying." Brian rapped on the table and spoke in the manner of a stage-direction. "Thunder and lightning. Enter Desmond Ferrier, slightly drunk and full of the devil. When he ripped out that line from *Macbeth*, the bottle jumped out of his wife's hand and smashed either by accident or design."

"By design?"

"Yes. It could have been a stage-effect; Eve herself could have planned it. That's why I don't know where to look."

"Haven't you got a *horrible* mind?"

"Possibly. We all have. Now consider the sequel. Nobody else had seen it happen; we bribed the night-porter to hush it up and get rid of the evidence. Mrs. Ferrier used the incident as a reason why Hathaway and Miss Catford should leave the hotel, luggage and all, for her villa. They didn't seem to be thinking very straight; they agreed. She next suggested we should get you too."

Audrey, in the act of lifting her glass, set it down that time untasted.

"But Eve Ferrier didn't know I was in Geneva a day early! Don't you remember? Phil hadn't let them know!"

"Well, Mrs. Ferrier knew. She said she'd heard it, and that it didn't surprise her. Did you tell anyone besides Phil himself?"

"No."

"Sure of that, Audrey?"

"Of course I'm sure!"

Brian watched her. The big room, after emptying of its first guests, had begun to fill again. Experimental squeals and plunks shook the orchestra-platform as the band tuned up. At the table behind Audrey, alone in vastness, with a fiercely apologetic look on his face and six bottles of beer in front of him, was Dr. Fell. A crutch-headed stick had been propped up against the table; waiters backed slowly away from him.

"Of course I'm sure!" Audrey repeated in a louder voice. "What was Mrs. Ferrier doing at the Hotel du Rhône?"

"Looking for her husband."

"And Mr. Ferrier?"

"He didn't say. Anyway!" Brian seemed to dismiss the point. "There were the five of us, in a sort of pandemonium. Mrs. Ferrier, I repeat, immediately wanted to take you with 'em. Since Hathaway was able to say you were putting up at the Metropole, I had to stop that one. I said you and Phil had gone to dinner, but that I hadn't any idea where you could be found afterwards or what time you would return."

"Oh?"

"Off they drove, with four or five hundredweight of luggage, in one private car and one taxi. Mrs. Ferrier 'phoned the Metropole at least twice before they left. By this time they'll have reached home; she'll be 'phoning the Metropole again."

"Well, why shouldn't she?"

The house-lights began slowly to dim. Brian raised his hand to a flying waiter.

"More champagne!" he said in French. "I take it," he added politely, "you can bear to sit through the show again? Usually there are eight or ten turns, some of them very good."

"If you think you're making me do something against my will," cried Audrey, "then you'd better think again. They *are* good, yes! Even if they're not very nice and my father wouldn't approve. You —you simply don't expect to find anything like it here. I always associate Geneva with John Calvin and righteousness."

"This is the French part of Switzerland. People tend to forget that. Look here, Audrey: do you seriously maintain you're in love with young Philip Ferrier?"

There was a pause. The blue eyes opened wide.

"I most certainly do maintain it," Audrey exclaimed, with every evidence of sincerity, "because it's true. Is there any reason why I shouldn't be?"

"I can think of a lot of reasons why your conduct is very peculiar if you are."

"Name one of them, please."

"With pleasure. When I got back from Paris this evening, I took a taxi straight from the airport to your hotel. I didn't even stop at my flat on the way."

"Dear, dear! That was very kind of you, I'm sure. But, as I said at the time . . ."

"Audrey, do you remember what you did say at the time? Stop and think. I was paying off the taxi when you came charging out of the hotel in a fine old stage of rage and near-panic. Before you realized you'd mistaken me for somebody else, you asked me what on earth 'I' thought I was doing. You said I was too early, and I'd spoil everything."

"All right! What about it?"

Brian answered her without raising his voice.

"This about it," he retorted. "Admittedly you were waiting for Philip Ferrier to take you out to dinner. But any woman who's expecting to be called for, even by her best boy-friend, waits in the foyer until he goes in to collect her. Or else she stays in her room until the reception-desk 'phones to tell her he's downstairs. She doesn't do what you did and she doesn't say what you said."

"I was only—"

"Shut up." And he rapped his knuckles on the table. "The implication was that you had mistaken me for Philip, wasn't it?"

"Of course! That's what happened."

"Oh, no. It couldn't have happened. I'm just over six feet tall, and nobody could possibly call me a heavyweight. Philip is more than half a head shorter, and he's on the chunky side. All you could see was the outline of a tall, rangy bloke in a Homburg hat, paying off a taxi in a semi-dark street. But it was enough to upset you badly."

And then, as he studied a face growing ghostlike in the dwindling lights, all Brian's anger began to change to a deep and desperate concern.

"Didn't you mistake me for somebody else? Didn't you mistake me for Desmond Ferrier, turning up at the hotel a good many hours before you expected him? And, if that's so, can you honestly claim to have any great affection for his son?"

VI

Every light in the room went out.

The thud of a tom-tom was joined by others, hammering in barbaric rhythm and swelling to a thunder that drowned out his voice. In total darkness he could not even see the white of Audrey's dress.

The beams of two spotlights, springing up at either side of the waxed floor, converged on the closed curtains of the stage. Of Audrey's expression, as the diffused glow touched her dark brown hair and set a mask on her face, he could read nothing.

It was perhaps ten seconds later, while tom-toms banged at the nerves, that Audrey began to slap at the table like a woman in a frenzy or a child in a tantrum.

"Oh, God save the lot of us and you most of all! You think I'm having an affair with Mr. Ferrier. Is that it?"

"It doesn't matter if you are."

"It does matter! It matters a great deal! Is that what you've been thinking?"

"Yes."

"And you were carrying a suitcase, so you imagined that meant . . . ?"

"We can't get anywhere if you slide away from every question. *Did* you expect Desmond Ferrier at the hotel? Was he supposed to be there at some time later tonight?"

"Yes, I did. Yes, he was. But it wasn't for that reason. If you ever breathe a word to Phil about this, or about my agreeing to meet him at all . . . !"

"I'm not going to tell anybody. But I'm too fond of you to see you involved in a situation that's going straight towards another murder with you in the middle of it."

"Brian, get me out of here. I won't go back to the hotel, if you're afraid they'll ring me up and lure me away; I swear I won't. Now please, please get me out of here!"

Brian stood up, taking out a note-case. Instantly a waiter appeared at his side and said something he could not catch under the thunder of drums.

The curtains swept apart. Half a dozen remarkably undressed young ladies, three to each side of the stage, coiled down a couple of steps and moved out close past the spectators for what the bills described as a pantomime of the jungle.

"Audrey! Wait!"

But Audrey, who now seemed to hate *La Boule Noire* as much as she had previously liked it, stopped only when Brian caught her arm. That was the moment when they both saw Desmond Ferrier.

He did not see them, or did not seem to. He had just pushed through the crowd to a table on the opposite edge of the floor, and he was striking a match to light a cigarette.

Evidently he had left his hat at the *vestiaire* on the way upstairs, as Brian had left a black hat of the same kind. The glow of the match-flame illumined his face: a strong face, with heavy-lidded eyes and hollows under the cheek-bones.

The nose was thin and aquiline, the mouth an elaborately mocking curve. Except for lines of bitterness or discontent stamped into the forehead or round the mouth, which Brian had observed at the Hotel du Rhône, that face showed as comparatively few signs of age as the ruffled dark hair a little shot with grey.

Clear in the match-flame, briefly kindled, Desmond Ferrier's eyes turned sideways towards a shapely brunette at the head of the dancers.

The tom-toms hammered, the smoky lights shifting colour from white to yellow and then to red. The match was blown out.

"Brian! What's delaying you?"

"Don't you see?"

"Yes, of course. Does it matter?"

"I think it might. The last time I saw him, he was driving home with the rest of the party. A few questions might be in order."

"Brian, no! You wouldn't dare!"

"Now why the devil wouldn't I dare? What special and particular privileges has *he* got?"

Angry voices were crying at them to sit down or get out of the way. Brian looked down at Audrey's eyes; he realized that he had no idea how much truth she was telling him, or how far he could trust her. When Audrey turned and bolted, through a group which made way for her, he followed her less because of indecision than because of a gesture made by Desmond Ferrier.

Ferrier, much more primed with whisky than he had been an hour or so before, was signalling across the floor. And he was signalling to Dr. Gideon Fell.

Meanwhile, as for Audrey . . .

To leave that room was a weight off the lungs and brain. Brian picked up his hat at the *vestiaire*. As he ran downstairs, as the noise receded, he found his wits steadying too. At the foot of the stairs a long and narrow room, set out with chromium chairs and black-topped chromium tables for a lower-floor bar, stretched in brooding half-light to the door giving on the street.

Audrey, flushed but steady of gaze, waited for him by one table with her wrap trailing from her shoulder. There was nobody else in sight.

"All right," said Brian. Automatically he began to shout; then lowered his voice. "Where do you want to go? My car's outside, round the corner from the Place Neuve."

"Your car?"

"Do you still keep forgetting I live here? In a flat not two hundred yards from the Hotel du Rhône? Where do you want to go?"

"I don't want to go anywhere. But I had to get out of that awful stuffiness before I fainted. Can't we—can't we sit down here? Won't this do?"

Again he conquered an impulse to shout.

"Anywhere will do, Audrey, provided you stop telling a pack of lies and explain why your great friend Desmond Ferrier was going to visit you at the Metropole tonight. Is he still expected there, by the way?"

"Mr. Ferrier is not my great friend. And I haven't been telling you any real lies at all," cried Audrey, "even if I didn't give away everything because I promised I wouldn't." A singular luminous fixity glazed over her eyes. "Brian, I do believe . . ."

"You believe what?"

She darted back past him. He thought she was going under the archway and back up the stairs; instead she sat down in a corner under a half-partition shielding the archway at one side, with a black-topped table in front of her and a sign advertising Cinzano above her head.

"You believe what?" Brian repeated. "And what, exactly, is your notion of telling the truth?"

"Mr. Ferrier wanted to talk to me about Eve! That's all there was to it."

"All?"

"All that's important. I told you at the hotel: my father keeps me under such ridiculous surveillance that sometimes I could scream. So I wanted to have twenty-four hours here on my own. Just to be free, if you can understand that! Or can you?"

"Never mind. What happened?"

"I wasn't even sure I wanted to see Phil. I did tell Phil in one letter I might be here a day early. I didn't say I *would*, I just said I might, and where I was going to stay if I did. And then, when my plane got to the airport in the middle of the afternoon, Mr. Ferrier was there waiting for me."

"Desmond Ferrier?"

"Yes." Audrey spoke every word with intense care. "I hadn't told him I should be there; neither had Phil. But there he was. He said he had something terribly important to discuss with me about Eve. He said he would be occupied, unfortunately, until late in the evening; but people didn't keep early hours here as they did in London. Couldn't he, couldn't he pretty please, drop in and take me out for a drink about midnight?"

"Midnight?"

"Brian, this is the truth!"

"I'm not denying it, am I?"

"Well!" Audrey spread out her hands. "He's terribly distin-guished-looking, and he's got a way with him, and he rather sweeps you off your feet. I didn't know what to say, so I said yes."

"One day, my girl, that may be your epitaph."

"For heaven's sake, Brian, will you *ever* take me seriously? There was no harm in it, was there? Anyway, I had hardly been at the hotel for half an hour when Phil rang up to see if I was there, and asked me out to dinner. I couldn't refuse Phil, could I?"

"No, you could not," Brian told her with some restraint. "But you mentioned to him, of course, you were seeing his father later?"

"I didn't, and you know I didn't. There wasn't anything wrong. Mr. Ferrier didn't do anything he shouldn't. That is . . . well, he didn't. But what if Phil got the wrong impression? So I asked Phil, on the 'phone, if he'd take me to a night-club or something after dinner. If he kept me out late, than I could change my mind and I needn't see Mr. Ferrier at all."

Brian drew out a chair and sat down opposite her at the table. The noise from upstairs, only a little diminished, sounded as though the house itself were stamping its feet.

"Now what did Mr. Desmond Ferrier do or say, Audrey, that might be misinterpreted?"

"Do you care? Do you really care?"

On the table there was an ashtray also advertising Cinzano. He resisted the impulse to pick it up and smash it on the floor.

"You're like Mr. Desmond Ferrier," said Audrey, "in more ways than one. Only you don't know it. You'll never learn it. Naturally I was frightened when I thought I saw him get out of the taxi!"

"But it wasn't the actor-hero; it was I. Weren't you disappointed as well as relieved?"

Audrey drew in her breath with a gasp.

"Disappointed? Desmond Ferrier positively infuriates you, doesn't he?"

"I never said—"

"*I* say it, though. And yet you don't mind Phil. You like Phil. Shall I tell you why?"

Brian seized the ashtray, but put it down again.

"Phil's a darling," Audrey continued passionately. "He's terribly good-looking; he's really well-meaning and good-natured; and yet, according to your standards, he's a bit of a fool. You don't mind that. But Mr. Ferrier is clever; and clever men irritate you because you're clever yourself. —Don't you *dare* hit me!"

"I wasn't going to hit you. We weren't discussing the short-comings of my character."

"No; it seems we were discussing the shortcomings of mine. All right! You turned up at the Metropole Hotel, and told me about Eve being accused of murder at Berchtesgaden. Then I heard about Mr. Ferrier's 'joke,' if it is a joke, about Eve wanting to poison him. At dinner . . ."

"Go on!"

"At dinner," and there were tears in Audrey's eyes, "Phil told me about an unexpected guest who'd got to their house at noon today. Phil didn't know much about him. But *I'd* heard of him. His name's Dr. Fell."

"Then maybe we're reaching a point of good sense at last. You saw Dr. Fell, didn't you?"

"Saw him? How in heaven's name could I see him?"

"Well, he's upstairs now. He was at the table next to ours. I rather think he's been watching you."

There was a pause.

"You don't mean a terribly and incredibly large man with a mop of hair over one eye? Who looks so absent-minded he doesn't even seem to know where he is? That's not Dr. Fell?"

"That's the man."

"But—!"

"He really is absent-minded, Audrey. You may have heard of the telegram to his wife: 'Am at Market Harborough; where ought I to be?' Unlike Gerald Hathaway, who never does anything by accident, Gideon Fell seldom does anything by design. On the other hand, finding him in a night-club is a little too unbelievable unless someone begged him to look you over."

It was as though the sheer unfairness of all created things took Audrey by the throat.

"But why? I—I haven't got anything to *do* with this awful business, whatever it is!"

"No; you haven't. And nobody is going to say you have. That's why you're flying back to London tomorrow." Brian stopped, glancing to the right. "Listen!"

Audrey began to speak, but thought better of it.

Roaring waves of applause from upstairs, rising and then dying away to silence, suggested that the jungle number had ended. This rather sinister ground-floor bar, with its framed photographs round the walls, was equally silent.

From beyond the archway, in the direction of the stairs leading up, issued sounds as though a well-grown elephant were trying to descend with the aid of a crutch-handled stick. Next they heard the unmistakable voice of Desmond Ferrier, notable for its jocularity and power as well as its clarity of diction.

"It wouldn't be chivalrous, Doctor, to say my dear wife has a slate loose. No!"

"Harrumph? Hah?"

"However, I tell you straight we're getting towards very dangerous ground." The voice broke off. "Damn it, man, can't you look where you're going? You haven't got the figure for negotiating stairs at night-clubs."

"Sir," intoned the wheezy voice of Dr. Fell, "I have not even got the figure for night-clubs. Especially since I don't know why I am here."

"You're obliging an old friend."

"In what particular way? If your son and Miss Page are engaged to be married—"

Desmond Ferrier spoke with mocking emphasis, like Mephistopheles.

"Ah, but we don't *know* they're engaged. A fairly close study of Miss Page's letters to my son, gained without his knowledge, leads me to believe they soon will be. Anyway, I hope they are."

"Why so?"

"Because it will prevent something unpleasant," replied Desmond Ferrier. "It will prevent my dear wife from poisoning Miss Page, from poisoning herself, or from poisoning me."

"Sir, you are not—?"

"Not serious? You say that too? My dear Dr. Fell! My formidable old King Cole! Stand where you are. Stand just where you are, here at the foot of the stairs!"

The lumbering footsteps ceased. The stub of a still lighted cigarette, flicked hard between thumb and second finger, sailed out from under the archway and lay burning in the middle of the bar floor.

"My dear wife firmly believes I have got my eye on Audrey Page; and, what is worse, that Audrey Page has got her eye on me rather than Phil. Perhaps with a view to divorce and then matrimony to follow."

Here the actor ruminated. Brian, looking past the side of the partition, could see him lifting his eyebrows and pointing a long forefinger at Dr. Fell.

"The first part, mind you," he added, "is not so bloody silly as some of my dear wife's ideas. The girl is very bedworthy. Strictly between ourselves, I shouldn't mind a bash. But I suppose the decencies must be preserved towards one's son's fiancée; she has money, and Phil needs that; finally, my dear wife's jealousy of any woman and all women has reached the point where all I want is some degree of peace and quiet."

"H'm," said Dr. Fell.

"You don't believe that?"

"Sir, I am waiting."

A fluid grin flashed in the semi-darkness beyond the arch.

"Then take the three possibilities in reverse order. One: Eve will poison me. That is as may be; that is with Allah; I can take care of myself. Two: Eve will poison herself."

"Harrumph. And how likely is that?"

"It's possible; my dear wife has threatened it often enough. But I can't see her doing it unless she finds a way of putting the blame on Audrey Page."

The band upstairs began a lively dance-tune. Audrey, as white as a ghost, flung herself across the table and seized Brian's arms as he was about to jump up. The ashtray slid across to the edge.

"Three!" continued Desmond Ferrier. "Three: she will kill Audrey Page. To be quite candid, I don't see that happening either. But it might."

"Oh, ah. And my role in this?"

"Whatever my dear wife may be up to," the other said with great clarity, "find out what it is and stop her. You saw Eve's pathological state today. She ended by carrying vitriol in a perfume-bottle this evening, as I've just told you. Either you or Phil has been close to the Page girl all evening; I've arranged it so. But this can't go on forever."

"My good sir, need it go on at all? Surely it would be simpler to warn Miss Page and send her home?"

"I had thought of doing that tonight. I had meant to warn her. But do I wreck Phil's marriage when my dear wife may only be bluffing?"

All the mockery fell away from Desmond Ferrier's tone.

"Eve and I are broke, Dr. Fell. My dear wife thinks she can return to the stage in triumph. She can't; she is finished. I myself am in no enviable position after years of retirement. The courage fails and the bones soften. I have things on my mind, believe me, which you would not find pleasant to think about."

"Sir," answered Dr. Fell, "I do not doubt it."

"Meaning what?"

The discarded cigarette had burnt itself away on the floor. There was a long, rumbling sniff from Dr. Fell's nose. Suddenly he loomed up huge beyond the partition which shielded Brian and Audrey from view.

Intent, back turned, muttering to himself, Dr. Fell lumbered towards the door at the front of the oblong bar. He had reached out one hand for the knob, shaking his crutch-headed stick in the other, when Desmond Ferrier moved after him.

"Yes, magister?" the latter inquired. "Do you care to state an opinion?"

Dr. Fell fumbled and bumbled at the door, having to set both leaves of it wide open on the street. Afterwards he wheeled round, face red and chins high.

"My mind, sir, is at present so clouded with facts as to be nearly useless. However, regarding Miss Page: does your son know what happened at Berchtesgaden seventeen years ago?"

"Up to tonight he didn't. Eve and I have been too careful. But I told you: with all these people unexpectedly in town, Gerald Hathaway and my dearest Catford and a chap named Innes, he certainly knows now. I don't doubt the Page girl knows too."

"Oh, ah. Yes. We may be sure of it."

"Answer me, magister! Shake not thy gory locks at me!"

"Answer you as to what?"

His back turned, oblivious of Audrey or Brian in the corner, Ferrier made a gesture of cynical self-ridicule.

"Let's have a little honesty, shall we? I can play a picturesque character-part with the best of 'em. Fortunately most people don't know a character-part is the easiest of all to play. But I'm no hero of the big bow-wow, unless it can be useful in getting a woman down to business; I'm a family man gone sour; I've got a bastard of a conscience and it worries me." The deep voice changed. "Did I make a mistake by not warning the little Page girl?"

"Possibly not."

"Possibly?"

"In my humble opinion, at least, Miss Page is in no danger. But, by thunder! It may be very necessary to warn someone else."

"Oh? To warn whom?"

Dr. Fell spoke a name, and nobody heard it. It was lost as he shouldered out into the Place Neuve, under the shadow of those bastions which once supported the fortress-walls of Geneva. Desmond Ferrier followed him. The leaves of the door swung creakily in a rising wind.

For perhaps ten seconds after they had gone Audrey sat motionless, with so curious a shining in her eyes that Brian was both puzzled and alarmed.

In the next moment Audrey slid her knees out from under the table and ran to the door. There she stood looking out, as though deliberately hiding her face. He hurried after her.

"Well, well!" Audrey whispered. "Who was it, my dear? *Who* have they got to warn?"

"I didn't hear. Any more than you. It can't make any difference to you, can it?"

"No; but—"

"How much does it take to convince you? You're not still thinking of joining their merry party, are you? Or do I have to sit up all night at your hotel and guard you until you take the plane?"

"No. No, cross my heart! You don't have to do that."

"If you're lying to me again . . . !"

She turned round in a pallor of earnestness, eyes raised.

"Oh, Brian, do you imagine I'm absolutely silly? There isn't anything on earth that could make me go. I'll do what you want me to. I'll be good. I'll take the first place I can get on a plane for London, whether it's tomorrow morning or later. I promise."

Audrey did not keep her promise.

These events took place on the night of Thursday, August 9. At eight o'clock on the following morning, when Brian had got less than four hours' sleep, the telephone rang in the sitting-room of his flat.

What he heard, tumbling up out of bed, struck the mist from his eyes and brain. It sent him downstairs after his car, to drive roaring out of Geneva by the rue de Lyons and the road to the French border. Only an hour later he discovered how much he cared for Audrey, lies and tricks and all. There was not even time to curse her. For terror gathered round at the Villa Rosalind, and the fangs of a murder-trap closed at last.

VII

The doorbell did not work, or did not seem to work.

"Hullo!" Brian called, and again rapped on the inside of the open door to the hall. "Isn't there somebody at home? *Hullo!*"

There was no reply.

He glanced back at his car, a battered M.G., in the drive before the villa. The silence weighted him down. Though it was only a quarter to nine in the morning, this thundery overcast sky might have been any hour of the day except for the hush in and around these trees on the ridge.

Almost as soon as he had left the outskirts of Geneva, turning right for the main road towards Annecy and Chambéry, the hills began to climb into a steep limestone ridge with almost the effect of mountains. The French frontier, if he remembered correctly, was six or eight kilometres away.

"The Villa Rosalind, monsieur?" his informant had shouted from a bicycle. "But certainly I know the Villa Rosalind."

"Is it far?"

"No, not far."

"How do I find it?"

"It finds itself. A white house, all alone and not high, with a gable in front and a *creuser* at the back."

He was fairly sure that *creuser* meant gully or ravine: an ugly image for this loneliness of trees, and the reality showed lonelier still.

Standing in front of the villa, which was unpretentious and undistinguished, of two storeys and perhaps fourteen rooms, he heard a prowling wind rise in the trees. The gable, or rather gable-outline, was unmistakable above the front door: the gable had a bull's-eye window, of vari-coloured glass, as one gaudy touch to overlook the door.

The wind rose and seethed. To the left of the villa was a lean-to garage for two cars, open and empty. The memory of last night, and particularly of the small hours when he last saw Audrey, returned with almost intolerable vividness now.

It had been past one in the morning when he drove her back to the Hotel Metropole. Audrey, hesitating at the entrance, had put out her hand.

"Good-night, Brian."

"Good-night."

"You—you look depressed."

"I am, a little."

For abruptly, instead of shaking hands as he was doing, there had come over him an impulse to take her in his arms: an impulse so strong as to be terrifying. Perhaps Audrey's intuition sensed this or perhaps not, but the look in her eyes changed.

"What's wrong? You don't still think that Mr. Ferrier and I . . . ?"

"No, I don't," he almost snarled at her. "It was an idiotic notion."

"If anybody 'phones me from the Villa Rosalind, Brian, I won't speak. I shall just not answer the 'phone at all."

"No; not that either. I want you to ring Phil. I promised him you would."

"Ring Phil?" She froze in the dim-lighted doorway of the hotel. "Brian! You didn't tell *him* you thought Mr. Ferrier and I . . . ?"

"God damn it, what sort of swine do you take me for? No. Just say I had a bee in my bonnet, like all these cursed temperamental people; say you're going to London, and you'll write from there. But listen! Don't talk to anybody else at that house. And, above all, don't talk to Madam Eve. Agreed?"

"Brian, what *is* wrong?"

"Agreed?"

"Yes." Her lips quivered. "Yes, yes, yes! Good-night."

He had driven off with a grind and crunch of gears which expressed his mood. Afterwards, in the sitting-room of his small flat on the sixth floor of a new block overlooking the Rhône, he smoked cigarette after cigarette, staring out of the window.

A sleeping-pill was necessary. The noise of tumbling green water in the river, rising to open windows through a city as silent as Pompeii, plagued him with problems of murder or attempted murder before the drug took hold. Nor was it only a problem of murder. He should not have been thinking of Audrey: at least (let's face it) in the way he did think of her.

Only an insistent screaming in his dreams, which became the ring of the telephone in broad daylight, banished bitter thoughts for worse ones. He stumbled into the other room; he had been listening to the frantic voice for twenty seconds before he realized what Audrey was telling him.

"Just a minute! Repeat that, will you?"

"Brian, for heaven's sake don't be cross! I'm only saying. . . ."

"*Where* did you say you are? You didn't go out to that villa after all?"

"I didn't mean to! I swear I didn't mean to!"

"How long have you been there?"

"Since last night. Since about an hour after you left me."

A clock on the low bookshelves, in a room of cream-stucco walls, indicated that it was just eight o'clock.

"You talked to your boy-friend? And he advised . . . ?"

"No. I didn't speak to Phil. They said it would be better if I—"

"Who said?"

"Brian, I'm sorry! I talked to Eve. And—and Mr. Ferrier called for me in a Rolls."

When suspicions return, darker and sharper than they have been in the first place, they are all the worse because you believe you are being played for a fool.

"All right, young lady," said Brian. There was a slightly sick feeling in his stomach. "You've made your choice. Now get out of it as well as you can."

"Brian, are *you* going to desert me?"

About to replace the receiver, he saw the curtains blowing at the windows and tried to clear barbiturate-fumes from his head.

"Audrey, did you plan this last night?"

"No, no, no! Don't be cross; oh, please don't be cross! If you desert me . . ."

"Nobody's deserting you. You've got a perfectly good boy-friend to depend on. Or you should have."

"He's gone to work. He works at Dufresne's Bank in Geneva. And there's nobody else here."

"Nobody else? At eight o'clock in the morning?"

"I mean there's nobody I can trust. You've got to come out and take me away from here. I did something foolish. I—I didn't think there was any danger, not really. But she's out of her mind. She really is out of her mind. Please, please don't leave me with her!"

Thunder-clouds were massing up to the east, throwing their shadows. Brian stared at the telephone.

"Brian! Please! Are you still there?"

"Hang on," he said. "I'll be with you as soon as I can."

And so, at a quarter to nine, on that lonely ridge where the white-painted house loomed with a bull's-eye window of multi-coloured glass, he took a few steps back to study its façade. But this told nothing. There were flowers in window-boxes. There was a strip of brick terrace in front of the open door. Otherwise . . .

"Hullo, there!"

Brian entered the hall.

A certain casual untidiness, despite the breath of polished floors and fresh curtains, lay all about him. A room to the left, a room to the right, opened under broad arches from the central hall with a staircase on the left-hand wall. As though for a deliberate touch of naïveté in the decoration, there was a brightly coloured wall-clock whose pendulum had the figure of a doll-girl in a swing.

The clock ticked loudly. The doll-figure, beaming over one shoulder, switched back and forth. And a voice said: "Yes?"

At the back of the hall a door in the polished panelling, evidently leading to a cross-passage through the width of the villa, had opened with some abruptness. The woman who hurried out was middle-aged and harassed-looking; she appeared to be Swiss, though she addressed him in excellent English.

"Yes? What is it, please?"

"Good morning." Brian restrained a jump of his crawling nerves. "I couldn't seem to—"

"Alas! It is difficult to hear. My fault. You wished?"

"Miss Audrey Page. Where is she?"

"Miss Page is not with us."

Tick-tick went the clock, the little Swiss girl-figure making two arcs of her swing before Brian realized he might be reading a wrong and sinister implication into the words.

"I am so sorry!" said the middle-aged woman, smiling briefly but with the harassed look still there. "Miss Page, I should say, is out. She has gone for a walk."

"A walk? When did she go? How did she seem?"

"It is perhaps half an hour ago. She was happy. I have heard her singing."

Several times more the jovial pendulum swung while Brian tried to control his expression. If that little devil had dragged him out here for a nonsensical reason, for a reason that was a lie, or for no reason at all, this time he was through trying to help.

Finished! Past it! She must . . .

Brian, regaining suavity, caught back his thoughts.

"I am a friend of Mr. and Mrs. Ferrier," he said, stretching truth on his own part. The woman gave him something that was between a bow and a curtsey. "But I understood . . . where is everybody?"

"Sir, we are disturbed today."

"Yes. Where is everybody?"

"Mrs. Ferrier is occupied. Mr. Ferrier and Miss Catford are not yet up. The gentleman with the title has borrowed the Rolls and driven to Geneva. And the very large and stout gentleman with the stick: ah, yes! I think he is in the cellar."

It was unnecessary for the woman, who had started a little, to explain that this last statement had not been a figure of speech. Heavy footfalls could be heard ascending invisible stairs.

The door at the rear of the hall did in fact lead to a transverse passage with back rooms opening from it. Brian observed this as Dr. Gideon Fell, in a black alpaca suit with a string tie and a smear of cobweb across the collar, loomed up in the passage behind the middle-aged woman.

Wheezing, less ruddy of face than he had been for several years, Dr. Fell maneuvered himself sideways out into the hall. He was sunk in obscure speculations; he did not even see Brian or anyone else.

"Bottle!" he said clearly. "Archons of Athens! Bottle!"

"My name is Stephanie," the woman cried out, catching a sort of psychic atmosphere. "I will go now."

And she hurried back into the passage and closed the door.

To Dr. Fell, standing in the hall and leaning on his crutch-headed stick, it seemed vaguely to occur that he had heard a noise or that someone had spoken. He rolled up a massive head, under the mop of hair growing ever more grey. Presently recognition dawned in his face.

"My dear Innes!" he protested, with rumblings of distress and apology. "How do you do? This is an unexpected pleasure at a doubtful time. Er—can I help you in any way?"

"Possibly. Who was the woman who just left us?"

"Forgive me; did a woman just leave us? Tut, now! Describe her!" said Dr. Fell, and woke up thoroughly as Brian did so. "Yes, to be sure! That was Stephanie, the servant."

"The housekeeper, you mean?"

"No. I am instructed to say she is 'the' servant. The only one. So, so? My statement appears to bother you."

Brian looked round him.

"It does, in a way. Dr. Fell, you've seen the cars this household maintains. Is it usual to keep a Rolls and a Bentley, but only one servant to attend to everything?"

"Sir, I am no authority on domestic arrangements in Switzerland."

"Neither am I; but . . . !"

"Hear me!" thundered Dr. Fell, with a violence that concealed apprehension. "This is a country of great charm and high civilization. But I am paying my first visit. I believe it has the lowest homicide-rate in the world. And yet one of the most celebrated of all murder-cases, the death of a certain woman, occurred at Geneva in 1898. Aside from this, unfortunately, my knowledge is mostly confined to misapprehensions gained from the music-hall. Not having either a figure for mountain-climbing or a taste for yodelling in the streets, I have hitherto neglected it. For all I know, the servant-problem may be as acute here as it is in Sunningdale or Hackney Wick. *Explicit;* here endeth."

"I wasn't thinking about the servant problem. Neither were you."

There was a silence.

"Oh, ah!" grunted Dr. Fell, suddenly lowering his defences. "Oh, ah! Well. Yes, it is revealing. Come with me."

He led the way into the drawing-room on the right.

"Last night, in here," he continued, "the amount of theorizing and loose talk about murder was enough to make my flesh creep. But we were civilized about it. By thunder, how civilized we appeared to be!"

"Including Audrey Page?"

"Oh, ah. Especially Audrey Page."

Audrey was not quite civilized, Brian had been reflecting. Neither, he suspected, was Eve Ferrier. Then he tried to drive the thought out of his mind.

Behind this room lay a dining-room where the remnants of several breakfasts still cluttered a table. The drawing-room itself, a comfortable place of overstuffed furniture in white slip-covers, had two high windows facing the front. Two more windows, in the east wall, overlooked a space from which trees had been cleared away to make a formal garden stretching along the side towards a stone wall bordering a ravine at the back.

And between these two windows, above the stone fireplace, hung a half-length portrait of Desmond Ferrier as Hamlet.

A little yellow light burned above it, the only light in the room. Its rich oils gleamed like Ferrier's face. Though the painter's signature was only a blur, you could see the date of 1926. Below the fireplace, on a table, Sir Gerald Hathaway's Guy-Fawkes hat lay beside the open brief-case and the photograph album.

The whole room seemed explosive with presences which were not there.

"Oh, yes!" said Dr. Fell, following Brian's glance. "If you are thinking of your friend Hathaway . . ."

"Where is he?"

"In Geneva, I presume. He took one of the cars. But last night he was all over me."

"What did he say? Did he explain how Hector Matthews could

72

have been poisoned when it wasn't possible to administer any poison?"

Dr. Fell reared up, hammering the ferrule of his stick on the floor.

"Unless we retire to Bedlam, sir, we must accept the word of a reputable German surgeon who swears there was NO drug or poison. We even telephoned to Stuttgart and woke him up."

"Very well: put it in any terms you like! Did Hathaway explain how any man can be made to jump off a balcony by witchcraft or black magic?"

"No, he did not. He merely outlined the factors of the problem; and even then, it seemed to me, he misstated one of them."

"*You* think it couldn't have been done?"

"I think so, yes. But I don't know. Archons of Athens, I don't know!"

Here Dr. Fell, with commendable restraint, lifted his stick but prevented himself from taking a swipe at Hathaway's hat.

"Let me commend to you," he added, "the virtue of humility. Up to about two o'clock this morning, at least, I felt convinced of one thing. If any murder-plot were in fact directed against someone in this house, the intended victim could be only one person."

"Oh? Which person?"

"Eve Ferrier, of course!"

"Why 'of course?'"

"I will not bore you," Dr. Fell said with dignity, "by stating my reasons now. Basically, and perhaps wrongly, I still think them valid." He looked harassed. "Nevertheless, when Miss Audrey Page was in some fashion persuaded to join us here at past one in the morning, these old snake-locks of mine curled with disquiet. Up to that moment I had not realized that Mrs. Ferrier hated her."

Brian stood very still. Outside long windows, over all these craggy hills, he could hear acres of trees seething under the wind.

"Last night—" he began. "Last night you swore Audrey was in no danger!"

"I did not swear it. I said it. How are you aware I said it?"

"Audrey and I overheard you. Never mind that! About an hour ago Audrey rang me up at my flat. . . ."

"Oh, ah? Well?"

"A first I thought it was a game of some kind. Then it scared me. Audrey pleaded to be taken away from here; she said Mrs. Ferrier had gone crazy."

Dr. Fell's expression, his mouth slowly opening under the bandit's moustache, had begun to change. By this time Brian was almost shouting.

"But then, when I did get here, it turned out to be a game after all. Or I thought it was. Audrey did go for a walk, didn't she?"

"I presume so. That was what Stephanie told me."

"Did you see her go?"

"No, I did not."

"Where's Mrs. Ferrier?"

Dr. Fell drew a deep breath.

"Sir, there is no need to alarm yourself! Mrs. Ferrier is in the room they call the study, and most assuredly she is alone. The lady seems obsessed by these memoirs of hers; she declares her 'new life' cannot begin until she has finished the book and told all. Let me repeat—" Here Dr. Fell stopped abruptly, as though at a new thought.

"Where is this study?"

"Upstairs, at the back of the villa."

"Dr. Fell, is there by any chance a balcony?"

Carefully, with an intense and cross-eyed carefulness, Dr. Fell put down his stick on the table beside the brief-case and the album.

"Attend to me!" he begged. "If you are thinking that history may repeat itself, put the notion out of your mind. It may be I have a glimmer of what Hathaway is driving at. Even in the unlikely event that he is right, there is no need to fear what happened before."

"*Is* there a balcony?"

"There is. There are three rooms upstairs at the back of the house, with a balcony running outside all three, and the study in the middle."

"Then I think I'd better go up there."

"Go up if you like. And I have made a fool of myself many times. But the balcony has no connection with this. The same thought had occurred to me; it must be rejected; it has no validity!"

"Probably it hasn't. All the same, I'm going up there."

"Oh, Lord! Oh, Bacchus! Oh, my ancient hat! 'Tell all.' Mrs. Ferrier hides herself away there; she will allow no one to enter. . . ."

Brian did not hear the last of this. He walked with every appearance of casualness into the lower hall, not wishing to make a fool of himself. Then he began to run.

There were sixteen steps, uncarpeted and painted brown, in the staircase along the left-hand wall. If he went up them two treads at a time, he made as little noise as possible. In the upstairs hall, where three closed doors faced him from a cross-passage through the width of the villa, his footsteps clacked so loudly on hardwood that he stopped.

It was all so normal-looking!

A vacuum-cleaner stood beside a linen-cupboard near the head of the stairs. A mop was there too. But it could do no harm if he knocked at the study-door. Brian ran at it, and lifted his hand to knock.

"You shan't have him," said the voice of Eve Ferrier. "Not after all these years. You shan't have him."

It was not loud, beyond that closed door, but it was not normal either.

"*I never looked at him!*" That was Audrey's voice. "*I never once thought of him!*"

"*Don't lie to me. It was all in a diary. I saw it yesterday evening. You pretended one thing, and you were doing another.*"

Brian seized the knob and wrenched it. But the door was locked or bolted on the inside. He shouted something, and never remembered what it was, just before he began to hammer his fist on the panel.

There was no reply. Then footsteps began to retreat, as though towards a window.

The realm of all nightmare, where dreams hold us helpless, and coalesced like a wall in front of Brian Innes. Twice more he banged his fist on the door, hearing the whispery voices continue inside. Next, looking left and right, he ran towards the door on the right.

That was unlocked. He flung it open on a bedroom, with two full-length windows opening towards the back on the balcony he sought. Before five strides had carried him to the window nearest the study next door, he saw an open suitcase—only half unpacked, full of women's clothes—lying on a chair near the foot of the bed.

But this impression went past on a flash before the wet breeze swirled in his face, and he reached the window. Outside lay the balcony, very broad if not very sturdy, with its hand-rail and lath-like supports painted green. Wooden steps, from an opening in its floor, led down to a narrow terrace; and below that, beyond a stone wall, the ravine tumbled outwards in massed trees.

Both Eve and Audrey were on that balcony. One of them did not stay there long.

"Audrey!"

They did not hear him. Both women had their backs turned to him, outlined against a vast dark sky. It was not as though Eve were attacking Audrey; it was as though Audrey were attacking Eve—if, in fact, any person touched her at all.

Audrey was the nearer to him, one hand flung up as though for an invocation. Eve, in a yellow house-coat and black slacks, with high heels that gave her grotesque stature, flung herself suddenly against the hand-rail.

Just as Brian reached Audrey's side, Eve threw out her arms as though to grasp something in the air. A streak of lightning shot jaggedly down the sky. And, at the same moment, Eve pitched head-foremost with her hands at her throat. If she screamed, he did not hear it under the long concussion of the thunder.

Nor did he hear any noise when her body, falling past the lip of the low stone wall on the terrace underneath, was caught and swallowed by trees some sixty feet below. Only the thunder rolled its echoes above the hills. He and Audrey were alone.

ACT TWO

"Any young fool of a player can humbug the town by appearing in tragedy, but comedy's a serious matter. You're not ready for comedy yet."

—DAVID GARRICK

VIII

Some twenty minutes later, with the shock still on his wits, Brian left the study.

He left by the door to the upstairs hall, which had been locked and bolted on the inside. Pain burnt up through his hand when he unlocked it.

Both his hands and his clothes were torn and dirt-stained from climbing down the side of a gully to see what must be seen there among the trees. Heart and lungs ached from the strain of climbing back. But physical shock counted for very little.

The lies in the story he now meant to tell—that is, if he could get away with it—had been planned already. At the door he took a last glance behind him.

"Is there anything contradictory here?" he was thinking desperately. "Anything at all? Anything that might trip me up?"

No!

Still the storm would not break. A wink of lightning opened outside the two open windows, beyond a green-glimmering balcony. Thunder shocked and tumbled up and down the sky.

But nothing in the study, with its apple-green walls and its many books and pictures, had been altered or even touched. On the writing-table, between a glass ashtray and a bowl of roses, the chromium desk-lamp shed down yellow light on that curious pile of manuscript-sheets written in dark blue ink. Eve's uncapped fountain pen lay beside them.

A strong draught rushed through the room, belling out white window-curtains, when he opened the door. A few manuscript-sheets fluttered to the carpet. That didn't matter, he decided. Brian glanced at the mantelpiece, where a clock showed twenty minutes past nine.

Then he closed the door behind him and went to the head of the stairs.

"Dr. Fell!" he called clearly. "Dr. Fell!"

His voice was shaky; he cleared his throat.

But for a moment only the thunder answered.

The upstairs hall was almost dark. From what he had been told, from what he now knew, he could understand the arrangement of rooms on this floor; he could try to remember who slept (or did not sleep) in each one.

At the front of the villa were two bedrooms separated by an enormous bathroom with that bull's-eye window of coloured glass. One bedroom had been Eve Ferrier's, one her husband's; the groping of his wits couldn't place them or straighten them out.

Then the oblong body of the hall, with a bedroom to the left and a bedroom to the right of it. One was Philip Ferrier's, one was Paula Catford's. Then the transverse passage which had a small bathroom at each end; and, behind that, the three rooms with Gerald Hathaway's at the left, the study in the middle, and Audrey Page's to the right.

And all this, Brian reflected, was aside from Dr. Fell's bedroom on the ground floor. The hardwood floor up here, a pale lake, vibrated to the hollow concussion of the thunder.

"*Dr. Fell!*"

"Hey?"

"Come up here, will you?"

Brian backed away from the head of the stairs.

Then, close at hand, a door opened almost in his face.

Paula Catford, in a close-fitting silk dressing-gown, her black hair tumbled from sleep, loomed up ghostlike with towel over her arm and a sponge-bag in her hand. The image she in turn must have seen, of death-pale face and taut jaws, sent her first forwards in a rush and then back with a start.

"You're not Desmond. You're not Desmond at all! Who are you?"

"Miss Catford, please go back to your room."

"Of course; I know! You're Brian Innes." Her eyes dilated. "What is it? There's blood on your hands."

"There's blood on somebody's hands. Keep out of this."

He saw her shocked look; she did not deserve it. But Paula, for all her gentle ways, had a femininity almost as overpowering as Audrey's.

"I'll keep out of it. I won't ask questions. But not unless you wash those cuts and put iodine on them."

"Miss Catford, for God's sake!"

The bathrom at the end of the passage was only ten steps away. Hot water rushed into the wash-bowl. There was no iodine in the medicine-cabinet, but Paula found a bottle of T.C.P. and used nearly half of it on his hands. A whole convulsion of creaks and cracks animated the staircase as Dr. Fell lumbered up. Paula glanced towards him, and back at Brian.

"Now, please! What is it?"

She flung down towel and sponge-bag on the edge of the tub as Brian went out, slamming the door after him. He halted Dr. Fell long enough to take the key from the inside of the study-door, lock it on the outside, and keep the key before hustling the Gargantuan doctor into Hathaway's bedroom on the left of the study as you faced the back.

Once more a door slammed, with its echoes in thunder outside. Even a less observant man than Gideon Fell would have read his companion's face.

"Mrs. Ferrier is dead. She went over the balcony out there," Brian pointed, "and she's as smashed up as anything I ever saw in World War Two. I'm going to tell you what happened; I'm going to confide in you. Then, I warn you, I'm going to tell the police every reasonable lie I can think of."

Dr. Fell, who had been standing with head lowered in a mood between incredulous shock and dismay, opened his mouth to roar. Brian stopped him.

"Wait!" he said curtly.

81

"But, my dear sir—!"

"*Wait.* This was murder. They're going to hear it was murder. That poor damned woman, and I say poor damned woman in more ways than one, was still breathing when I found her. You can't forget things like that."

"Then why should you lie?"

"I'll tell you just what I saw and heard when I ran up here."

Brian did so, from the first sleepwalker's cry of, 'You shan't have him,' to the fall headforemost with Audrey's hand stretched out in touching-distance. Again he saw Eve's back and hands as she plunged over.

The bed in Hathaway's room was still unmade. A large ivory crucifix hung over it. Dr. Fell, wheezing heavily, sat down on the bed.

"Miss Page, then, did not go out for a walk?"

"Yes. She went for a walk. But she came back hardly five minutes before I got here. She was too frightened not to go out, and yet too frightened to stay out when she had gone."

"Sir, will anybody believe that?"

"No. They won't believe a word she says. That's why—" Brian stopped.

"But who saw her return? Did Stephanie see her?"

"Nobody saw her. Look here!"

He strode towards the windows, both of which were closed and locked. He unlocked and raised one of them, so that a gush of air dispelled mustiness as well as a faintly sweetish odour. Dr. Fell, whose shock appeared to be passing as his scatterbrain awoke to ghoulish activity, struggled up from the bed and joined him.

Brian pointed along the balcony towards the far bedroom. He also indicated the green-painted wooden staircase going down through the balcony floor to the terrace below.

"As I understand it, Audrey arrived here for the first time at well before two o'clock this morning. Desmond Ferrier drove her in the Rolls. Mrs. Ferrier gave her that bedroom there."

"I am aware of it, sir."

Anger kindled in Brian Innes like the pain of torn hands and a wrenched shoulder.

"These aren't statements; they're questions. As I also understand it, five of you had breakfast by seven-thirty. You and Audrey couldn't sleep; Hathaway had some errand in Geneva; Philip had to go to wark; and Eve was mad-obsessed by the book that 'told all.' Is that true?"

"Oh, ah. Quite true."

"Then listen!" Brian snapped. "At eight o'clock Audrey rang me up from an extension-'phone in that bedroom. She had been frightened to death ever since she saw Mrs. Ferrier's altered behaviour towards her when she got here."

"One moment." Very gently, poised as though hanging there and hardly breathing, Dr. Fell touched his companion's arm. "Miss Page, then, was not frightened of Mrs. Ferrier before she arrived?"

"Yes; she was frightened before." Brian looked him in the eyes. "It began at the night-club, when we heard Desmond Ferrier tell you—what he did tell you."

And he recounted it, together with everything Audrey had told him at *La Boule Noire*.

"Then why did she consent to come here?"

"I don't know."

"Did Miss Page refuse to explain?"

"No, she did not refuse. But a few minutes ago she was so hysterical that she barely made sense." Brian paused. "You may say, of course, that she has been having an affair with Desmond Ferrier. That she couldn't resist him. That he had only to whistle and she ran here immediately, after promising me she wouldn't. That's what they'll all say."

"*Gently! Go gently!*"

Brian clenched his fist, feeling blood ooze between the fingers with the odour of antiseptic stinging his nostrils.

"She denies," he said, "that there was anything, anything at all, between her and Desmond Ferrier or any other man. She denies it incoherently but absolutely."

"Do you believe that?"

"Yes. I believe it."

"Yet it must have been a powerful reason which brought her here?"

"Yes. It must have been. I suppose so."

Brian's gaze did not waver. Dr. Fell, fiercely intent, made a little gesture as of one who encourages. And Brian went on.

"At eight o'clock, I repeat, she was in that bedroom there. Audrey knew Mrs. Ferrier was in the study, writing furiously at this book which 'tells all.' Audrey says she could 'feel her.' She says she couldn't bear to be near her. You see that outside staircase?"

"I see it."

"Audrey put on shoes with heavy crêpe soles. She crept out and down the stairs: inches at a time, she says, aching in case she made a noise. By the time she had reached the terrace down there, she tried to act defiantly in spite of the fact that she ran. She hummed or sang; she isn't sure what it was, as you or I might whistle in a graveyard. That must have been the singing Stephanie spoke about.

"Anyway, she ran. She walked along the main road, south-west, towards the French border and the Haute-Savoie. She couldn't stay away, because she was expecting me. At the same time, when she returned, she couldn't resist the frightening fascination of Mrs. Ferrier's presence. She couldn't resist torturing herself, as you or I might press an aching tooth to feel it hurt. She returned by way of the balcony. She crept along to peer in at the window unobserved. And Mrs. Ferrier caught her."

"Caught her," repeated Dr. Fell.

Smoky, wet-looking clouds moved along a grey horizon above the tossing of the trees. Brian stared at the balcony. In imagination he saw Audrey there: he saw her eyes and her mouth, and the brown tweed suit and the tan stockings and crêpe-soled shoes.

Brian drew a deep breath.

"Caught her," muttered Dr. Fell, who seemed miles away in a tense dream. "Go on!"

"Mrs. Ferrier had been writing. She looked up and saw Audrey. She shouted at Audrey, and dragged her into the study by main force. I interrupted while that lunatic scene was still going on. When Audrey heard me pound at the door and call out, she ran for the balcony. Mrs. Ferrier ran after her."

"And then?"

"Let me quote Audrey's exact words. '*I never touched her. It was as though the lightning struck her, and she threw out her arms and went over.*' That's the end of it. That's how Eve Ferrier died."

"Where is Miss Page now?"

"She's gone. I sent her away."

"Where did you send her?"

"Look here: Audrey was in no fit state to talk to anyone, let alone the police. She said they wouldn't believe her. She said they wouldn't believe me. She was quite right."

"Sir," and the ferrule of Dr. Fell's stick banged on the floor, "they would NOT believe her. That is true; but it is not the point now. Where did you send her?"

"To my flat. I gave her the key. And I sent her by way of the Hotel Metropole."

"By way of the Hotel Metropole?"

"Yes. For some reason, when Desmond Ferrier picked her up at the hotel, she didn't give up her room. She left her luggage there: everything except one suitcase, which is in the bedroom here. She said she was going back—"

"Going back? Did the young lady explain why she did that?"

"No. Don't snort! It gave me the way out to provide her with a story."

Dr. Fell waited. Brian moved away from the window, closing his eyes and then opening them again.

"Eve Ferrier's manner towards Audrey changed from the moment she got here. Audrey was scared; and everybody saw it. Correct?"

"And if it is?"

"So her story is that she bolted away from here at not much past eight o'clock this morning. She was seen to go out; nobody saw her return. Or, at least, we hope nobody saw her. Officially, she was never in that study at all. She doesn't deny Eve Ferrier had a lot of mad ideas, because they'll question her about it; her story is that she ran away before anything had happened. And I testify Mrs. Ferrier was alone in the study."

"Alone?"

"Yes."

"But you heard two women quarreling in there. That was why you banged on the door and ran through the other bedroom to the balcony. How do you account for your own conduct?"

"Don't you see? My story is that Mrs. Ferrier was talking to herself, rather wildly—I couldn't distinguish any words—and didn't answer my knocking. So I ran through in time to see her fall."

"Oh, ah? Suppose the police ask how anybody could have pushed or thrown her from the balcony, if she was all alone there?"

"Dr. Fell, nobody *did* push or throw her!"

"Nevertheless, suppose they ask that? Or think you yourself must have attacked her?"

"Then they've just got to think so, that's all. But it isn't what happened. That woman was poisoned: just as, in some mysterious way, Hector Matthews was poisoned at Berchtesgaden seventeen years ago! With an honest investigation, and there'll be an honest investigation in this country, they'll discover the truth."

"Purely for the sake of argument, what if they find no drug or poison was used? What then?"

"God knows," Brian said after a pause. "Understand this!" he added bitterly. "I'm not taking any self-righteous attitude about lying. I'm dead sure that's what really happened; but it's not the real reason why I say it. Now go on! Preach a moral lecture; call me a selfish and insensitive swine. If you choose to tell the police and give the show away, I can't stop you and I couldn't even blame you. But there it is."

Dr. Fell, who had been turning away with a more startled and cross-eyed expression than any he had yet shown, suddenly wheeled back and reared up.

"Tell the police? Give the show away?"

"Yes."

Dr. Fell surveyed him up and down.

"Sir," he declared with polished courtesy, "you might be called many things, all of them more temperamental than you believe yourself to be. But selfish or insensitive you are not. And do you really take me for such a pious Goody Two-shoes as all that?"

"I only said—"

"Hear me!" interrupted Dr. Fell. "Is formal observance of law so mighty and potent a ritual? Does upholding the status of Big Brother count one featherweight in the balance against protecting the foolish or shielding the innocent? The strong ones of this earth, the Gerald Hathaways for instance, can take care of themselves. But the weaker ones, the Audrey Pages and the Desmond Ferriers . . ."

"Ferrier? Are you calling him weak?"

"By all the Archons, I am! But I promised him help. To conceal the presence of Miss Page, in my humble opinion, is the best possible way of doing that. Now we had better have a look at the study."

"Dr. Fell, we can't leave her down there any longer. We've got to ring the police!"

"In a very short time, yes. Meanwhile, since we insist on committing perjury, there is no headlong rush to commit it. Will you lead the way?"

Instantly Brian stepped out through the open window. The other more gingerly followed.

Though not a drop of rain had fallen, the continual thunder still rolled and split its echoes down the sky. Their legs felt shaky on the open height over a gulf. The wind swooped into their faces, blowing the ribbon on Dr. Fell's eyeglasses as he lumbered towards the two windows of the study.

"Now then! Just where did this happen? Where did Mrs. Ferrier go over?"

"Here." And Brian took up a position about four feet to the left of the far window, facing the hand-rail. "Just where I'm standing now. With her back turned."

"With her back turned towards Miss Page?"

"Yes."

"Could you see her face?"

"No. Not at any time."

"Take care!" Dr. Fell said sharply. He touched the hand-rail. "This balustrade is uncommonly shaky. A sudden shock against it might send anybody over, and Mrs. Ferrier was a tall woman. Hang it all, though! It should have been at least waist-high for her?"

"She was wearing high heels, as I told you."

"With slacks? Is that customary for any woman?"

"Not unless she's in a very unusual state of mind. Which we know Mrs. Ferrier was."

"Which we know! Which we know! Oh, ah! Now be good enough to describe what happened. Describe it again."

While Brian repeated it, Dr. Fell glanced past him through the window into the study. He looked at the big writing-table against the east or left-hand wall, where a chromium desk-lamp illumined a pile of manuscript-sheets in dark blue ink. His gaze travelled across to the west wall and the mantelpiece, where a white-faced clock pointed at twenty minutes to ten. He looked towards the closed door opposite the windows.

And then, in a terrifying instant, values shifted. Over Dr. Fell's face went an expression of such utter and complete dismay that Brian, who had known him for fifteen years, felt cold to the heart.

"What is it? What's got into you now?"

"Sir, I greatly fear—" Dr. Fell began. His throat seemed to close up. "A while ago, I believe," he added with some violence, "you locked that door and put the key in your pocket? Will you unlock the door now? Unlock it!"

"Unlock the door? Why?"

"Because I am afraid," replied Dr. Fell, "that I was terribly wrong and Hathaway was terribly right. Whether we like it or not, Miss Audrey Page can't be kept out of this affair after all."

"*What are you saying?*"

"I say what I mean: no more and no less. You have just stated a factor that changes everything. You cannot possibly tell the story you had meant to tell."

Whereupon, with a rush of emotion like the rush of the thunder, he in turn saw Brian's face.

"In the name of Almighty God," Dr. Fell said in a voice he very seldom used, "will you try to believe me for Miss Page's sake? You must not deny she was here or that she saw Mrs. Ferrier fall to death. If you deny it, you let that girl walk straight into a trap and you are doing the very thing you have been trying to avoid. Will you take my word for this?"

"No, I will not. If there is so much objection to falsifying—"

"On the contrary! There is none. But you must not use *that* story, which will get her arrested, when I can provide you with another. Listen to me!"

The savagery of his tone struck Brian silent.

"What is one really damaging point against Miss Page? It is the open quarrel with Eve Ferrier, the accusation that she was stealing Mrs. Ferrier's husband, the row which threatened to end in violence. This must never be told; it should not come out in any case because it is so damnably misleading."

"For the last time—!"

"WILL you listen?"

The ferrule of Dr. Fell's stick banged on the floor of the balcony.

"Eve Ferrier," he said, "made no accusation in front of the others. Miss Page *was* frightened, as everybody knew. She *did* telephone you at eight; this you admit freely. Now shall I tell you the rest of what you say?"

"Go on."

"You arrived here to take her away. You spoke to me, and I told you where to find her room. You went upstairs to her room. You rapped at *that* door; you entered when there was no answer. Miss Page was standing at the window and looking to the left in horror. You ran to her side in time so that both of you saw Mrs. Ferrier fall.

"There is no unconvincing tale of a woman 'talking to herself' in the study. Instead it provides an alibi, both for you and for Miss Page, which no questioning can shake if you hold to it. Is this, or is it not, a better account than your own?"

Ten seconds crawled by, while thunder assaulted the balcony.

"Yes. Yes, it's better." Brian's old sardonic mood surged back. "You've had more experience, of course. But Audrey ran away! And I told her to!"

"Oh, no. *I* told her."

"You—"

"The girl was shocked and hysterical; she could do no good. I advised her to leave while you and I took charge. I am slightly acquainted with M. Aubertin, the Director of the Police; he has visited London half a dozen times. Can you trust me in the matter, as you and others have trusted me before?"

"It's not a question of trusting you! Dr. Fell, do you know the real explanation of this business?"

"For some part, yes. I think I do."

"Will you tell me that explanation?"

"Yes! As soon as we can leave here without suspicion, I must question Miss Page and you will learn the truth. I could not hide it if I would; everybody will learn in less than twenty-four hours. If you agree, I can protect the girl with whom you are so obviously in love. If you refuse—"

"God's truth, how can I refuse? But Audrey—!"

"Oh, ah! Miss Page must agree with the story." Dr. Fell wheezed heavily, moving his shoulders and groping within his scatterbrain. "She left here, you said, at about twenty minutes past nine. What, exactly, did you tell her to do?"

"Audrey can't drive a car, or she could have used mine. But it's only three kilometres, less than two miles, to the outskirts of Geneva. She was to walk there and get a taxi."

"We must speak to her before the police do. You understand that?"

"That's simple. She can't be far away. I can drive after her and—"

"No! Every move of ours will be scrutinized later. Never chase a witness after you have dismissed her as guilelessly unhelpful. Somebody will report it and the authorities are going to wonder. By the same token we can't leave a message at the Hotel Metropole or have her ring this house. Did you tell her not to speak a word of this to anyone until you saw her?"

"Yes."

"Then that should suffice. Or I hope it will. I hope so!"

And yet Brian, as the other persuaded him through the window into the study, hesitated amid all the fangs of uncertainty.

"Oh, ah!" grunted Dr. Fell. "If you say you have no relish for this affair, your liking is still ecstatic compared to mine." He spoke with a kind of sick violence. "But I failed miserably to prevent one tragedy. There must not be another. Now unlock that door before they think us the conspirators we are. And if, unfortunately, we must probe into Miss Page's relations with a certain actor . . ."

Conspirators.

Another tragedy.

Miss Page's relations with a certain actor.

The girl with whom you are so obviously in love . . .

Well, it was true he was in love with her; he couldn't deny it to himself, now, though he might deny it to others. And Audrey's image never left him.

The light of a chromium desk-lamp shone down on a manuscript, leaving most of the study in shadow. Brian went over to the door, taking the key out of his pocket. An enormous crash of thunder, rattling the glass ashtray and the bowl of roses and every picture-frame round the walls, struck at them as he unlocked the door.

Just outside, knuckles raised as though to knock, stood Desmond Ferrier.

IX

Desmond Ferrier.

He wore pyjamas, slippers, and a brocaded dressing-gown. Tall, unshaven, hair tousled in morning light, he looked every minute of his fifty-eight years. But the intense vitality remained, though the swagger and the smile had vanished.

It was almost as though, behind that lifted hand, his eyes awaited or expected something he dreaded to hear.

The echoes of the thunder died away. Dr. Fell, who had been standing with his back to the windows, lumbered forward in a mood of heavy and lowering distress.

"Sir," he said gravely, "I have news which will come as a very unpleasant shock. And yet, in a certain sense, it may be that the news is not unexpected. Your wife, as you see, is not here."

The Adam's apple moved in Ferrier's long throat. A fixed kind of look, almost a glare, sprang into his eyes before it was masked.

"Last night," continued Dr. Fell, "you said Mrs. Ferrier might try to kill Audrey Page, might try to kill herself, or might try to kill you. I believed, if you recall, that the danger was to Mrs. Ferrier."

The famous voice went a little off-key.

"Eve's a decent old girl. Always has been. What is it?"

"However, even if I warned you, it does not excuse my stupidity in failing to see—"

"Oh, so-and-so! What's happened?"

"No!" said Dr. Fell, as the other took a step forward. "Not in here. Let us go down to the drawing-room, and I will tell you. Mr. Innes!"

"Well?"

Brian spoke curtly as he watched Ferrier. When he thought of Audrey Page in this man's arms, his mind grew as poisoned with jealousy as Dr. Fell's had grown poisoned with self-reproach. And yet he couldn't really hate the man, and he wondered why. Then he saw something else.

Paula Catford, a look of horror and compassion on her face, stood not five feet away in the hall. She was fully dressed, her nails red-varnished, her hands clasped together.

"Mr. Innes," roared Dr. Fell, "in Miss Page's bedroom there is an extension telephone. Be good enough to get in touch with the Bureau of the Police at Geneva. Ask to speak to M. Gustave Aubertin, and say you have a message from me. No matter how difficult it may be, have no traffic with anyone else. When you speak to M. Aubertin, tell him as much or as little as you think fit."

"Sweet Christ!" said Desmond Ferrier, from deep in his throat. "Have you got to do that?"

"Yes!" retorted Dr. Fell. "You asked for my help, and you shall have it. But this must be done in good order." He controlled himself. "Mr. Innes?"

"I'm listening, thanks."

"Speak to M. Aubertin, please, and then join us downstairs."

Emotional currents, in that group, were as heavy as the pressure of the freak weather. Brian stalked out, suddenly conscious of his stained and dishevelled appearance. He went into Audrey's room, or the one they called Audrey's room, and closed the door.

It was here that Audrey had told him most of her stammered, faltering story. The one small suitcase she had brought—open, but not fully unpacked—lay where he had first seen it on a chair near the foot of the bed.

She had committed no murder, of course. That ought to have satisfied him. But it didn't.

The telephone was on a small table at the head of the bed. Reaching out to pick it up and dial zero, he hesitated.

A whole genie-bottle of images swam in his head. Audrey's presence remained as vivid as Paula Catford's eyes or as Eve Ferrier's haggard air. It was the recollection of the unmade bed in Hathaway's room and of the ivory crucifix above it, curiously enough, which gave him the strongest sensation of evil flowing out from a source he could only feel: not see.

Stop this!

The time must be getting on. At his flat, in the Quai Turrettini, Madame Duvallon would have come in at nine-thirty to get his breakfast. . . .

Breakfast, Madame Duvallon. Madame Duvallon, that stout and hearty elderly woman, who was as loyal as a bull-terrier and could be trusted with anything.

Brian sat down on the bed and dialled his own number. The ringing-tone had hardly buzzed before he heard Madame Duvallon's voice.

"It is you, monsieur?"

"It is I, madame. No, no, I shall not be there! But listen: a young lady will be there, I cannot tell how soon. Will you wait for her, if necessary? Will you give her an important message?"

He hardly needed the instant attention or shivering assurance.

"Say to her, 'My dear, our plans are changed.' Say that she is not to leave the flat or speak to anyone until I arrive. She is not to speak by telephone or open the door if anyone rings. Madame Duvallon! When you yourself go, leave your latch-key in the mailbox downstairs. Is it understood?"

Though Madame Duvallon's nerves must have screamed with curiosity, you would never have told it from her poised voice.

"Very well understood, monsieur! That is all?"

"Except this. Should you ever be questioned about the young lady, you never saw her and you have never even heard of her. That is all, thanks."

Brian sat back.

His next call, to the police, took him surprisingly little time. For all the delay he expected, he was soon speaking to a sharply intelligent voice whose suavity changed to concern. Afterwards he hurried downstairs. What he heard from the drawing-room, before he could see anyone, halted him in the middle of the staircase.

"—and that, sir," said the voice of Dr. Fell, "is a reasonably full account of Miss Page's and Mr. Innes's testimony. That is what they saw from the window of the bedroom."

Desmond Ferrier, though shaken, uttered a ringing oath.

"So that's it! Just like old Hector What's-his-name at Berchtesgaden?"

"Apparently, and I stress the word apparently, that is the case."

"Eve was alone?"

"In a certain sense, yes."

"So the poor old girl committed suicide? Chucking herself off the balcony?"

"At first glance, and also let us stress at first glance, your wife could have killed herself in that particular way."

"Then why do you want to question *me?* Anyway, I can't tell you anything about this morning. I was sound asleep until Paula knocked on the door and said she thought there was something wrong."

"That's true," cried the voice of Paula Catford.

"Sir," roared Dr. Fell, "I am not much concerned with this morning or even late last night. I am concerned with certain events from yesterday afternoon to yesterday evening. Above all I am concerned with certain diversions (let us politely call them affairs of the heart!) which have been occupying a number of people."

Dead silence.

The drawing-room, in semi-darkness except for the yellow light above the portrait of Desmond Ferrier as Hamlet, had taken on a somewhat wild quality like that of storm-clouds outside the eastern windows.

Ferrier, nervous and drawn of countenance, stood beneath the portrait with his back to the fireplace. Paula stood at one side of him. Dr. Fell, throned in an overstuffed chair whose white slip-cover stood out against gloom, sat partly facing them and held an album of photographs. On the mantelpiece lay Sir Gerald Hathaway's hat.

Brian's footfalls were distinct on hardwood as he entered. Dr. Fell addressed him without turning round.

"Did you reach Aubertin?"

"I did. M. Aubertin presents his most distinguished compliments, and says he'll be here in half an hour."

Ferrier snatched his hands out of the pockets of the brocaded dressing-gown.

"Half an hour? They're really going to—?"

"Why shouldn't they?" asked Brian. "He also presents *you* his most distinguished compliments, and his condolences on the death of . . . the rest of it."

"I'm a bastard and I admit I am," said Ferrier, looking straight at Brian. "But there's no need to stress it as much as that."

"Nobody is stressing it. Nobody is even saying it."

"Have a drink?"

"Not now, thanks."

It was Dr. Fell who intervened at this point.

"Let us return," he suggested, "to Mrs. Ferrier. And to a certain flaming love-affair. And to what happened yesterday that led towards an explosion. We have just half an hour for talking frankly among ourselves."

"All right, if you insist." Ferrier took a packet of cigarettes out of his dressing-gown pocket. "Is it important?"

"Is it important? Oh, my eye! You are an intelligent man, my dear sir. You know it is."

"Well?"

"What happened yesterday," said Dr. Fell, "I have tried to piece together from various matters that were told me and others I overheard and some I saw. I need not detail them. But much of it is still dark and o'ermisted.

"Indulge me, now! I arrived at this house about noon. You and your wife and I, only the three of us, had an excellent lunch at half-past one. Your wife was then in the gayest of spirits. She was almost radiant. You remember?"

Ferrier nodded. He took out a cigarette, but did not light it.

"Some time afterwards you made your excuses, without saying where you were going, and drove away in the big car. I believe," Dr. Fell raised his eyebrows, "I believe you drove to the airport and met Miss Audrey Page?"

"Yes."

"You also asked whether you might drop in at Miss Page's hotel, about midnight the same evening, so that you could talk to Miss Page about your wife?"

"Yes."

Taking a lighter out of his pocket, Ferrier snapped it on and touched it to the cigarette and inhaled with a great gust: all in one flashing movement, his face illumined under the illumined portrait.

"This was, in fact, to warn Miss Page that Mrs. Ferrier was in a dangerous mood of jealousy?"

"Yes."

Paula, in a primrose-yellow dress contrasting with a curious steely expression about her face, went over and sat down on the sofa opposite Dr. Fell. Ferrier did not even seem to see her.

"But you did not keep your appointment for midnight? You did not warn Miss Page?"

"No. You know damn well I didn't. I was with you at midnight, and I told you about it anyway."

"Good!" said Dr. Fell.

"The rest of that same afternoon," he went on gently, "I myself spent here in the drawing-room with Mrs. Ferrier. She remained in the best of spirits. She brought down her press-cutting books; one of them is still here in the room.

"You returned before six o'clock. Your son, Philip, had already returned from Dufresne's Bank. Officially, neither you nor your wife was supposed to know of Philip's plan for taking Miss Audrey Page to dinner. Now Mrs. Ferrier knew it; she confided it to me, with much pleasure and some archness, in the course of the afternoon. Did *you* know of it?"

"My dear old boy," said Ferrier, with a broad and curling grin, "I hardly see how it matters."

"Then let me refresh your memory. I am leading up to the explosion."

The glow of Ferrier's cigarette pulsed and darkened.

"Let us imagine," said Dr. Fell, his eyes unwavering, "that it is yesterday evening at shortly before seven. Philip has gone upstairs to dress. You and Mrs. Ferrier and I are not changing: no, we are having dinner at home. We are here in the drawing-room, again the three of us. You and Mrs. Ferrier are having a cocktail, and I a glass of sherry."

"Speaking of that point—"

"No!"

Dr. Fell's uplifted hand halted Ferrier as he started for a sideboard between the two front windows. The latter remained where he was, still smiling.

"I will drop the present tense," said Dr. Fell. "Quite suddenly you put down your cocktail glass on that coffee-table over there. You said to your wife, 'My dear, I have just remembered that I must go out.' She cried at you, 'You must go out before dinner?' 'Alas,' you said, 'I must go out for dinner itself.'

"There then followed," pursued Dr. Fell, "what I shall be forgiven for describing as a blazing and embarrassing family row. You were accused of deserting your guest. I protested, with truth and vehemence, that it did not matter.

"Philip, on his way to the Hotel Metropole, attempted to intervene and was sent packing in the Bentley. Your wife asked you flatly where you were going. You smiled, as you are smiling now, and said you meant to have dinner alone. Presently you drove away in the Rolls-Royce. Where did you go, by the way?"

Ferrier drew deeply at the cigarette.

"I had dinner alone," he answered.

"Where?"

"I'm afraid I've forgotten. By the way, Fell, was this when I decided to murder my wife?"

"Oh, no," said Dr. Fell.

He sat back in the chair.

"If we adopt a joking tone, sir," he added politely, "the others must still understand we are both deadly serious. You and I know that, don't we?"

"We do."

"Your wife was not yet angry. Not really angry. Not raging, and half out of her mind. That had yet to come. When Mrs. Ferrier and I sat down to another admirable meal prepared by the maid, she was under a strong nervous tension: no more than that. I beg you to observe she did not really hate anyone, including Miss Audrey Page.

"But she was wondering. She was speculating. I wished I could read her eyes. As we sat here having coffee after dinner, I in this chair and she on the sofa where Miss Catford is sitting now, something else occurred to her. She sprang up without a word, and walked out of the room.

"I was not disturbed. Life among artists can be a fascinating business. How long a time elapsed, while I sat and mused in my customary half-witted fashion, it is impossible to estimate. It may have been an hour, or it may have been very much longer. But I was somewhat startled to hear high heels rapping down the stairs where informal low heels had gone up. I glanced round towards the hall there. Need I tell you what I saw?"

Two voices spoke out.

Paula Catford said: "No; it won't be necessary to tell us."

Desmond Ferrier snapped: "Paula, my sweetie-pie, you'd better take a little care. You may not know what you're saying."

"Oh, I think I know what I'm saying!"

Paula, all slenderness, her clear complexion flushed under steady hazel eyes, got up from the sofa and addressed Dr. Fell.

"You saw poor Eve in a raging fury, didn't you? She had put on a blue-and-silver evening-gown. She absolutely reeked of perfume, as she usually does nowadays. Probably she'd rung for a taxi without even telling you. The taxi had driven up, and she ran out and drove away. Isn't that so?"

Dr. Fell leaned forward.

"Bull's-eye!" he said. "Whang in the centre of the target. Now, then! Can you draw any further inferences from the facts?"

"The time of night," declared Paula, with the startled look of one remembering, "the time of night was about ten-thirty. Wasn't it? Eve took a taxi and drove straight from here to the Hotel du Rhône, where the rest of us saw her."

"Good! I was not at the Hotel du Rhône, but I have no doubt you are right. Anything else?"

"Eve did that because she had just thought of something—or, more probably, had just discovered something or got proof of something that sent her into such a rage. Of course! We should all have seen it for ourselves, last night, if we hadn't been arguing so much about how a murder could have been committed at Berchtesgaden!"

"Well, well, well," observed Desmond Ferrier. He flung away

his cigarette into the fireplace. "Don't stop there, sweetie-pie. Don't turn it up now. Go just a little step further, Paula, and you'll land me in more trouble than Job ever knew with all the boils on his bottom."

Paula started back. "What on earth are you talking about? Trouble? How?"

"Ask Dr. Fell."

"Sir," Dr. Fell said with fiery embarrassment, "I take no pleasure in all this."

"Ask him, Paula!"

"Yes? What is it?"

"No sooner had Mrs. Ferrier driven away in the taxi," said Dr. Fell, "than her husband here came roaring back in the Rolls-Royce. He could scarcely have missed her by a minute. Those two cars must have passed each other close to this house. I encountered new surprises and had new glimpses into the artistic temperament."

"In what way?"

"When I told Mr. Ferrier what had happened, he went off the deep end too. He insisted on driving straight back to Geneva, and taking me with him. He would answer no questions or meet no objections. He said that Miss Audrey Page was at a night-club off the Place Neuve; he left me at the night-club, ostensibly to 'watch' Miss Page, while he followed his wife to the Hotel du Rhône."

Paula's eyes first widened and then narrowed.

"But that's absurd!"

"What's absurd about it?" inquired Ferrier. "There are some things so obvious I didn't even see them when I was gassing about them. Just ask yourself some of the questions the coppers are bound to ask me."

After a moment of being shaken, it was plain he had begun to take heightened and super-theatrical pleasure in his own position.

"How did I know Eve had gone to the Hotel du Rhône? That's one question. What had Eve discovered, undoubtedly in my bedroom, which made her run to that same hotel in pursuit of me? Above everything else, if I really believed Eve might try to kill Audrey Page because Audrey and I were having a roll in the hay, why did I let Audrey come to this house last night?"

Outside the windows of the drawing-room, above a formal rose-garden, the sky had become so dark that it was barely possible for them to see each other's faces by the little yellow light over the portrait.

Thunder-thick air pressed down the heat and would release no burst of rain. Paula Catford pressed her hands against her cheeks.

"*Audrey Page?*"

"Don't be wilfully obtuse, Paula."

"I am not being obtuse, wilfully or otherwise. I am asking—"

"The cops' answer," Ferrier said brutally, "may well be murder. Eve thought, or told me she thought," and his eyes speculated, "I was trying to beat Phil's time and marry the girl myself. I wasn't supposed to be in love with her, but then I never am in love with 'em, am I? So Audrey and I got together and settled Eve's hash. It's happened before, once or twice in this world. Isn't that the position, Dr. Fell?"

"Oh, ah! Yes. I greatly fear they may have some such notion."

Paula's tongue crept out and moistened her lips.

"But you—you didn't do it, did you? My God, you *didn't?*"

"No, I did not. I hadn't a damn thing to do with it. The point is, how do I answer the charge when they say I did?"

"You—you *weren't* having an affair with her? Audrey Page? That over-intense and over-romantic young lady who's so mad about Brian Innes that she let herself be persuaded to come here in the hope he'd follow and take her away?"

Nobody spoke for fully ten seconds.

Dr. Fell, leaning back, was watching Desmond Ferrier with absorbed attention. Ferrier's smile had grown broader and more than a little cruel. But Brian, who hardly saw either of them, strode towards Paula. And she turned to face him.

"Now really, Mr. Innes!"

"Yes? You were saying?"

"Do I have to say it? Aren't you, who must be a reasonably civilized sort of person, the one who's being a little obtuse now? That's what the girl did, you know. Every word she said about you, and I daresay every word she said to you as well, made that plain to anyone. When she 'phoned this morning and actually asked you to take her away, surely you guessed it for yourself?"

X

"Didn't you guess it, then?" Paula insisted in a louder voice.
It was though she talked less at him than at herself, a lonely and slender figure, outlined against a long window. But she met Brian's gaze steadily.

"Forgive me if I sound rude," she begged. "It happens to be true. A woman like Audrey Page can't really fall for anyone except someone older than herself and someone she can glamourize. Like you. Or like that man over by the fireplace who thinks everything so very funny. Didn't it *ever* occur to you: about yourself?"

"Yes, it occurred to me," Brian said honestly. "It occurred to me more than once. I hoped it was true; I'm still hoping so. But it seems to me the person who gets the poor deal in this business is Philip Ferrier."

The man by the fireplace laughed.

"Never try to be a gentleman, old boy. It doesn't pay. Take what you can get and be thankful you can get it." His tone changed. "Marriage is a different thing, though. We'll have to prevent you from marrying her."

"You think you can?"

"I think I can try."

Paula, as though she found all men past hope when their vanity or arrogance happened to be roused, went on to something that appeared to concern her more.

"Desmond, stop this! If poor Eve thought you wanted Audrey Page, it explains a lot I couldn't understand. I couldn't understand why the girl was so frightened. I couldn't understand why Eve was so sweet about her until Audrey actually walked in here. But stop acting, please! This isn't funny in the least."

"Acting, eh? Do you imagine I think it's funny?"

"You seem to."

"Then think again, angel-face. I'm laughing, if you could call it that, because my story is bloody silly and yet every word of it is the truth. I've played parts like this; I never expected to do a real one. Question me yourself: why don't you?"

"Desmond, I . . ."

"Come on, Paula! Those big eyes of yours don't fool anybody. You've pried some statements out of people who never knew how indiscreet they were being until they saw themselves quoted on the front page. Have a whack at it; try your technique on me!"

"Desmond, I can't! Not now."

"Then somebody ought to do it, just to see how I behave." Ferrier turned a savage face towards Brian. "What about you, old boy? Care to question me?"

"There's nothing I should like better."

"Then fire away. That is, unless Dr. Fell . . . ?"

But Dr. Fell was saying nothing. Absorbed, intent, a trifle eerie-looking, his gaze moved from Ferrier to Paula and back to Ferrier again. If it badly disturbed Paula, it had no effect at all on the latter. Ferrier's personality, brocaded dressing-gown and all, dominated the room like Othello's.

"The oracle and augur is silent. He won't be drawn. The field is clear for the paint-mixers and the lesser amateurs. That is, if you know how to question a witness."

"I'll try." Whereupon Brian, in rage and haste, blundered at the very start. "Were you, or weren't you, having an affair with Audrey?"

"Ho! That's all he can think of!"

"Were you, or weren't you?"

"No, I was not. Anything else?"

"Yes. Mr. Ferrier, do you keep a diary?"

There was a silence as sudden as the stroke of a gong. Paula looked up quickly. Dr. Fell's eyes moved back and forth.

"Yes, I keep a diary. I've kept one for twenty years. Why do you ask?"

"Are you willing to hand that diary over to the police?"

"No, naturally I'm not. Any more than I want it published in the Continental edition of the *Daily Mail*. Who would?"

"You left this house just before seven o'clock yesterday evening, and didn't return until half-past ten. Where did you go?"

"As I told Dr. Fell, I was having dinner alone. If you can call it a dinner."

"Where were you?"

"At the Cave of the Witches."

"The Cave of the Witches? What's that?"

"Oh, no! I'm answering questions, old boy. I'm not teaching you what you already ought to know."

"Why did you suddenly decide to have dinner alone?"

"Because I couldn't take my dear wife's affectations any longer. Or her jaw. Besides, I wanted to think about somebody."

Paula, clenching her hands and with a little gasp as though she saw only hopelessness in his attitude, turned away and hurried to the sideboard between the two front windows. There, reaching out towards a decanter of brandy, she stopped before touching it. Ferrier watched Brian with a fixed, agreeable smile.

"At half-past ten, when you heard Mrs. Ferrier had rushed away in a taxi, you drove straight to the Hotel du Rhône. Please answer your own question: how did you know she had gone there?"

"I didn't."

"Oh?"

"But it was a natural enough assumption," Ferrier retorted swiftly. "Eve went to the dining-room, they tell me. I frequently had dinner there; so did all the rest of us. It was the natural place for her to look for me."

"And you to look for her? When she'd already had dinner at this house?"

"Why not?"

"That was the only reason you went to the hotel?"

"Yes!"

"Very well. If you thought Audrey was in danger, why did you let her come here?"

"Because I was pretty sure my dear wife was bluffing. I didn't think there was any real danger. Audrey herself didn't think there was any real danger; ask her!"

"How do you know what Audrey thought?"

"Ask her, I tell you! Well, we were both wrong: my dear wife killed herself and tried to put the blame on Audrey. Eve hadn't any cause for being suspicious, but she believed she had." The same fixed look, almost a glare, returned to Ferrier's eyes. "Their so-called murder was a suicide; the only crime those cops will ever find."

And Brian, on horns and hooks of doubt, couldn't make up his mind.

"By the cream-faced loon of Dunsinane," Ferrier exclaimed softly, and snapped his fingers, "I'm getting rather good at explanations. Leave the police to me."

Paula whirled round from the sideboard. "Desmond, for heaven's sake be careful!"

"Leave 'em to me, I tell you!"

"Look here," said Dr. Gideon Fell, "this has got to stop."

The sharpness of that common-sense voice, falling on heated nerves, brought silence without bringing peace. Slowly, with infinite labour, Dr. Fell rose to his feet.

"Sir," he said with thunderous earnestness, "you had better face the fact that your wife's death was murder. I cannot help you, nor can anyone else, if you brought me all the way from London to practice a piece of deception. Have you anything to tell me now?"

"No."

"Let me repeat," said Dr. Fell, caught between wrath and deep worry, "your wife's death was murder."

"Sweet Christ," Ferrier breathed, "*I* didn't want her to die!" Very briefly his self-control skidded; tears sprang into the eyes of Paula Catford; afterwards Ferrier had himself in hand again, urbane as ever.

"Your wife's death was murder. . . ."

"Have you got to go on saying that, magister?"

"I fear so. The police are a deadly enough danger, to begin

104

with, if you care for your neck at all. You walk amid other dangers too. They are not the only persons threatening you."

"Who else is?"

"Sir Gerald Hathaway. Or, at least, he is threatening me. I am almost sure he knows how this murder was committed. Do you know how it was committed?"

"No. I'll work that one out in good time. Besides, what has Hathaway got against me? I never saw the bloke in my life until last night."

"He has not necessarily got anything against you. But if he can show me up for the fool and the duffer I undoubtedly am . . . !"

"Magister, are you sure he's not bluffing? Look here!"

Moving away from the fireplace, Ferrier looked round him and discovered the table which had served as a sort of fire-screen when Brian first entered the drawing-room. Pulling the table back to its former position, he took the photograph album from Dr. Fell's hands and put it down on the table. On the floor beside another chair he found a large book of press-cuttings, which he set beside it. Plucking Hathaway's hat from the edge of the mantelpiece, he dropped the hat beside both.

"Hathaway is quite a card, isn't he? Until three o'clock this morning he stood just here and lectured us like a professor before a class."

"I need no reminding," said Dr. Fell.

"He very coolly accused Eve of poisoning that rich boy-friend, Hector Matthews, and assumed she wouldn't kick him out of the house for saying so. In which, to do the old girl justice, he was right." Ferrier gnawed at his under-lip. "You say you agree with him?"

"About what?" Dr. Fell asked sharply.

"He showed," retorted Ferrier, "all the ways in which Matthews *couldn't* have been poisoned. Matthews couldn't have swallowed poison, to begin with, because he took nothing to eat or drink. Matthews couldn't have been injected with poison, because witnesses were standing or sitting beside him all the time. Matthews couldn't have inhaled poison, because it would have affected others too. In short, there wasn't a way left."

"So it seems."

"And yet, if we're to write down Matthews's death as murder, we've got to cover and explain all those points against it?"

"Sir, need you belabour the obvious? Yes! We must do just that."

Ferrier pointed, like Mephistopheles at Faust.

"So if you're thinking they're certain to pitch on me as the murderer of my wife, don't be so afraid for my neck. They can't see through a millstone. They can't see what isn't there. *I* wasn't at Berchtesgaden in '39."

"Tut! The murderer of your wife was not necessarily at Berchtesgaden either. You know that as well as I do."

"What do you mean, I know it?" The blood jumped into Ferrier's forehead-veins. "If I killed Eve, it must have been for the sake of Audrey Page. I made out the case against myself. Don't be misled, any of you," and he looked at Brian, "by a pleasant house or an easy style of living or two expensive cars in the garage. The house runs on credit; the Rolls was bought on credit; the Bentley's mine, but I've had it since I played Hamlet at the old Royalty Theatre in '26. That's why—"

Ferrier stopped abruptly.

Dr. Fell, with the expression of one struck across the back of the head with a fairly heavy club, was staring at a corner of the ceiling.

"The motor-cars," he breathed, in a hollow voice. "The motor-cars! Hour after hour in a spiritual abyss, endless searching of rooms and even of a cellar, and all because I neglected to think of the motor-cars."

Here Dr. Fell, fastening on his eyeglasses more firmly, blinked round towards Brian and made incoherent noises, both of thanks and apology.

"You must forgive me," he said, "for not being alert to your hint. You yourself reminded me of the motor-cars earlier in the day. Once upon a time, incredible at this may seem, I owned a car too. I could get inside it; I could even drive it. I might not understand the mechanism, but at least I owned a car."

"Is this supposed to mean something?" asked Ferrier, who clearly did not understand. "It would be more interesting to see the mechanism in your head."

Dr. Fell's mood changed.

"You are welcome to see it, insofar as it concerns you. By

thunder, you've got to see it! Time is running out. We can't wait much longer."

"For what?"

"For a little frankness on your part. First, look out for Hathaway in more respects than one. It's true he gave us a lecture publicly. You also observed, no doubt, he had something of a conference with Mrs. Ferrier in private?"

"With Eve? When was this?"

"Shortly before we all turned in. They were in the dining-room there, having an earnest talk and not too much at daggers-drawn. Come! Surely you noticed it?"

"I wasn't myself, magister. I'd taken a good many drinks."

"In candour, so had I. Hathaway and Mrs. Ferrier were stone-cold sober. I strongly suspect Hathaway's errand in Geneva this morning has something to do with a cable-office. He may be trying to get some information which I obtained, before I left London, from Scotland Yard."

Paula Catford, plainly puzzled as well as startled out of her wits, straightened up at the sideboard. The effect on Ferrier was even more pronounced.

"Lord of high hell!" he said, as though addressing a prayer. "A month ago I went to England especially to see you. I told you several things in confidence when I asked you to visit us. And you repeated 'em to the police?"

"No, I did not. Nobody has betrayed you. It might have been better if someone had."

"I am asking . . . !"

"So you are. Actually, you told me very little except the story of Berchtesgaden and a hint that your wife might try to poison you. You were not being frank then. You are not being frank now."

"Will you tell me how?"

"I intend to do so. Sir, you never feared your wife would try to poison you. That was childish; the whole approach was childish. There was no need to shield Mrs. Ferrier (yes; shield her!) by what at first sight seemed to be an accusation. Nor is there any need to blacken your character in order to whitewash hers."

Ferrier appealed to the ceiling. "Paula, do you understand what this maniac is talking about?"

107

"No! Do you?"

"I think he does," interposed Dr. Fell. And he looked at Ferrier. "Your statement a moment ago, that you might have designs on Miss Page because of her father's money, is less childish than grotesque. Your reputation, let's face it, is as notorious as it is well-deserved. You would cut the throat of an actor or actress who stepped on your lines or spoiled a scene. You would cheerfully seize any woman from fifteen to fifty, and think it a good day's work. But marry for money you would not do."

"Have you got through accusing me of virtue? What *is* all this?"

Dr. Fell spoke with a sharpness much in contrast to the black worry and distress of his manner.

"Miss Catford is quite right," he said. "Stop acting; come off your high horse and doff the buskins; or they will land you in prison for the rest of your natural life."

"Get to hell out of my way," said Ferrier, and strode towards the archway into the hall.

"One last question, then! All information from the police is not about crime or criminals. Hathaway was right on another point too: the key to this problem is in your late wife's character. Why didn't you tell me she had been married twice before she married you in 1943?"

Once more Brian had the feeling that his wits were flying loose and that nothing made reasonable sense.

This, apparently the most harmless and even irrelevant of questions, stopped Ferrier just under the archway.

"Why should I have told you?" He swung back again. "Those things are common knowledge. What difference does it make?"

"Still, you kept it to yourself?"

"I didn't mention my opinion of the weather. It never occurred to me—"

"It has occurred to some others. Deputy Commander Elliot had a few remarks to make on the subject."

"Such as?"

"About her first husband, whom she divorced in '36, I have learned little so far. But there was a very good reason why she would not have announced her 'engagement' to Hector Matthews three years later."

"Why?"

"Because her second husband, whom she married in '37, was still alive and still her husband. On the outbreak of war he became a fighter-pilot in the R.A.F.; he was killed during the Battle of Britain in '40. This does not seem to have been generally known. Certainly it did not affect Matthew's legacy."

For a short space it was so quiet that the clock in the hall, its pendulum, the fair-haired doll, cheerfully and idiotically swinging, marked the seconds in loud beats. Then Paula hurried towards Ferrier; she put her hand on his arm before she turned and faced Dr. Fell.

"Are you coming back to the accusation," she cried, "that poor Eve in some way killed Mr. Matthews after all?"

"Ask Mr. Ferrier."

"I won't believe . . . !"

"Ask Mr. Ferrier. Ask him what it may well mean."

"Paula," said Ferrier, and added a word seldom heard in polite society, "you keep out of this."

"Miss Catford may keep out of it. Oh, ah! So may you. If imprisonment means nothing, or unjust suspicion means nothing, is there no other consideration at all?"

Ferrier, lifting his shoulders, shook off Paula's hand and pressed long fingers over his eyes.

"I don't want more trouble, God knows. But there's no danger of—"

"Of what? And are you sure of it?" roared Dr. Fell. "I have tried to use discretion so far. Hathaway may not be so discreet."

"I don't know," said Ferrier. "I don't know. I need five minutes, just five minutes, to think it over!"

Dr. Fell had moved towards him. So had Brian. All three heard the noise of motor-cars turning in at a gravelled drive and sweeping up outside the villa. Stephanie, the maid, anticipated anything else when she hastened into the drawing-room.

"Mr. Ferrier," she said, "the police are here."

XI

Eight o'clock in the evening, growing dark again.

And he had hoped to see Audrey hours before this.

Heedless of the wet road's slipperiness after the rain, Brian sent his car bucketing down towards the outskirts of Geneva.

The greatest wish of those who spend a good part of their lives in travelling, he had often reflected, is to hang or shoot or otherwise exterminate all people occupying any kind of official position.

This, admittedly, was unfair. The officials couldn't help it. And, since the purpose of so many governments nowadays is to make life as complicated and irritating as possible, he should be grateful for the Swiss method of letting you do exactly as you pleased so long as you didn't interfere with anyone else.

Nothing could have been more polite or considerate than the police questioning. But nothing could have been more thorough, over nearly ten hours. What the other witnesses said Brian did not know. They were kept in separate rooms like separate compartments. The tireless Stephanie got these witnesses a meal at half-past one. The thunderstorm, breaking in a deluge of rain shortly after the arrival of the police, made a background in accord with Brian's mood.

His sense of frustration, he knew, came from another source.

"You tried to be too clever," he thought bitterly. "And, as usual, you cut your own throat."

So far as he could tell, nobody doubted his story—or, rather, Dr. Fell's story—that he and Audrey had been together when they saw Eve Ferrier fall from the balcony. Nobody expressed surprise or wrath at the statement that Audrey had been sent away from the villa because she was suffering from shock.

M. Aubertin, suavely tri-lingual in French, English (and German as well, he understood), had merely nodded.

"But that is only natural, Mr. Innes."

"Don't you want to question her?"

"Presently, it may be. We have fully enough to occupy us for the moment."

"I've told you everything I know, and told it twice over. Can't you let me get away from here now?"

"In good time, Mr. Innes. You will appreciate the necessity for thoroughness. Of course you wish to—er—reassure yourself about the young lady?"

"Yes. I do."

"Where is she now?"

"I am not sure. She may be at any one of a number of places."

"Well, it is simple. Telephone to whatever place or places you think she may be, and say you will be delayed."

But that was precisely what he couldn't do. First consideration: he did not dare risk speaking to Audrey until he had seen her alone and they could arrange to tell the same story; this invitation might be a gentle trap. Second difficulty: if she had received his message from Madame Duvallon, she wouldn't answer the 'phone even if he rang.

All sorts of other uncomfortable possibilities had occurred to him; certain further words of Dr. Fell, just before the entrance of the police, churned uneasily in his head.

The necessity for seeing Audrey, which he hid behind a manner of a suavity as great as M. Aubertin's, had grown to something like a mania by the time they released him. He was also looking forward to the explanation Dr. Fell promised, when the Gargantuan doctor had said he would accompany Brian to the latter's flat and explain the technique of a murder as soon as he had questioned Audrey.

And Dr. Fell couldn't go with him.

"Sir, it is impossible! I cannot leave here just yet."

"Why not?"

"Take my word for the fact that it is impossible. I will try to join you later."

"Is there more trouble?"

"Not from the authorities, I hope. Let us trust there will be none from another quarter."

At eight o'clock, through a new-washed world of wet foliage and dampness, he drove at high speed down the limestone ridge towards the lights of Geneva.

A few red embers of sunset, promising a fine day tomorrow, lay in the trees behind him. This promise concerned only the weather. People won't behave as they ought to behave, or as they think they should. At least, he told himself when he slowed down to a decent observance of traffic-signals and turned at last into the Quai Turrettini, at least he would find Audrey.

Or would he?

His block of flats, a comparatively modern one, wore its usual stone face of dignity and somnolence. By craning his neck from the street, he could see a light burning in the two windows which marked his sixth-floor living-room.

He parked his car in the little cross-street beside the building, near a sign saying it was absolutely forbidden to leave vehicles there. In the darkish entry to the flats, the yellow metal surfaces of the letter-boxes gleamed faintly.

He had given the key of his flat to Audrey. He had told Madame Duvallon to leave her latch-key inside the letter-box. His fingers shook as he fumbled in his pocket for the tiny key which opened the letter-box. If the latch-key wasn't inside . . .

It was there.

He took the lift up through dead-quiet floors, where dim little lights in passages shone on rough-stucco walls painted dark grey.

And Audrey was there too. Her cry of, "Who's there?" he heard at very nearly a scream as soon as he opened the outer door of the flat. She was in the little entrance hall, evidently ready to go out, but shrinking back at the noise of the key in the lock.

They looked at each other.

Instinctively Audrey began to run towards him. She had not taken a step before she checked herself; she paused, covered with the same sort of pouring self-consciousness he himself felt. Their eyes communicated; each knew, and was aware the other knew.

Instantly, of course, they both pretended they didn't know.

"Take it easy," said Brian, snapping out the words. "You're not in any danger, you know."

"I thought I was."

"Danger from whom?"

"From her."

" 'Her?' "

"*You* know. Eve. Or from—" Audrey stopped, eyes widening.

"Now just a minute! This is a worse case of nerves than I thought. Eve is dead."

"I know she is. But I've been hearing her outside that door every time somebody walked past. What's happened? Where have you been all day?"

"I couldn't get away any sooner."

"What's going on at the villa? Do they think I did it?"

"No, they don't. Get that notion out of your head once and for all. First, though, did you see Madame Duvallon? And have you had anything to eat?"

"Yes, yes, yes! There was a lot of food in the fridge. I couldn't eat much, but your Madame Duvallon kept insisting and I had to."

"In that case, you're going to have a drink now. Then, after I've explained what you must tell the police when they do question you, we're both getting out of here for a while."

Except for small entrance-hall, kitchen, and bathroom, the flat contained only two smallish rooms, living-room and bedroom, set side by side. Brian had a studio at Vesénaz where he did his work. This flat, a symbol of his rootless life, only emphasized the presence of Audrey now.

She backed away from him into the little living-room, where the light of lamps shone against cream-coloured stucco walls. Again he was watching her as he went to the cabinet which contained the portable bar. She wore the same tweed suit, with tan stockings and crêpe-soled shoes.

"You got to town before the rain caught you, I see?"

"Yes." Audrey watched him in turn. "And you—you've had a wash and brush-up since you climbed down to look . . . to look at what happened to her."

"I have. By courtesy of the police."

"What do they say? What do they think?"

"I wish I knew. Here."

He poured out a brandy and soda and gave it to her. Between the two windows, above low bookshelves, hung a black-and-white sketch of Audrey he had done from memory. She carefully refrained from looking at this at any time while he told her everything.

"—so Dr. Fell's conclusions, whatever they are, seem to have been based from the beginning on information he got from Scotland Yard before he left London."

"Then Eve," Audrey asked incredulously, "had two husbands before she married Mr. Ferrier?"

"That seems to surprise you."

"It does, rather. I—I don't know why it should."

"Never mind that! Can you remember what you're supposed to have said and done this morning? Can you repeat this new story without being caught?"

"Oh, I can repeat it. I ought to be used to lies and deceit by this time. And I'm not in the least frightened now you're here."

Audrey took a gulp of the brandy and soda, in some mood between bitterness and another he could not define. She set down the glass on a bookcase.

"I didn't speak to Eve at all or go into the study at any time. Is that it?"

"That's it."

"When we'd finished breakfast at half-past seven, I went up to my room. I was frightened of Eve. I did 'phone you and go for a walk afterwards. When I returned, I went straight to my room by that outside staircase. I was in my room, looking out on the balcony, when I saw Eve run out on the balcony. And you were with me when we both saw her fall. Dear God! That might almost have been true, everything about it! But . . ."

"But what?"

Audrey made a baffled gesture.

"Well, I keep thinking about Eve. Brian, why is so much being made of this second husband of hers?"

"I can't tell you."

"But surely Dr. Fell said something that would indicate—" She stopped.

"No. Dr. Fell didn't give one detail about the second husband except that this chap had been killed in the war. He didn't even mention the man's name. Wait a minute, though! Just before Aubertin walked in, he did add that the second husband seemed to have been the one great love of Eve Eden's life."

Audrey's eyes shifted, as though she were again running away. Brian, putting down the latch-key on the portable bar, poured whisky for himself and hesitated as he was doing so.

"Audrey, you had a lot of talk with Eve I didn't overhear. Is there something you haven't told me?"

"No! Truly there isn't!"

"You're sure of that?"

"I'm positive. But I was just wondering . . . is it possible this second husband could still be alive?"

Brian counted ten before he spoke.

"No, it's not possible. It's not possible Eve herself is alive, either. She struck head down between a couple of trees; she was dead a few seconds after I found her. You're not being hypnotized by any kind of morbid fancy, are you? Or thinking Eve might come back after you and tap at the door?"

"No! No! Brian, you've got to listen to me."

The odd thing, he decided, was that for all Audrey's wild talk she seemed to have grown up a good deal since that morning. He could not define this sense of maturity which, rightly or wrongly, he felt was there. But he could have sworn to it.

"I was only wondering," and Audrey seemed to grope among scattered impressions, "if I could have misunderstood what she said to me."

"How?"

"You talk about being hypnotized by—by ghosts or whatnot. Do you know what I first thought, when Eve began raving at me? I thought *she* was hypnotized. That's what she looked like and sounded like."

"After everything else we've been exposed to, you're not bringing in murder by hypnosis?"

"I wonder."

"There is enough of weird-sisters atmosphere already, believe me, without importing more of it. Let's forget that, shall we?"

"Brian, listen! If you just say 'murder by hypnosis' and don't add anything else, of course it sounds silly. But that isn't all."

Audrey straightened up.

"I've been very silly, you know, and I've behaved about as stupidly as anyone could behave. I've given you an awful lot of trouble because I was trying to prove something to myself and to you too. All the same, there's one thing you've *got* to understand whatever else you think as long as we're both alive. There never has been any kind of affair, any kind, between me and Desmond Ferrier."

Here her voice went up.

"Oh, I know!" she added before he could speak. "I know what you're going to say. You've told me before it doesn't matter if there is. You've said that so often I can quite believe it doesn't matter to you."

"Audrey, stop this blasted coquettishness. It means everything in the world to me, and very well you know it. I've been in love with you for years."

"No, don't come near me. Don't touch me. Not now! I've got *some* little vestige of pride left, even if nobody could possibly think so."

"I don't mean to touch you. Not until this business is over. And then, damn your soul, I'll touch you and more than touch you with a thoroughness you've probably not experienced in your life."

"Well, I hope you do. But can't you even s-say you love me," Audrey cried out at him, "without swearing at me and looking as though you wanted to strangle me?"

"No, I can't. That's how you affect people."

"All right. I don't mind; I love it. But you say 'people,' and that's what I mean too. I'm going to prove to you there's nobody else and never has been. So *will* you listen?"

In another instant the emotional temperature would have been out of all control. Brian finished the whisky and whacked down the glass on top of the bar.

"I am all attention, madam. As Hathaway would phrase it."

"If you're making fun of me again—!"

"Will you get it through that pretty little head, my dear, that no-body is making fun of you? Or has ever wanted to? You're a female devil, a succubus of near-thirty masquerading as nineteen."

"That's not a very nice thing to say, now is it?"

"Who cares whether it's a nice thing to say? We're beyond that; I love you; I've been looking for you all my life. Now what is it you wanted to explain about the murder of Eve Ferrier?"

The word 'murder' fell between them and stayed there.

Audrey, her colour high, turned away from him and then turned back.

"Eve," she said, "was raving at me about—about stealing some-body. Naturally I thought she meant her present husband. But she never actually mentioned a name; a lot of what she told me didn't make much sense. Suppose she meant a previous husband?"

"A dead one?"

"Presumed dead, then. And there was a first husband, according to you. What did Dr. Fell learn about him?"

"Not a great deal. You can ask him." Brian began to reflect. "Any-thing is possible, admittedly. He thinks the question of the second husband is the most important factor of all. So does Ferrier, though neither of them will say why. And, since Dr. Fell's helping Ferrier as well as helping you—"

"Brian, why should Dr. Fell be helping me?"

"Because he doesn't want to see you get arrested for something you didn't do. He's like that. The weakness of the first-or-second husband theory, if we're looking for a murderer, is that Eve seems to have gone off the deep end because of something she read in a diary."

"Well, why shouldn't that be? *I* keep a diary. So does everyone else at that house. Everything you write in a diary isn't necessarily a confession about yourself. Mr. Ferrier could have written informa-tion about somebody else."

"Meaning yourself? The information concerned you, remember."

Audrey went pale.

"So you think I did kill her after all?"

"I don't think anything of the kind!"

"And, of c-course, Mr. Ferrier and I . . . ?"

"Stow it, will you?"

"If you don't think that," Audrey said suddenly, "there's only one other possibility." It was as though inspiration came to her. "Maybe I *can* help you! Maybe I *can* justify myself!"

He seized her by the shoulders; and then, warned by the hysterical look of determination in her eyes, he remembered overwrought states of mind and released her. The ticking of the clock on the bookshelves drew his eyes.

"There's no need to justify yourself. You're tired; we're both tired. Do you see what time it is?"

"T-twenty minutes to nine? What about it?"

"Near here, in the rue du Stand, there's a quiet restaurant where they serve very good food. We're going there, and we're going to try to forget murder for a while."

"Yes. You're right. I'm sorry."

"Then get ready. After we've had a good dinner, with enough wine to aid it, we may be able to think rationally about a problem that seems to have no meaning at all. We'll also drop your suitcase at the Metropole."

"Suitcase?"

"You haven't forgotten you left a suitcase, only half unpacked, in the room they gave you at the villa? I brought it with me. It's downstairs in the car."

"But, Brian—!"

"Is anything wrong?"

"Not wrong, exactly. Only I can't go back to the Metropole! Or, at least, I don't want to. It would look awfully funny."

"Why? Haven't you still got your room there?"

"Not now. When you sent me here this morning, by way of the hotel, I was still badly upset. I thought you just wanted to hide me until I could get out of the country. So I gave up my hotel-room and sent the rest of my luggage on to the airport. Now I don't want to go. Will the police think I've run away?"

"You can't have run away, my dear, if you're still very much present. But you'll need that suitcase. I'd better go down and bring it up."

"Brian, darling, I can't stay with you here! I mean . . . !"

He made no comment on Miss Audrey Page, would-be woman of the world. She was too deadly serious, and so was he. Brian did not even smile.

"Yes; I know what you mean. And yet it might be the best way of preventing more trouble. In any event you'll still need the suitcase. Half a minute, now!"

The outer door of the flat slammed after him. He took the lift downstairs. But he was not to be free, even for thirty seconds, from forces that had begun to gather for a last evil pursuit.

The block of flats lay almost in the shadow of the Pont de la Coulouvrenière, a grey-white shape amid the Rhône's seven bridges. Against a fine clear night, not too warm, its lamps threw reflections into rushing water.

But the little side-street was almost dark. A street-lamp on the quai showed him that someone, a mere furtive-looking shadow, had opened the back door of his car and appeared to be groping in the back seat.

Brian charged. He gripped somebody's wrist, heaving the intruder out and round towards the street-lamp as though in a game of crack-the-whip.

"Now what the devil," cried a familiar rasping voice, "do you think you're doing?"

Brian dropped the wrist, cursing in a discovery of anti-climax, as the tubby little figure staggered and almost fell. Gerald Hathaway, hatless against the glow of the lamp, stared at him in bouncing exasperation.

"Yes, my fine friend? What do you think you're doing?"

"What do you think *you're* doing, if it comes to that?"

"You live here, don't you? This is your car, isn't it?"

"Yes to both questions. How do you know so much?"

"I know you live in these flats," Hathaway retorted, "because I called here last night. A Madame Duvallon or Duvallet, who said she was 'opening' the flat for you, told me you would be back from Paris. And I know it's your car because this morning, before I could call out and stop you, I saw you drive away in it. But do my eyes deceive me?"

"How?"

"Is this the ultra-conservative and pompous Mr. Brian Innes? Behaving as though he saw a gangster behind every bush? It's that girl, I imagine?"

"Yes. I suppose it is. As for the skittish Sir Gerald Hathaway—"

Only Hathaway's own dignity prevented him from doing a kind

of dance on the pavement.

"You ruddy idiot," he raved, "I was going to wait for you because I'm a fellow of some considerable delicacy. You've got her upstairs, no doubt."

Though these words had the inflection of a question, they were rather a statement than a question. Brian met them as an attack.

"What makes you think she's there?"

"Don't be evasive, my friend! She's not at the Metropole; she's not at the Villa Rosalind. There's nowhere else she could be."

"Deducing again? Hathaway, just why were you waiting for me?"

"For one thing, to warn you. If you've got any fondness for that girl, you'll be careful. Have you seen the evening newspapers?"

"No."

There was a folded newspaper in Hathaway's pocket. He took it out and waved it, though Brian could see nothing except the outline of his bald head and his bristling beard.

"It's splashed all over the place. The press here," Hathaway said bitterly, "seem to have almost as few inhibitions as they have in France."

"I still don't understand—"

"De Forrest Page is a friend of mine too. You were asked to take care of his daughter, not get the police after her. This won't make pleasant reading for her father when the news gets to London."

"Audrey's name isn't mentioned in the press?"

"Isn't it? Take a look at this! And that's not all. Don't trust Gideon Fell too far. To judge by the reports you can read any-where, he's talking nothing but riddles and he's concealing a lot of vital information."

"Whereas a fellow named Hathaway never does that? And forget what the newspapers say. What do they say at the Villa Rosalind?"

"I don't know what they say at the Villa Rosalind. I haven't been there."

"Since when?"

"Since I left very early this morning."

"Hathaway, who's scatty now? Do you want the authorities after you too?"

The other man drew himself up, shivering with excitement. His high, harsh voice sang out in triumph.

"I have beaten Gideon Fell. I have beaten him all hollow. Part of this case may be explained by one substance: oil of vitriol. The other part of the case may be explained by another substance: oil of bitter almonds."

"Oil of bitter almonds? What's that?"

"The poison that killed Mrs. Ferrier. Come here!"

XII

Unpredictable, between triumph and obscure fear, Hathaway darted across the road to the quai-side above the river. Brian followed him. There Hathaway stood fully under a street-lamp, holding up the newspaper.

"If you will read this description," he began with some vehemence.

"I don't want to read anything. What's oil of bitter almonds?"

"It's also called nitrobenzene."

"It sounds like a prussic-acid derivative. Is that what it is?"

"Tut! Your ignorance of criminology! Read Murrell on Poisons. The point I want to make," enunciated Hathaway, holding the newspaper rather like the Statue of Liberty with her torch, "is that Gideon Fell has been telling us lies."

"About what?"

"If you had been at the villa late last night," snapped Hathaway, "you would have heard him say (well! you would have heard him intimate) he first learned of Hector Matthews's death from Mr. Desmond Ferrier a comparatively short time ago in London."

"But he didn't?"

"He heard it from *me*. And at a meeting of the Murder Club some years back."

"Will you try to make sense?"

"The Murder Club," Hathaway spaced his words, "is a discussion-group which meets at Beltring's restaurant in Soho. I was once its guest. When I attempted to interest your elephantine friend in the story of Hector Matthews, he pretended there was little in it."

"So your vanity was scratched?"

"Young man, I resent that."

"Thanks for the 'young.' Isn't that what happened, though?"

"I refuse to listen to mere insults. Still!" Hathaway swallowed hard. "Could I have expected Mrs. Ferrier would be killed this morning? Hardly. The most astute man alive could never have expected it. Therefore—"

"Now look here," Brian interrupted in some desperation. He nodded towards the block of flats across the street. "Audrey's over there alone; I must get back. But you came to me for reassurance, and I'll try to reassure you. Just tell me what's on your mind."

"This morning (do you follow me?) I sent a cablegram from the Hotel du Rhône."

"No; I don't follow you."

"It was well known at the Savage Club," Hathaway cried, "that Ferrier had consulted Gideon Fell. If Fell wanted more facts, about Mrs. Ferrier or about anyone else, where would he have gone? To Scotland Yard; any fool could have guessed as much. His colleague Hadley has retired. Almost certainly he'd have spoken to Deputy Commander Elliot. Agreed?"

"Well, that's what he did."

"Ah! Fell admitted this?"

"There's no question of admitting it. He told us so this morning."

"Ah! But they'd not have been so indulgent with *me*. So it seemed better to wait until Fell was here in Geneva, and then send Elliot a cable of inquiry signed with Fell's name."

"Holy God! This is better and better. You've been sending fake cablegrams to Scotland Yard?"

"*A* cable. *A* cable! I could make certain, at the hotel, of having any reply delivered to me. Admittedly there was a certain amount of risk."

"I'll bet there was. They're supposed to take a fairly poor view of forgery."

"This childish sarcasm . . . !"

"Hathaway, I'm not blaming you. We're all liars in the same boat. But if you're afraid of the consequences . . . ?"

Hathaway, really amazed, glared back at him.

"Consequences? Tut! Do you imagine I referred to a risk like that? No, no, no! I was compelled to send a message in far too general terms. 'Have you any further information on the subject we discussed?' Fell might not have seen Elliot. Or Elliot might not have answered, even with a hundred words reply-paid. Or he might have answered only through official channels. Risk!"

"So he didn't answer?"

"Oh, he answered." Hathaway gripped the newspaper in both pudgy hands. "He and Fell, evidently, had been discussing the lady's two previous husbands. When I investigated those two husbands, long ago, I paid no attention to them because both were poor men from whom she couldn't have inherited a penny. That was a mistake on my part."

"Then Elliot's reply was about her second husband? A fighter-pilot in the R.A.F.?"

Hathaway looked him up and down.

"Now how, my fine friend, were you aware . . . ?"

"Never mind! It was about her second husband, wasn't it?"

"No, it was not. It concerned her first husband. I already knew he had been a very young and unstable analytical chemist employed by the Ferndale Aniline Dye Company. In March of '36 she divorced him. A month later he committed suicide by swallowing a poison called nitrobenzene. That was the information in the cable. Can anyone now doubt this woman spread suicide or murder wherever she went?"

Brian turned away.

The buildings of the Quai Turrettini showed dark grey against street-lamps and under a rising moon. Brian glanced towards the lights of the Hotel du Rhône; he hesitated, and looked back at the staring face in front of him.

"Laugh at my deductions. Laugh!" said Hathaway. "They were right in every way."

"I'm not laughing. This nitrobenzene, or oil of bitter almonds, is the same stuff that killed Mrs. Ferrier herself?"

"It was. A post-mortem will prove it was."

"In that case, why are you here?"

Now it was Hathaway who shied back. "I don't understand."

"I think you do understand. Why aren't you out at the villa, triumphing over Dr. Fell and the police too? Why are you standing here and shivering as though you didn't want them to ask you questions?"

"The fact is, my dear fellow—"

"Well?"

"The fact is, my dear fellow," Hathaway answered in a loud voice, "that I don't want them to ask questions. There! I can prove every bit of the trick that was used to kill Mrs. Ferrier. But I can't explain the trick used on Hector Matthews."

"Matthews? Matthews at Berchtesgaden? That's the very trick you've been saying you *could* explain! You've been shouting it at everyone since last night!"

"I was over-optimistic: merely that. I can explain all except one very small, relatively minor point. And I don't like being challenged or sneered at. In short . . ."

"In short, you were the one who deliberately lied?"

Hathaway threw the crumpled newspaper over the parapet into the river. Even his bald head had taken on a look of furious earnestness.

"I did not lie," he said, "and I resent being told I did!"

"Then what do you call it? Nitrobenzene, presumably, leaves traces in the victim's body?"

"Naturally."

"So there isn't any real mystery about the way in which Mrs. Ferrier was killed? It was a different method from the one used on Matthews?"

"No mystery? A different method?" Hathaway, in danger of strangling from his own sincerity, had to gasp for breath. "I would have you know, my fine friend, it was exactly the same method for both of them. I was with Mrs. Ferrier at the breakfast-table this morning. She did not eat or drink anything, any more than Matthews did on the other occasion. She was not injected with poison. No one

125

came near her with poison. The miracle, if you wish to call it so, remains just as it was."

"Then why can't you explain both deaths? Don't fume: answer me! Why can't you explain both deaths?"

"Because—"

Again Hathaway stopped, but from a different cause.

He had looked down towards the Hotel du Rhône in an abstracted sort of way. Then his gaze grew rigid. A police-car, moving fast, swept up and stopped just outside the hotel. Out of it climbed Philip Ferrier, M. Gustave Aubertin, and Dr. Gideon Fell.

Brian knew the last two of them were coming to question Hathaway, which meant that very shortly they would be questioning Audrey. Automatically he looked across at the block of flats just opposite, and raised his eyes towards the lighted windows in the sitting-room of his flat on the sixth floor.

But those sitting-room windows were now dark. Nor was there a light in any window of his flat.

Cold panic touched him. After counting windows, up and across, he made sure there was no mistake. That was his flat; those were the windows. A similar blank blindness swam across his wits.

Hathaway, leaning forward to touch his arm, had gabbled a sharp question. Brian did not hear it. Unheeding, eyes raised towards those windows, he ran across the street in the path of an oncoming car whose horn screamed before it swerved and missed him.

He did not glance backwards as he entered the building. He had reached the lift before he remembered there was a question he had been wanting to ask Hathaway since early morning; and, of course, he had failed to ask it.

This hardly mattered now. Concern for Audrey, as well as another panicky discovery, drove it from his mind. He was in the sixth-floor corridor, and groping in his pockets for a key to the outer door of the flat. But he found no key at all.

Fool! Idiot!

Vividly he remembered putting down Madame Duvallon's latch-key on the portable bar. He had neglected to pick it up again. When he went downstairs for Audrey's suitcase—also forgotten, in the tumult of meeting Hathaway—the spring-lock of the door snapped shut after him. If anything had happened to Audrey . . .

Brian stood still. He was in a familiar corridor, haunted by the ghosts of so many cooked meals. You sensed the presence of people all about you, though you never saw any of them. In somebody's flat a television set throbbed with muffled life; he knew it was a television, not a radio, from the hoarser, heavier sound.

If anything had happened to Audrey . . .

"Nonsense!" he said aloud.

But he pressed the door-buzzer, he pressed it for many seconds and heard it clamour inside. He called Audrey's name. There was no voice or footstep in response.

His first thought, that Eve Ferrier might have returned to carry away Audrey in the dark, was morbid and unlike him. Yet he seized the knob of the door, twisting it and pushing. And the door yielded, almost flinging him into an unlighted entry.

It had been closed but unfastened, its spring-lock set at the open position. That must have been done by Audrey herself, who could easily have left unseen while he was talking to Hathaway. He began to believe this as he ran from little room to little room, switching on lights. He knew it for certain when, in the bedroom, he encountered a message scrawled in lipstick across the dressing-table mirror.

"I love you too," ran Audrey's message. "Please forgive what I'm going to do."

The city's night-noises, through open windows, made a reedy cacophony above the rushing of the river. Brian returned to the living-room.

Nothing seemed disturbed there, including the glasses he and Audrey had drunk from, until his frantic eye studied the telephone. Though the telephone did not seem to have been moved either, the little note-pad had been pulled to one side.

There was nothing written on that note-pad. Nor could you distinguish any marks, either, until you held it tilted beside the light of a lamp. Words written by a sharp-pointed pencil, on a thin top-sheet torn off, had left their imprint on the leaf below.

From his desk Brian took a blunter pencil of soft lead. Putting down the pad on the desk, he gently began to black out the surface of the under-sheet so that the writing might emerge in the white of its indentations.

"Desmond Ferrier. Desmond Ferrier. Desmond Ferrier."

That name, written three times, emerged as Audrey must have scrawled it as she sat by the telephone and poured out what was in her mind. He could almost see her writing it while she waited for the number she had dialled.

The grey-black surface crept down on the paper. Next, sharply written in the middle of the sheet, emerged an address she must have received over the phone. The words were also underscored.

Caverne des Sorcières,
16 rue Jean Janvier
Twenty minutes.

There were no more indentations.

Caverne des Sorcières. Cave of the Witches. He knew where he had heard that name before.

Cave of the Witches.

Brian tore off this sheet and put it in his pocket. When he looked up at the black-and-white sketch of Audrey Page, yearning at him from the wall between the windows, he neither cursed her impetuousness nor raved at her tendency to face danger even though she might be in mortal terror of it. He was thinking of Dr. Fell's warning.

"I failed miserably to prevent one tragedy," Dr. Fell had said. "There must not be another."

This was the point at which the clamour of the door-buzzer, piercing through his thoughts, made him jump up from the chair beside the desk.

It could only be the police.

If there had been any other way out of the flat, Brian would have bolted. They were not going to keep him from Audrey. On the other hand, they were not going to learn of this address until he himself had discovered what Audrey thought she was doing.

The door-buzzer went on shrilling. It wouldn't stop; it wouldn't leave off piercing his nerves. Presumably Dr. Fell and M. Aubertin had seen him, as he had seen them. He could hardly pretend not to be there, and he had no means of leaving the flat except through that clamouring door.

It was not the police, as he discovered when he opened the door. Paula Catford, seeming perhaps a little less good-natured and sympathetic, hesitated only a moment before she brushed past him without any invitation to enter.

"You must forgive this intrusion, Mr. Innes." She wheeled round in the entrance-hall, her colour high. "I'm afraid I must see her. Where is she?"

"If you mean Audrey . . ."

"Please, please! Of course I mean Audrey. Don't tell me she's not here. There's nowhere else she could have gone."

"That," Brian answered bitterly, "is what everyone else says. Have it your own way: she was here, right enough, but she's gone out."

"Where?"

"I don't know. And I'm afraid I have got to go out too. Immediately. I don't want to seem inhospitable, but will you excuse me?"

"No. I can't excuse you. Murder isn't a joke; there's somebody with a sick mind among us; the police are getting closer for an arrest."

"Do you think I don't know that? Anyway, what do you want with Audrey?"

"Mr. Innes, why did she telephone to Desmond Ferrier a little while ago?"

Brian looked over at the clock on the bookshelves. It was nearly ten minutes past nine, much later than he had expected.

"Quite by accident," said Paula, "I picked up an extension-'phone and heard them talking. That's easy to do, with so many extension-'phones at the villa. I put it down immediately, of course. But why did she ring up? Why did Desmond go out?"

Paula, at least, was harmless. The clock-ticks grew more imperative. Brian made up his mind.

"I can tell you what I think, at least, if you'll answer something in return."

"Anything, believe me! Oh, anything!"

"What, exactly, is the Cave of the Witches? Did Ferrier really have dinner there last night?"

"I—I beg your pardon?"

"Ferrier said he did, though he added 'if you could call it a dinner.' That doesn't sound the sort of name any restaurant would adopt. He also seemed to think, for some reason, I ought to know of the place."

"The Cave of the Witches!" Paula looked badly startled. "Is that

129

where he and Audrey went tonight?"

"Answer the question, will you?"

"The Cave of the Witches! It's in the rue Jean Janvier, off the rue de l'Hotel de Ville in the Old Town. That's why Desmond must have said you ought to know it; he was joking."

"Believe it or not, I am getting a bit fed up with the sort of remark Desmond Ferrier seems to think is a joke."

"Please!" Paula spoke sharply. "In the eighteen-eighties and eighteen-nineties, here in Geneva, there was a painter who used the pseudonym of Jean Janvier. I did a story about him. Didn't you ever hear of Jean Janvier?"

"No."

"He wasn't a very good painter, they say. But he was colourful. He specialized in witchcraft, vampirism, and all kinds of sadistic horrors as well. The work fascinated a lot of people. In the early nineteen hundreds there was a little museum of his paintings; but some said they were indecent and others lost interest. Janvier pictures were a drug on the market.

"Then, after World War Two, somebody had a brand-new idea. A man named Lafargue bought up a job lot of the lurider canvases, and opened a combination restaurant and night-club in the street where Janvier lived. It's mainly an odd kind of night-club, though you can get a meal of sorts in the evening. The—the attractions go on later."

"What attractions?"

Paula dismissed this.

"It doesn't matter! Many people get a terrific thrill out of waitresses and other attendants who have good figures but papier-mâché skulls for heads. It's mostly crude, of course, but some of the effects can be quite frightening."

"And that's supposed to be an entertainment?"

"Yes. Like a very sophisticated version of the Ghost Trains and Haunted Mills at amusement parks." Some emotion not remote from fear had begun to gather in Paula's expressive eyes. "Please tell me!" she added. "Did Desmond take Audrey there?"

"I don't know. I honestly can't tell you. I wasn't here when she 'phoned him. Why should he have taken her there?"

"That's what *I* don't know! You see. . . ."

"Go on!"

"It was a favourite place of Eve's. They even modelled a mask of her face. Mr. Innes, have you told anyone about this?"

"No; I've just discovered it. Everything's happened in less than half an hour."

"Then don't tell anyone! Will you promise?"

"Why?"

"I can't tell what sort of mood Desmond may be in. Your Audrey Page seems quite a pleasant sort of person; I'm sure she is, and I know you're very fond of her." Paula's voice rose up. "But she *has* caused quite a lot of trouble. It may be Desmond is—is trying to punish her by frightening her a little."

Brian's tone changed. "Is he, now? And that's his idea of a joke too?"

The words held a compressed, controlled violence; it was as though he had struck her in the face. For once the alert and fragile-seeming Paula, so sensitive to the reactions of others, must have misjudged the effect she wanted to produce. It was evident that she knew it. Paula sprang forward.

"Wait! Where are you going?"

"You know where I'm going."

"No. You mustn't. I won't let you."

The outer door of the flat still stood wide open, admitting more reminders of past meals. The television set talked distantly and hoarsely. Paula, running to the door, slammed it shut and set her back against it.

"Brian, I beg and plead with you! You don't understand everything!"

"I don't understand anything. Get away from that door."

"The police—"

"Never mind the police. Last night, when oil of vitriol splashed the floor, I had to pick you up bodily and swing you round from it. Must I do the same thing now? Get away from that door!"

"I hate saying this, please believe I hate saying it. But you've got to mind the police, after the plain, simple untruths—there's no other word for it!—you and Dr. Fell have been telling M. Aubertin about Audrey Page."

"What do you mean?"

131

"Have you forgotten I was upstairs at the villa this morning, and very much alive and awake, when you were in Sir Gerald Hathaway's room with Dr. Fell? And you confided in him what really happened in the study before Eve fell to her death? If the police hear what did happen, and what Eve said to Audrey just then, won't Audrey go to prison as perhaps she ought to go?"

XIII

And it stopped Brian in his tracks. It was the only check which could have held him back.

He looked at Paula, studying her.

As though challenging him, she had twisted the knob of the spring-lock and pulled the door a few inches open: still holding it behind her, guarding it, while he heard the familiar noises from the corridor outside.

Paula's expression grew even more intent.

"You're going to call this blackmail. I can't help that. Yes! I did listen outside Sir Gerald's room this morning. No! I haven't told the police and I don't want to, though I did ride to town in the same car with M. Aubertin and Dr. Fell and Phil Ferrier a little while ago. Call me anything you like! I'm fighting for something that's very dear to me; I'll do whatever I must."

Brian did not reply.

"What is it?" she asked suddenly. "What are you doing?"

Still without speaking, he hurried away into the living-room. This had a broad doorway; and, beside the doorway, an arched opening through which you could see the whole of that room from the entry.

He felt an inexorable sense of time rushing past, of minutes fall-ing into eternity while Audrey was being "punished" and fright-ened by some grotesque claptrap in a cellar of the rue Jean Janvier. The knowledge of this did not soothe his wrath.

From the portable bar he picked up Madame Duvallon's latch-key. It was as though, by turning away, he had yielded and lost the game. Paula knew he hadn't.

"*What are you doing now?*"

Brian put the key in his pocket and returned.

"Once before, when I went out of here, I forgot this key. Now I'm going out again."

"You're not!"

"All I propose," he said, "is a visit to a public night-club in a public street. Is there any reason to use such heavy threats in trying to stop me?"

"Yes; I'm sorry to say there is. Your precious Miss Audrey Page, as though you didn't know it, has caused far too much trouble al-ready. She must have threatened and devilled Desmond Ferrier until he hadn't any choice but to meet her there."

"At the Cave of the Witches? Audrey asked him to do that?"

"What else?"

"My dear Paula, come off it. I'll give you ten to one Audrey's never even heard of the place."

"Well, she was the one who rang him up! She was the one who made him look like death when he left the villa. I tell you, I won't see him unhappy any longer! He's suffered far too much already."

"Suffered? That fellow?"

The lash of contempt sent Paula momentarily out of all control.

"My God, how stupid you are! How little you understand! With an out-and-out nymphomaniac like Eve—"

"Nymphomaniac?" There was a dead silence as Brian interrupted. "Isn't that a change from your tune last night? Isn't it a considerable change from being the woman's greatest friend and champion?"

"I am her friend. I always have been. Eve was never, *never* like that in the old days before she lost her looks." Paula flung back her head, hands clenched. "Did you ever notice that the truly beautiful women in this world, and often the ones who seem to put the most accent on sex, are the very ones who aren't much interested in sex after all? They can't be; they're too vain; they're interested only in themselves. Oh, God, what am I saying?"

"Not much that's relevant. Will you answer the question?"

"What question?"

"Why do you want to keep me away from the Cave of the Witches? And keep the police away too?"

"I—"

"Is it because I might ask questions? And the police certainly would ask questions? And discover Ferrier wasn't anywhere near the place yesterday evening?"

"That's it, yes. But that's only partly it. You don't understand!"

"Then tell me something else. I had intended to ask Hathaway, but you'll do just as well. It's been understood you were to have dinner with Hathaway yesterday evening, but somebody put off that engagement. You didn't see Hathaway until you met him with me, in the foyer of the Hotel du Rhône. Isn't that true?"

"Of course it's true. I don't see what. . . ."

"You will. Hathaway said he telephoned you at the hotel and cancelled the dinner-date. Did you actually speak to him, or did he only leave a message?"

"He left a message. I wasn't in my room. I was downstairs buying cigarettes."

"You weren't in your room. Were you even at the hotel?"

"At the . . . ?"

"Yes! When Desmond Ferrier can't account for a blank of several hours yesterday evening, isn't it because he was with you?"

All the colour receded from Paula's face, making her vivid eyes enormous. The door, two inches open behind her back, swayed in a gentle draught.

"Mr. Innes, this is the most sickening and insufferable thing I ever heard! Do you accuse *me* of—of being concerned in poor Eve's murder?"

"No," roared Brian.

"Then what are you saying?"

"You're a Thoroughly Nice Girl in capital letters. You're whirling along in a rat-race of journalism when all you really want is a husband and a home."

Paula Catford went as white as though he had accused her of an act much worse than murder. She stood very straight, lips parted.

"Your conscience *has* bothered you about Eve," Brian said. "Very probably Ferrier *is* in love with you. Otherwise I can't see him telling lies so gallantly about a mere episode in his amiable young life. If you don't mention Audrey's lies, I don't mention yours or Ferrier's. Now get away from that door. I'm going out to find him and do something about it if he's been frightening Audrey."

"Oh, I'll be quiet! Do you imagine that will help you?"

"Why shouldn't it?"

"Listen!" And Paula held up her hand.

Moving aside from the door, she pushed it wide open. Through the corridor, from beyond a door with a glass panel at the far end, rose the wiry hum of the lift ascending from the ground floor.

"You've left it too late," said Paula. "That's the police."

One long step carried him into the passage. Beside the lift-door, a little to the right, he could see another door to the enclosed staircase. The lift, slow and asthmatic, would take thirty seconds to reach the sixth floor. He could be on his way down, completely unseen, long before then.

Her next words, in a hurt and hating voice, briefly stopped him again.

"If you think you're going to hurt Desmond or make more trouble for him, I don't think they'll let you. It certainly won't help when they arrest Audrey."

"Arrest Audrey? Are you crazy?"

"Oh, I don't think she did it! But Aubertin does. I can tell."

"Because you've been listening at doors again?"

It was even more brutal than his last attack, but Paula did not flinch.

"Yes, if you must know! Who's had more experience with the ways the police question people in any country, you or I? Dr. Fell's shielding Audrey too much. He's given her an alibi; he says he was with her before breakfast this morning."

"Before breakfast this morning? What's that go to do with it?"

"I'm afraid I haven't the least idea. It doesn't sound true, though. If you want to take care of her, you'd better stay and do it. You can't avoid Aubertin now."

"I think I can," Brian retorted—and was off down the passage as the hum of the lift rose to a singing whine that drowned out even the hoarseness of the television set.

The light inside the glass panel, to show the presence of the lift, was not yet in sight when he caught the heavy staircase-door beside it.

A last glance over his shoulder gave him a glimpse of Paula, the back of her hand pressed hard against her teeth, as she stood in the entry. He would have given much to recall his words; the hurt, hating look on her face was one of a woman wounded and in despair. The memory of it stayed with him on his way downstairs.

So did other memories: of Hathaway on the quai-side, of Hathaway's bewildered air and sagging shoulders when he realized a murder case in real life was different from an academic one.

Brian tried to drive away fancies. He couldn't tell Paula that Dr. Fell had been doing fully as much to protect Desmond Ferrier (why: damn Ferrier's hide, why?) as he had been doing to protect Audrey. An image of Ferrier's countenance, Mephistophelian yet feverish, crowded out all other images except that of Audrey.

So this distinguished gentleman was "punishing" Audrey, was he? Gently punishing her, with a light and expert touch, by arranging for her to be frightened?

The enclosed staircase, a concrete shell round concrete metal-bound treads, set up a clatter of echoes as Brian ran down. Wrath had become fury. The echoes rained round him in hollow din, past each little landing-window.

He mustn't let this cloud his judgment, though. He mustn't . . . .
Steady.

He reached the lowest step, beyond whose landing a heavy door with a head-high glass panel led out to the ground-floor passage and the entrance. He seized the knob of this door, began to open it—and came almost face to face with Gustave Aubertin, Director of Police for Geneva.

Some other tenant must have been using that lift when he and Paula thought they heard the police. In front of the lift-shaft, ground-floor level, stood Sir Gerald Hathaway, Philip Ferrier, Dr. Gideon Fell, and Aubertin himself.

That he could hear their voices, as well as see them through the panel like faces in an aquarium, was due to the compressed-air device which kept these doors from slamming. The piston of the air-lock, above the door, held it not quite closed.

Aubertin, a thin-faced greying man, very well-tailored, stood in the background with his eyes on the glass panel as though he could see Brian. But he was preoccupied, the latter realized; he was listening to the others, poised and waiting.

"Sir," Dr. Fell was thundering to Hathaway, "let us hope you are being no more inconvenienced than the rest of us."

"Less," Aubertin said softly.

"The question," and Dr. Fell reared up, "most vitally concerns all of us who were at breakfast this morning. You must be aware of that?"

"Indeed and I am aware of it," Hathaway said in a cold and bitter voice.

"Oh, ah! Now the dining-room at the villa is on the east side of the house, as the drawing-room is. Both of them overlook the garden. You are in a position to help us. Who went into the garden at shortly past seven o'clock in the morning?"

"I've already told you. Mrs. Ferrier herself. She went for a stroll there."

"Was Mrs. Ferrier the only person?"

"She was the only person I saw," replied Hathaway, peering up sideways. "Does that tell you nothing?"

"Sir, we would have *you* tell us something."

"What, for instance?"

Over all that little group, quiet and as though huddled by the lift-shaft, hung the tense air of men expecting some kind of explosion. There was a policeman on duty at the entrance to the flats: Brian could see his silhouette against a street-lamp.

The lift-shaft was silent, because the lift itself had stopped at some upper floor. Dr. Fell reached out and pressed the recall-button. Its buzz echoed out resonantly and ended in a whir as the lift began to descend; but Dr. Fell, a mountain of worry with a red face, kept on fiercely pressing the button after this ceased to be necessary.

"Yes?" prompted Hathaway.

"Harrumph, hah! Am I correct in assuming, Sir Gerald, that you yourself were a trifle excited when you took the Rolls and drove to town after breakfast?"

"Excited? I? Tut! Who says I was?"

They were barks like a terrier's. Dr. Fell blinked at him.

"I referred merely," he said with some politeness, "to the fact that you left your hat behind. You have not got it even yet. When

a man neglects even so fine a property as that hat, on which I con-
gratulate you and even envy you, it is safe to assume he is as excited as is Mrs. Ferrier (for instance) in wearing slacks and high-
heeled shoes."

"Is it? Say what you mean!"

"That is well recommended; say it!" interposed M. Aubertin.

Dr. Fell, fiercely apologetic, addressed the Director of Police.

"Sir, I beg your pardon for all this. You have kept me muzzled
the whole day, as it is only right you should. But I can't question
your witnesses. I can't run with the hare and hunt with the hounds,
which is what I have been doing."

"Yes, my friend," said M. Aubertin, "I think you have been doing
just that."

The hum of the lift grew louder.

Philip Ferrier, with hollows under his eyes and in a desperation
like Brian's own, made the gesture of one who would arrest a run-
away engine.

"Now look!" he began. "As far as Audrey is concerned—"

"We are going to see Miss Page," the Director of Police interrupted sharply, "in good time. That can wait. As for you, my
friend," he said to Dr. Fell in an ever sharper voice, "it is plain you
have been trying to guide us. But I also think you want the truth.
Ask your questions."

Dr. Fell hesitated for a moment.

"In actual fact, then, there are only two questions. Every other
point is merely an elaboration of those two. Very well." He looked
at Hathaway. "The first question (and oh, by thunder, it's important!) is for you."

"Ah! It is about this morning, undoubtedly?"

"No," Dr. Fell told him with rounded emphasis. "It is about the
photograph album you have been carrying, and the death of Hector
Matthews seventeen years ago."

Every mention of Hector Matthews touched Hathaway like the
flick of a whip.

"When you were giving us a lecture last night," said Dr. Fell,
"and recounting all the ways in which the man *wasn't* killed, you
flourished that album like a talisman of triumph. If it meant anything at all, it meant you must have found your evidence in some

139

photograph taken at Berchtesgaden. But I have pored over the album until I am misty of wits; I can see no evidence in a photograph of the scenes there."

"Quite right," Hathaway said coolly. "There was none."

The lift, humming at its loudest, slid down to the ground floor. The light inside illuminated all their faces through its glass panel. Dr. Fell, who had started to open the lift-door, let it close with a slam.

"Oh, ah? Then your famous and still-unexplained theory was based on no more than a random guess?"

"Oblige me," snapped Hathaway, "by refraining from mere insult. My theory was based on other photographs—others!—of Mrs. Ferrier's tour in Germany. If you had listened to me, years ago at the Murder Club, you would have heard the essential clue. I also mentioned it to Brian Innes."

M. Gustave Aubertin, for all his flawless English, spoke with a sudden guttural harshness, whose effect was like a baring of teeth.

"Would it be too much, Sir Gerald, if you mentioned it to us now?"

"Stop!" said Dr. Fell.

"My friend," said M. Aubertin, "there is a limit to one's patience."

"Stop, I say," roared Dr. Fell, his eyes squeezed shut. "I see now what he means. And it does much to clear underbrush from our path." For a moment Dr. Fell remained with his eyes closed. "Now the second and equally important question," and he looked at Philip Ferrier, "is for you. I urge you, I beg you, to think with extraordinary care."

Philip, head lowered, merely nodded. This all-too-formal young man, with his formal black coat and formal striped trousers and formal hard collar, wore a look not far from sheer tragedy. He had been badly treated and he knew it. He had done his best, and it wasn't good enough. Now, in doggedness and determination, he was trying to understand.

"Look!" he said. "Do you know what killed Eve?"

"Yes," replied Dr. Fell, after exchanging a glance with M. Aubertin. "We have every reason to think we know."

"I'm not trying to dodge your question," Philip said with fierce clarity. "I've been answering a long string of 'em ever since I got back from the bank. Here's what I mean. It doesn't seem to be any secret, from what you two have been saying, that Eve either killed herself or was killed with poison?"

"Yes, young man," answered M. Aubertin. "We are almost certain it was poison."

"Ah!" murmured Sir Gerald Hathaway.

"So all this business about what happened at breakfast—"

"Or before breakfast," Dr. Fell interposed.

"All right; or before breakfast! When it comes down to brass tacks," Philip cried out, "you're saying she was poisoned either at breakfast or before then?"

"In a sense," Dr. Fell agreed gravely, "that is quite true."

"But it can't have been. It's damn silly! Eve didn't have any breakfast. She was at the table, and sometimes she'd have coffee and rolls. But this morning she didn't."

"In this particular instance," replied Dr. Fell. "she had no need to take breakfast in the ordinary way. That is the subject of my question."

A brief, chilly little silence coiled round the group. Hathaway stared at the floor.

"Five of us," continued Dr. Fell, "straggled down to breakfast at various times. 'Down,' in my own case, is a misnomer. I was sleeping on the ground floor, also on the east side. But let the statement stand."

He paused very briefly.

"At whatever times we descended, all of us—you, Mrs. Ferrier herself, Miss Page, Sir Gerald Hathaway and I—had all left the table by seven-thirty. According to Sir Gerald Hathaway, Mrs. Ferrier went for a stroll in the garden at shortly past seven o'clock. Did you see her there?"

"No, I didn't see her. But I'm certain she did."

"Why are you certain?"

"She always did. Every morning since she's been working on that book."

"When and where did you first see her this morning?"

"When I went downstairs, about a quarter past seven. She was coming out of the study."

"Out of the study?" Dr. Fell raised his voice. "Out of the study? Are you quite sure of that?"

"Yes, of course I'm sure," cried Philip, with both an astonishment and a sincerity it was impossible to doubt. "Why shouldn't she have done that? She said she'd sit with us and smoke a cigarette before she began work."

In the midst of a dead silence, while Brian Innes stood rigid behind the door, the silhouette of the policeman moved at the entrance to the flats. Footsteps rang first on tile and then on the concrete of the corridor floor. Marching up to M. Aubertin, the policeman saluted.

"Mr. Director," he said in French, *"the signal has been given."*

"Good!" announced M. Aubertin, with a sharp little smile. "You may go. Into the lift, if you please, with the rest of us. We must see Miss Page."

"But look—!" Philip began.

"Into the lift, please! We can all manage it, I think, at something of a crowding. Miss Page is upstairs; the signal has been given; we have very little time."

The policeman stalked away, leaving Brian's road clear. But he did not move, even after the others had gone up in the lift. He did not move, in fact, until a voice spoke from the stairs just behind him.

He was later to remember that a signal had been given, a baton had been lifted, for a loosing of other forces that would not end until a certain evil scene the next morning.

Meantime, at a time when all his wits groaned with exasperation, he heard Paula Catford speak from the stairs.

She stood halfway down the last concrete flight, gripping the iron railing, under a caged electric bulb whose light threw harsh shadows on a gentle face. He never forgot her there, lithe and slender in the yellow dress, with stockings and shoes (he suddenly noticed) of the same tan colour as Audrey's. Then Paula ran the rest of the way down.

"I wasn't sure I could overtake—" She paused. "Please forgive me for what I said a while ago. I didn't mean it; I didn't mean any of it! If you're going to the Cave of the Witches, so am I."

Exasperation grew still greater. Yet it was not easy to escape the pleading of her voice and her lifted eyes.

"I don't want to seem ungallant, but have you got any special reason?"

"Yes! Every reason!"

"For Desmond Ferrier's sake?"

"For yours too. I wasn't quite frank with you, but then I couldn't be. I couldn't possibly be!" The pleading of her eyes had become almost a hypnosis. "May I go with you?"

"If you promise not to interfere."

"I promise not to interfere at all," said Paula, "in the way you're thinking. But you don't know what may happen there unless I do go. You don't know what may happen," and she touched the lapels of his coat, "at the Cave of the Witches."

XIV

Against the rearward splendour of the moon, above the rue Jean Janvier, a black shape which marked the outline of the Hotel de Ville rose above lower roofs in the streets on top of the hill.

"You've been talking of impossible murders," Paula's voice breathed out of the gloom, "and yet you don't know the name of Aubertin?"

"It's vaguely familiar. I've heard it somewhere."

"You should have. I'll bet Sir Gerald knows it."

"Hathaway knows everything. Why should he know this particular event?"

"It happened in Geneva," said Paula. "A dead woman walked."

Brian, parking the car at an upwards and backwards angle against a little blind wall where it shouldn't have been parked, heard dirt spin under the rear wheels; the car humped and its engine stalled. Paula, in the seat beside him, leaned round and looked into his eyes.

You couldn't see much of the eyes except their faint gleam. Ten o'clock had rung from the bell called Clemency. Aside from the distant barking of a dog, the streets were as quiet as they seemed deserted. Brian inclined his head politely.

"Was it any particular dead woman?"

"I'm serious!"

"So am I. Where is this Cave of the Witches, by the way?"

"You could throw a stone and hit it." Paula leaned still closer. "Shall I show you?"

Brian climbed out of the car. He went round to the other side, opened the door, and almost yanked her out.

"All right. Show me where old Jean Janvier lived. Just because we're going to a night-club with a name like that, there's no need to drag in a ghost or a walking corpse."

"It isn't where Jean Janvier lived. It's a cellar where they've got a lot of his bigger paintings. And, whether you believe it or not, I'm telling the truth about the woman who died. She was the Empress Elizabeth of Austria, wife of the Emperor Franz-Joseph, not quite sixty years ago."

Under the eye of the moon, in a sloping little street with a dim lamp at ground-level, Brian paused as he heard that name.

"The Empress of Austria," said Paula, "had travelled across the lake by steamer from Caux. She was staying incognita at a hotel overlooking the Quai du Mont Blanc. The next afternoon, when she was walking back along the quai to the steamer, a young Italian named Lucheni got up from a bench and ran at her.

"Nobody, including the Empress herself, saw any weapon. The witnesses thought Lucheni made a grab at the watch she was wearing on her breast; his first struck her; then he ran away. The Empress said it was nothing, and walked on to the steamer with the Countess Sztaray. —You remember the case now, don't you?"

"Yes."

"The Empress didn't know it, but she was already dead. She'd been stabbed through lungs and heart with a knife-blade so thin she never felt the internal hemorrhage until afterwards she collapsed and died."

"Another of your journalistic reconstructions? Why mention it now?"

"Don't you see? The Commissary of Police was called Aubertin. It's only a coincidence in names; and, anyway, our present Aubertin is the Director.

"That's all? That's the only reason for mentioning it?"

They were standing close together. Paula looked up again. Either she had forgotten herself in some obscure excitement which made her eyes glisten, or else she remembered her attractiveness all too well and played a deliberate siren-game even with a man whose ideal woman was Audrey Page.

From somewhere near at hand, muffled, the music of an accordion broke out a thread of sound. There were voices, too: little more than a hum or a rustle, yet the sound had depth and grew heavier as the accordion-note soared up.

"Is that the only reason?" Brian demanded.

"You know it's not."

"Well?"

"We're almost there. Those are the steps leading down to the cave."

"I see them. Do you think we're going to meet a dead woman?"

"Oh, don't be absurd! When we see Desmond and your little girl-friend, if we do see them at all, will you let me do all the talking at first? Will you?"

"No."

"You're not very helpful, are you?"

"In getting Audrey arrested for murder?"

"She's not going to be arrested. Will you at least not speak," and Paula seized the lapels of his coat, "until I've said one thing to Desmond? Just one thing? No; don't answer! Don't answer! This way."

The accordion-music, the buffet of voices, smote them as they stumbled down the steps, past a heavy door which Paula opened, along a corridor, and down a few more steps on the right.

"Madame and monsieur," a woman's voice shrieked in French. "Be welcome. Be very welcome among us."

Brian's first impulse, which was to laugh at the incongruity, did not long remain.

In a fairly large cellar built to resemble a rock cave with grottoes and thick pillars, six or seven earnest couples were dancing to the bleat of the accordion. Except that a few were middle-aged, they might have been enthusiastic young men and women at a dance-hall in Hammersmith or Tottenham Court Road.

Then Brian saw the wall-decorations. He also saw the hostess.

A muffled, morbid beat stung the enthusiasm even before accordion had been drowned out by drum, trumpet, and piano.

Grotesque effects, even claptrap ones, are gained through the emotions of those who see them. These dancers were captivated.

In very dim light the hostess, whose thoroughly displayed figure contrasted with her bloodless face and wide-open mouth and the mark of the sword-cut through her neck, swam up at them and looked.

"A table? A table for monsieur and madame? A table?"

You did not notice that the hostess wore a mask until she thrust her face into yours. Paula, taking fright for all her casualness, shied back.

"They're not here," Brian said. "Audrey and *your* boy-friend. They're not here."

"They're bound to be here!"

A shriek of discordant laughter, uttered by a machine like most of civilization's laughter, shook out above that music. It gave Brian the impression, fortunately only for a moment, that the people were not human either.

"Well, look for yourself," he shouted above the din. "You can see every—"

"There! Under the painting of the three vampires with their victim."

"A table?"

"Yes, a table." He was about to ask whether they could get something to eat, but changed his mind. "Over there! The one over there."

Somebody, who had taken too much to drink, fell over one of these tables. They were ranged round the pillars or against the walls. Audrey Page and Desmond Ferrier sat facing each other, their heads together, Audrey talking quickly and her companion seeming to deny every word she spoke.

"Wait!" said Paula.

Brian did not wait. He stalked past the hostess and reached that table by the wall. He could not hear Audrey's last words, or the exclamation Ferrier uttered.

But he saw Audrey's scared, startled countenance as she looked up. He saw Ferrier's expression, one of guilt and near-consternation too spontaneous to be hidden. Rising up so that the chair fell over behind him, Ferrier said one full-throated word which was lost in the crescendo of the music.

147

And then the music stopped dead. Every hostess (there were six of them, in various states of mask and dress) inexplicably vanished as though she had never existed. Soft greenish light broadened and brightened under the grottoes.

And every illusion vanished too. Except for those curious paintings round the walls, the cavern became a commonplace night-club full of rather unfashionable suburbanites applauding the music and chatting their way back to tables covered with red-and-white cloths.

"Good evening, old boy," Desmond Ferrier said agreeably. "Quite a surprise, seeing you here. Sit down, won't you?"

Brian, whose head swam a little from the heat or some other cause, did not answer.

"Sit down, won't you?" Ferrier invited again. "They won't serve a meal after ten o'clock, but you look as though you could do with a sandwich. Care for one?"

"Thanks," said Brian, matching his tone.

"Something to drink?"

"Thanks."

But such a brittle surface must crack under strain; the atmosphere was wrong for it.

Despite thrifty visitors nursing a small brandy or a glass of beer, despite metal ashtrays stamped in practical Woolworth fashion with *La Caverne des Sorcières, 16 rue Jean Janvier*, the big paintings would not be banished.

They lined the walls. They were softly lighted. For all their bad drawing, for all their too-lurid colours and too-intricate detail, they had a clumsy power which breathed images into the mind. Young witches and old crones adored Satan. There was one canvas, on the would-be nursery subject of Bluebeard and his wives, which gave Brian bad dreams several times in the future.

"Sit down, won't you?" Ferrier repeated in too loud a voice.

"No. I don't think either of us will sit down just yet." It was Paula who intervened. "Desmond, this can't go on. I've been talking to Brian here." She paused. "He knows."

"Knows what?"

"This morning," Paula replied in a thin voice, "you told me not to be wilfully obtuse. I wish you wouldn't be obtuse either. If Brian guesses, the police have guessed too. Why don't you tell them that yesterday evening, at least between a little past seven and a

148

little past ten, you were with me in my room at the Hotel du Rhône?"

Nobody spoke while you might have counted ten.

Audrey Page rose slowly to her feet. Paula, after an effort to speak those words without being self-conscious of them, had gone pink in the face and stood rigid. But Ferrier, instead of treating this lightly, made the motions of one who fights through fog.

Gaunt-seeming, drawn up in a fuzzy dark suit and black tie, with his hooded eyes and aquiline nose and broad mouth no longer mocking, he stood outlined against the flesh of vampires on the canvas behind him.

"Now why don't I tell 'em, eh?" he demanded. "What about yesterday afternoon? Why don't I tell 'em that yesterday afternoon, between whatever hours you like, I was in Audrey's room at the Hotel Metropole?"

"*Desmond!*" screamed Paula.

"I don't tell 'em that," Ferrier shouted, "because it's not true. Neither is your story about the Hotel du Rhône."

Paula stared at him.

"There's no need to shield . . ."

"Who's shielding anybody?" asked Ferrier, with his face in a paroxysm and sweat on his forehead in the dim greenish light. "I've played in many things in my time, but never in bedroom farce. Can't you two women think in terms of anything else?"

"And yet," intervened Brian, who was looking hard at that curiously contorted expression, "that's just what it is. It's murder; it's the most serious crime in the world; but it's a bedroom farce that depends on a missing husband."

"What are *you* talking about? What concern is it of yours?"

"It's no concern at all of mine. You can sleep with as many damn women as you like." Suddenly Brian seized Ferrier by the collar, twisted the grip round, and flung him back against the wall. "But what's this about you wanting to frighten Audrey?"

Ferrier's gaunt shoulders whacked against the painting, which slid partly sideways. A bottle went over on the table. And then, after that brief explosion of violence, when several spectators thought it amusing byplay and applauded, both of them controlled themselves.

Ferrier, a man half out of his wits, stood straightening his necktie with the world also beyond all control.

"Frighten Audrey? Are you scatty?"

"I said it," Paula cried out, "but I didn't really mean it. I mean, I didn't know it was the truth. That is—"

Paula stopped, evidently not knowing what she meant.

"Mr. Ferrier," Brian said formally, tugging at his own collar, "I beg your pardon. We don't seem to be acting like civilized human beings."

And Ferrier suddenly shouted with his old laughter.

"That's fair enough, old boy. But I'm glad you said it. For honour's sake I should have had to have a crack back at you; and I'm not as young as I once was."

Then, though he was still mocking himself, his whole voice and bearing altered. It took on a terrifying air of the regal and the stately; even his features seemed to alter in that dim light.

> *Soft you! a word or two before you go.*
> *I have done the state some service, and they know't—*
> *No more of that. I pray you, in your letters,*
> *When you shall these unlucky deeds relate,*
> *Speak of me as I am. Nothing extenuate,*
> *Nor set down aught in malice. Then must you speak*
> *Of one who loved not wisely, but too well;*

Whereupon the voice dropped to its normal tone, shattering illusion with a twist of sarcasm.

"Or, as Othello didn't say, a poor bastard who seems unwisely to have loved everybody in sight. I wasn't frightening Audrey, you clot. If anything, she was frightening me."

"What's that?"

Audrey's exclamation of, "This isn't funny," was instantly cut short.

"I agree it isn't, little one." Ferrier looked at Brian. "She's been questioning me like Aubertin and Dr. Fell themselves."

"Yes, I've been asking him questions," Audrey said in despair. "But I haven't heard much in return, even though I've been utterly and absolutely frank to make him speak. And I *have* been frank about this morning, Brian."

Once more the threat of disaster spread its wings. Or was it really disaster?

"You told him . . . ?"

"I told him I was with Eve in the study. I told him Eve and I had the most awful row. I told him Eve accused me of stealing her husband, though I'm not sure now she meant Mr. Ferrier. I told him Eve ran after me out on the balcony. I've admitted I was alone with Eve when she fell."

Paula said nothing; Paula only looked. After all, she knew the whole story.

On the table between Audrey and Ferrier lay the remains of a sketchy dinner together with two bottles of Burgundy. One of these bottles, empty, had been knocked over. Ferrier, picking up the other bottle without troubling about a glass, tilted it to his mouth and seemed less to swallow than to inhale.

"Have a drink!" he suggested, and thumped the bottle down. "By the way, Innes, what do they do to you in this country if you're convicted of murder? There's no death-penalty, is there?"

"Not yet."

"What do you mean, not yet? Are they reversing the English process and introducing a death-penalty instead of abolishing it?"

"Never mind! The point is—"

"The point is," said Ferrier, who was reasonably tight already, "I didn't realize the dense extent of my trouble this morning. If there was a hypothetical case against Audrey and me twelve hours ago, it gives me green goose-pimples to think what would have happened if Aubertin and Dr. Fell had known all the rest of it."

"Dr. Fell did know."

"Hey?"

"I said Dr. Fell did know. He promised to help you, and he's made me promise too. Don't complain too much; you've had in-credible luck so far."

"So I've had incredible luck, eh? I've had incredible luck, the joker says! When in walks my dearest Paula, not five minutes ago, and blows the gaff on certain alleged relations at the Hotel du Rhône. Whether I'm convicted of murdering my dear wife because of one sweet charmer at the Hotel Metropole, or convicted of murdering her because of another sweet charmer at the Hotel du

Rhône, it won't make very much difference when the jury bring in their verdict."

Paula, hardly breathing, began one speech and ended with another.

"You can't think of anyone but yourself, can you? And all the time, all the silly, romantic, devoted time, *I* thought . . . !"

"You thought what?" Ferrier asked quickly.

"It really doesn't matter."

"Get this straight, my pet." Ferrier spoke with a sick, ironic intensity. "I am your utter and single-minded bond-slave. I kiss your ankles—and vertically."

"Stop! Stop! Stop!"

"Oh, no. I've never deceived you. I never will. But I can't see any way out of this mess without landing in chokey. Who the hell can help any of us now?"

"Possibly I can," said Brian Innes.

"Ho? With all due respect, old boy . . ."

("So now," Brian was reflecting with some irony, "I am nobly going to the rescue of the man I wanted to jump on with both feet, just as in the melodramas he used to play.")

But none of this showed in Brian's manner.

"Listen to me," he said aloud. "This situation may not be as bad as you think. Audrey was asking you some questions, was she?"

"Yes! What about it?"

"Right. If you'll tell the truth about a few things here and now, and Audrey feels up to telling us about breakfast this morning . . ."

"About breakfast?"

"That's what I said. If both of you will do that, we may be able to nab the murderer independently of the police and even of Dr. Fell."

Paula glanced at him quickly. Audrey kept her gaze on the table. Ferrier, picking up the bottle again and draining it in one monumental swill, gave him a hard, wary look before putting down the empty bottle.

"Did I invite any of you to have a drink?" he asked. "No; wait. We can't get service until the lights go down and the witches return. But look here: if you're assuming the role of Great Detective, lately played by Sir Gerald Hathaway . . ."

"I'm not assuming the role of great detective. I can't pretend to it."

"Have it your own way, old boy. All the same! How do you get round the fact that they may arrest Audrey for chucking Eve off that balcony?"

"Audrey didn't throw anybody off a balcony. By this time the police know it. Your wife was poisoned, Mr. Ferrier."

"Ho?"

"Your wife was poisoned, I repeat, either at breakfast or before breakfast this morning. That lets you out, because you didn't come down to breakfast. It lets Paula out; she wasn't there either. Finally, if Audrey had really poisoned Mrs. Ferrier, would she have hung about to watch the poison work and get suspicion thrown straight at herself?"

Abruptly, through that imitation cave, the laughter-machine in some grotto uttered its brazen screech of ha-ha-ha. Pleasurable little squeals and cries greeted it from the women guests. Audrey sat down at the table and put her face in her hands.

"Eve was poisoned?" demanded Ferrier, taking out a silver cigarette case. "How do you know that?"

"I heard Aubertin and Dr. Fell say so."

"Ho? And how was she poisoned?"

"They didn't honour me with their confidence. But there's one possibility, at least. What about the cigarette she was smoking at breakfast?"

XV

"Cigarette?" Ferrier repeated incredulously.

The sight of his own cigarette-case caught his eye. In a still more feverish mood he put it back in his pocket without opening it.

"As you've been pointing out, old boy," he added, "I wasn't at breakfast this morning. I never heard one word about any cigarette. What makes you think it was that?"

"I don't think so, necessarily. Maybe the police don't think so either. The poison may not have been administered at breakfast. Dr. Fell only intimated that; he didn't say it in so many words. On the other hand, he did indicate it and it's our only lead."

If Brian's fingernails had been longer, he would have gnawed at them.

"There's also the possibility," he said, "that the police are hiding the trumps in their hand until they can scoop up everything."

"Meaning what, old boy?"

"That she may not have been poisoned at all."

"Now take it easy!"

"Mrs. Ferrier," said Brian, "may have been stabbed with a knife-

154

blade so thin that not a spot of blood showed, and they didn't find any wound until the police-surgeon examined her. As in the case of the Empress of Austria. Dr. Fell swore this morning that the whole world would know the truth within twenty-four hours."

Ha-ha-ha rang the demoniac blare of laughter from its metal throat, quivering amid tables and bottles.

Paula Catford made a shivering movement that was too calm for anger.

"This isn't helping us, and it's just a bit silly. Desmond, will you dance with me? I want to talk to you. *Will* you dance with me?"

"I can't dance with you, sweetie-pie, until the band gives us some music. But that merry ha-ha means the effects are beginning; the lights will go down and the band will begin at any minute. Meanwhile, who's the Empress of Austria? What's she doing in this?"

"Nothing," Brian admitted. "We won't go into that, because it might bring the guilt straight back to Audrey. Let's take a more reasonable line. Mr. Ferrier, did you ever hear of a poison called nitrobenzene?"

And, clearly, Ferrier had.

He did not attempt to evade or deny. Leaning down to pick up the chair he had knocked over when he first jumped up, he set it back carefully on its legs.

"Yes, I've heard of it. My dear wife's first husband committed suicide with the stuff. You heard that from Aubertin, didn't you?"

"From Aubertin?"

"Naturally." Ferrier's voice held a shade of impatience. "When they questioned us in separate compartments for most of the day, Aubertin startled my ears off by knowing it."

"No; I heard it from—"

About to mention Hathaway's name, Brian stopped. Ever afterwards, when all truths were plain, he was to remember Paula Catford and Audrey Page as his questions proceeded: Paula standing tall and dark-haired, in a tight-fitting yellow dress, close beside him; Audrey, smaller and more rounded, in brown tweed suit and orange sweater, sitting at the table and suddenly looking up. They spoke almost together.

Audrey said: "Her *first* husband?"

Paula said: "I'm not the only one, it seems, who listens at doors."

Ferrier gripped the back of the chair.

"A minute ago, old boy, you were blabbering something about a bedroom farce. . . ."

"And a missing husband. Yes."

"You don't think one of my late wife's husbands had anything to do with this?"

"I think that's the key to the secret, if we can find it."

"Lord of high hell," intoned Ferrier, with a roll in his voice as though he were again playing Othello, "those blokes are dead. D-e-a-d, dead. They could no more have come back than Eve herself could come back."

"Don't talk like that!" cried Audrey.

"Let me ask the questions, will you?" Brian begged. He did not take his eyes from Ferrier. "Your wife smoked, didn't she?"

"Yes. Fairly heavily."

"I thought so. In the study, just to the left of the manuscript she was writing in some kind of purple ink, there was a big glass ashtray."

"What about the manuscript?" Ferrier asked sharply.

"Just a minute! Did you ever use that study?"

"No, never. It was Eve's particular domain and nobody else's."

"But I understood you were writing your memoirs too?"

"I tried." Ferrier moved his neck. "I began it. I tried, so help me! I sat on the terrace and chewed a pencil. And yet, when I looked back over what they call a great theatrical career, the only scenes that stood out in my mind were incidents that were funny or incidents that were bawdy."

Paula cast up her eyes. "Please, Desmond! This is hardly the time . . . !"

"I can't help it, my pet. That's how I am. Only the other day a couple of earnest interviewers nearly blew their stacks when they were questioning me about my conception of the character of Hamlet. 'We feel, Mr. Ferrier, that we have solved every problem of this play except one. Mr. Ferrier, did Hamlet seduce Ophelia?' 'In my day,' I said, 'invariably.' "

"*Desmond!*"

"I keep telling you, my pet: I'm like that! You wouldn't have me any other way. But I don't feel such stories add much to Shakespearean commentary, or would greatly improve my reputation if I wrote 'em down."

"Desmond, haven't you maligned yourself enough?"

"Possibly he has," snapped Brian, and Ferrier's eyes changed a little, "because we're going on to the murder. This *is* a question of murder."

"Why is it? If my dear wife committed suicide, or else . . . Look here, Innes: could the poison have been in a cigarette?"

"I think it could have."

"Nitrobenzene?"

"Without Dr. Fell's or Hathaway's encyclopaedic knowledge, I do seem to remember one or two facts about that poison. It's used commercially for dyes and—and other things. If you soaked cigarette-tobacco in a preparation of the stuff, and you could somehow conceal the odour, I think the smoke might be damnably dangerous."

"Are you sure of that?"

"No! But we've got to thrash it out.—Audrey!"

Audrey sat up straight.

"Yes? What is it?"

The light which illumined the Cave of the Witches had begun to dwindle and fade slowly among the pillars. Appreciative "Oh's!" and "Ah's!" from other tables greeted this approach of darkness. The paintings would remain faintly visible: like that, behind Ferrier's back, of the three vampire women taking their blood sustenance from an apparently dead young girl in a churchyard. And therefore the faces at this table remained visible too.

"Here we go again," observed Ferrier, "for more ghost-and-corpse effects in the dark." He struck the back of the chair. "Can anybody tell me why my late dear wife liked this place so very much?"

Audrey, lines of fatigue under her eyes, twitched her head round with the glossy brown hair trembling against her cheeks.

"Do you mean to say you don't know, Mr. Ferrier?"

"Easy, little one!"

"Even if people do think I'm stupid, I can tell you that without any trouble. She loved thinking of herself as a . . . as a *femme fatale*, or a witch-woman, or any of the kind of parts she played in those old films they're always reviving."

"Dear, dear, dear!" Paula breathed out of the gloom. "That's very perceptive. Imagine your noticing it!"

"I notice a good deal, thanks very much," said Audrey. "Do you mean to say *you* don't like the place, Mr. Ferrier?"

"Yes, I like it. In more elegant language, so what?" Again Ferrier's voice grew to a shout. "You sound like the coppers this afternoon, cornering me in the drawing-room and grilling me like a sole. I was here for dinner yesterday evening, was I? Did I like the Cave of the Witches best when I dined out? Did other people prefer it too?"

"What did you say?" asked Paula, raising her voice too.

"Eve liked it best, yes. I like it, right enough; but give me a good meal at the Béarn. Phil doesn't like it; he prefers the Globe or the Hotel du Rhône. You, Paula, like it a good deal better than you've ever admitted to anybody on earth—"

"That's absurd!"

"All right, call me a swine again. I was rattled; it's not as easy as being questioned by Innes here. Innes, what do you think you can find out from Audrey?"

"I can find out what happened this morning," said Brian. "That is, if Audrey's up to it?"

"Darling, I'm not so frail as all that," Audrey cried. She looked up at him with a strength and intensity that made his heart turn over. "But I don't understand what I can tell you. Nothing *happened!*"

"Maybe a good deal happened. Think back. At what time, before breakfast, did Mrs. Ferrier go out into the garden?"

"Eve? Into the garden?"

" 'Now the serpent,' " Ferrier proclaimed, " 'was more subtle than any beast of the field which the Lord God had made. And he said unto the woman—' "

"Ferrier," Brian yelled, "for the love of Mike keep out of this. Audrey, please answer me. At what time did Mrs. Ferrier go out into the garden?"

Audrey, with wide-open blue eyes, looked back at him uncomprehendingly.

"Brian, I don't understand what you're talking about. She didn't."

"Didn't what?"

"She didn't go into the garden at any time."

"But she was seen there!"

"Who saw her?"

At the far side of the cellar, on a long note, the accordion swept up its music for the beginning of more dancing. Chairs shuffled back in the gloom. These four, at the table for four beside the wall, remained motionless.

"Let's get this straight!" Brian insisted. "As I understand it, she usually went for a stroll there before breakfast?" He glanced at Ferrier. "Isn't that so?"

"Yes, she always did. But don't ask me anything about this morning. Paula and I weren't up. Consequently, as you yourself have pointed out—!"

Audrey looked from one to the other of them.

"D-darling," she said to Brian, commencing to stammer and then correcting herself, "all I can tell you is what happened."

"Well?"

"I was the first downstairs. I hadn't slept a wink; I feel like death now. D-Dr. Fell knocked at my door at about a quarter to seven. I was already dressed, and we went downstairs. That maid (Stephanie, is it?) was laying the table."

"Go on."

"Sir Gerald Hathaway joined us about five minutes past seven; Eve was with him. Sir Gerald asked if he could borrow the Rolls to go to Geneva. She said yes. She wouldn't sit down at the table; she kept looking at me like fire. When Sir Gerald asked if she wouldn't have something to eat, she said no. But she said she'd got some cigarettes in the study, and she'd have a cigarette. She went upstairs; I thought, 'Oh, God, what's she up to?' and I ran out and looked up the stairs after her. All she did was go into the study, and come out again with a packet of ordinary Players' cigarettes, and run downstairs to the dining-room. She smoked one, yes. But . . ."

Here Audrey, staring at memory, let her voice trail away.

"Brian," she added, "why do you think it's so frightfully important? About the garden, I mean?"

"*I* don't think so. Dr. Fell does."

"Why?"

"The Lord only knows. Listen! When she went up to the study to get her cigarettes, couldn't she have gone down to the garden by way of the outer staircase? And back up to the study again?"

"No. There wasn't time. Anyway, there's a high stone wall on the east side between the rear terrace and the garden. She couldn't have climbed over it: not a woman like that. What's more, there's another thing too."

And here Audrey cleared her throat.

"I—I don't know about poisons and such things. But I'm quite definitely certain she couldn't have been poisoned by that cigarette."

Paula Catford, who had been waiting quietly, now spoke with great clearness.

"Audrey's right, you know."

"Easy, my pet!" snapped Ferrier.

"Desmond, please use your common sense. Could poor Eve have smoked a poisoned cigarette, at a table with all the rest of them there, without anybody else getting a whiff of it? Or, if she smoked it before seven-thirty, would its effect have been delayed until nearly nine o'clock? Any more than that could have happened to Mr. Matthews at Berchtesgaden?"

Silence. And checkmate.

More people were going out to the dance-floor. Drum, trumpet, and piano joined the accordion. The mechanical laughter blared above it. Out of the murk towards their table swam a death's head face above the body of a woman in a semi-transparent red-gauze robe, making Paula start in spite of herself and Audrey suppress a scream when the death's head bent down and looked at them.

Ferrier was giving some order which Brian couldn't hear. Paula tugged at his arm.

"Desmond, I want to dance. And I simply must talk to you."

"Half a tick, half a tick! For a second, there," Ferrier said to Brian, who had lowered his head in bitterness, "I was almost convinced you'd got it. There must be *some* solution to this business."

"Yes; there must be."

"Desmond!" begged Paula.

Half reluctantly, with a strained and pinched look round his nostrils, Ferrier took Paula's hand; they moved away into the dark. Brian looked at Audrey.

"I don't suppose you'd care to dance too?"

"I'd love to." Audrey sprang up instantly. "Stay beside me; stay as close as you can; don't ever go far."

"In that case, I trust you'll remember your own prescription. If you disappear again into the blue, as you've done twice before . . ."

"Brian, don't be cross! I won't disappear. However did you find me? And do you realize this is the first time you've ever danced with me? This is the first time you've ever condescended to?"

"Condescended to? The new dances aren't much in my line; I'm all for the fox-trot of twenty years ago. But this is an old-fashioned waltz anyone can manage."

Old-fashioned waltz or not, it was not being played quite like one. Nor was the spirit which swayed and swept through the cavern as they whirled out with the half-dozen other couples. Audrey's eyes, those intent blue eyes a little slanted up at the outer corners, were fixed on him. With or without intention, they circled from right to left round the circle of the cavern: widdershins, some would have called it.

"Wrong!" he muttered. "That solution of mine. All wrong! And yet—"

"No. I don't believe that! Do you remember my saying, earlier this evening, that when Eve stormed out at me she sounded as though she were hypnotized?"

"Yes?"

"A closer word," said Audrey, "would be groggy or drunk. Which is why she wasn't making much sense. She was poisoned then; she must have been."

"Yes; I thought of that. When I heard her talking through the closed door, she sounded like a woman sleepwalking. Afterwards, when she ran frantically at the loose edge of the balcony, she put her hands up to her throat as though poison had got her."

Audrey shivered in his arms. The music beat faster. In that dim greenish light, seen under the arches of the grottoes with comparatively few couples round them, the parade of Jean Janvier's paintings showed madness or death in their most exaggerated forms.

"Brian!"

Looking past his shoulder, she lost the beat of the music; both of them half-stumbled, recovered, and automatically moved on as Brian glanced over his own shoulder towards the direction of Audrey's gaze.

Paula Catford was leaving the Cave of the Witches.

There could be no doubt it was Paula.

Some thirty feet away, under another arch, Brian could see the five steps leading up to the corridor by which he had entered. Despite the bad light he could see Paula with reasonable clearness. There was nothing furtive about her leaving; she hurried up the steps and was gone.

"Of course," Brian began, "it might be—"

"If you're thinking of the ladies' room, no. That's in the other direction."

"Where's Ferrier?"

"I don't know. I can't see him."

It should have been easy to see him, since the cave was only sparsely filled. But they had little time to think even of this. The hollow shuffle of dancing feet, the dedication of faces swirling past, grew into something like an act of worship as the band's tempo became faster. What little light remained sank away until it was totally dark except for a vague phosphorescent glow round the pictures.

The music soared up and ended with a triumphant drum-roll. Yet no applause followed; only an excited whispering from dancers and spectators.

"Brian, I don't like this. What's happening?"

"Well, the music's stopped. People seem to be going back to their tables. We'd better go back to ours."

"But what is it?"

"Probably some kind of floor-show. You'll seldom find a night-club without one. Take my arm."

A man's harsh voice, from the direction of the orchestra, had in fact begun to speak at that moment, though the continuing drums obscured what he was saying. These words were also blurred by the rustle of murmurs rising hollowly under the roof. Holding Audrey's arm, Brian guided her in the other direction: towards a faint luminousness which marked the vampire-painting above their table beside the wall.

He now had no doubt it would be a floor-show. Vague shapes, spectators standing up and pressing a little forward round the circle of the arches, seemed to be staring towards the band-leader while Brian pushed Audrey past them and through the ranks towards what he imagined as the shelter of their table.

On the table, when they reached it, had been put down an

opened bottle of brandy and two clean glasses. But Ferrier wasn't there.

"He'll be here," Brian assured Audrey. "Or, at least, I hope he will be. Whatever night-club we go to, we never seem fated to finish the drinks somebody's ordered. Not that I particularly look forward to anything to drink. I'm too hungry."

"Darling, are you really hungry?"

"No. To tell the truth, I'm not. There's only one consolation: they've stopped that blasted mechanical laughter."

They had stopped the mechanical laughter, it was true. He had not expected other ingenious devices, and Audrey had not experienced them before.

The vividness of the artificial lightning, opening in a dazzling white series of winks, was followed by thunder-peals which exploded as though close above their heads. Brian's first feeling was irritation, then wrath at such tomfoolery.

"Ferrier ought to be here," he said. "He'd enjoy it. This is like the witches' cavern in the fourth act of *Macbeth*. I never saw Beerbohm Tree's famous production at Her Majesty's; it was before my time. And there doesn't seem to be any boiling cauldron. Otherwise it's reminiscent. 'Thrice the brinded cat hath mewed—' "

"Brian, let's get out of here."

"It's all right!"

"I daresay it is. But let's get out of here. It's too much like this morning, with the thunder over the balcony when Eve . . ."

They stood alone by the table, in an aisle of pillars with deserted tables covered in red-and-white cloth. Again Brian swore it was all right. At the same time, the thought darted into his brain, he was much too angry at a mere stage-device. If you became as furious as all that, if you cursed it too much, it was because your wrath hid some creeping tentacle of fear.

Then Audrey screamed.

The lightning held too long, like a frozen dazzle, before the stunning reverberations of the thunder. He and Audrey were standing close together. That was when they both saw the face of Eve Ferrier looking at them round the side of a pillar.

He knew it was only a mask, of course. At least, he knew this after the first blankness of the shock. He did not expect to see someone's hand, in a glove, rise up and point at them.

Three shots, from some very small-calibre weapon, were fired at them from a distance of less than ten feet. Even Brian did not hear the shots, whip-lashes lost under the ensuing thunder-noise; nobody else heard them at all.

He did not see the figure behind the pillar as the cave went dark. But he did see, by the evil luminescence round the vampire-painting, one result of those shots.

Audrey reeled and fell across the table. An empty wine-bottle, jarred by the fall, rolled off and smashed on the floor.

ACT THREE

". . . *Thou shalt not live!*
That I may tell pale-hearted fear it lies
And sleep in spite of thunder."

—MACBETH

XVI

Brian Innes dreamed a dream.

Instead of being asleep at his own flat in the Quai Turrettini, in the early hours of the morning on Saturday, August 11—which was actually the fact—he dreamed he still stood in the Cave of the Witches when those shots were fired.

Perhaps it was right that the dream should have been so much like reality. For, in that cellar on Friday night, reality had been so much like a dream.

In a nightmare, no matter what happens, nobody around you is ever surprised at it. You yourself may feel all sorts of emotions, from anger to terror; but nobody else seems to feel any emotion, or even much notice what is occurring.

You stand in a crowd, beside the girl with whom you are in love. Commonplace circumstances, a rather tawdry night-club which puts on a show you know to be a show, have dissolved into grisliness because of one extra touch.

A real human being, wearing a mask of rubber or papier-mâché, has altered that pattern by trying either to kill you or to kill the woman beside you.

167

Nobody turns round to look. And you, though you may feel the wind of fear, yet you aren't surprised either. Is it because, subconsciously, you have half recognized who the murderer is?

Brian knew he was dreaming. But that doesn't help, in the eerie morning hours when sleep wears thin and sweat starts out on the body.

In his dream, somebody screamed.

Startled awake, he sat up. It might have been yesterday morning. The telephone was ringing.

"Yes?" he said aloud, to the air.

He wasn't in the bedroom. He lay stretched out, leg-and-neck cramped, in pyjamas and dressing-gown, on the sofa in the little living-room with its cream-coloured stucco walls. Clean sunlight flooded the room, where curtains blew at open windows.

Brian picked up the 'phone with the effect of strangling it; at least it gave him silence. His, "Hello," in a tentative voice, was greeted by a throat-clearing of worry and ominousness both together.

"Sir—" began the voice of Dr. Fell.

"Sh-h-h!" urged Brian.

"What's that?"

"Sh-h!"

"I trust," observed Dr. Fell, "you are quite sober?" Brian could imagine the doctor's countenance, half ferocious and half pitying, close against the other mouthpiece. "Yes? Then may I ask what happened to you and Miss Page last night? Aubertin and I called on you."

"I know you did."

"Oh, ah? You will remember, perhaps, that the door of your flat was wide open? But nobody was there, and no message had been left?"

"There was a little trouble."

"There may well be more. Where were you?"

"Sh-h!" Brian glanced round the room, where his clothes lay scattered on the furniture. "I haven't time to tell you all of it over the 'phone. Briefly, Paula Catford and I went to a night-club called the Cave of the Witches."

As he sketched the rest of the story, Dr. Fell's breathing over the 'phone became more laboured and more wheezing.

"It wasn't Mrs. Ferrier's ghost or her corpse. It was an unpleasantly lifelike head-mask with fair hair, shoved round the side of the pillar and looking through eye-holes. I couldn't see anything at all of the figure, especially in that light."

"Who was hit?"

"Nobody. Three bullets went wild, diagonally, through a painting above our heads. The marks looked very small, about the size of a .22."

"And Miss Page collapsed, you say?"

"Audrey fainted. Less from fear than from shock on top of complete exhaustion. I didn't think she had been hit. There seems to be a general impression, from films and television," snarled Brian, "that you've only got to point a weapon in the general direction of someone, and pull the trigger. Presto! Some magic of firearms lets you kill at any distance, with any kind of snap-shot, and in any kind of light. It's a little more complicated than that."

"Where is Miss Page now?"

"Sh-h! She's here. She's asleep; she's in my bedroom. Just a minute."

"Sir—"

"Just a minute, confound it!"

Carefully Brian put down the 'phone. Groping for his slippers, he looked at the clock as he tiptoed out into the little hall. The white-painted door to the bedroom, where Audrey lay in exhausted sleep, was still reassuringly closed. At ten minutes past nine, on a fine Saturday morning, it was as though you could taste the sparkle of the air.

He returned to the 'phone.

"I'll answer your next question, Dr. Fell, before you even ask it. No, I did not set up a hue and cry after the person who fired the shots. Under the circumstances, would you have? I picked Audrey up and carried her out of there."

The telephone was silent, as though pondering.

"Did you hear?" Brian asked.

"Sir, I heard."

"Nobody in the place had seen what happened. The only person who approached was a hostess-waitress who rather gleefully said,

'Ah, the poor little one,' and indicated that people were constantl
fainting at such a delightful show. As for Paula and Desmon
Ferrier . . ."

"Oh, ah?" The other voice was casual and poised.

"They'd already gone. Both of 'em. Paula was the only one w
saw go. When Audrey and I went back to the table, we'd foun
an open bottle of brandy and two clean glasses. Under the bottl
was a note from Ferrier, though I didn't notice it until Audre
fell across the table."

"A note?"

"Paula was more upset than she'd admit. The note just asked t
to excuse them; it said the brandy had been paid for, and wouldn
we drink a toast to them *in absentia?*"

"Is Miss Page all right now?"

"Yes, I'm glad to say. But it wasn't likely I'd let her spend th
night alone at any hotel." Brian's conscience, never far fror
haunting him, intruded like the vision of the face round the pilla
"Anyway, whether I acted rightly or wrongly, it's done. There i
is."

"As you say, sir, there it is. Now tell me: was the weapon use
by the masked figure by any chance a Browning .22 automatic, o
the sort which used to be manufactured in Belgium?"

"It could have been. I didn't get a close look at it."

"And was the mask," Dr. Fell spoke with muffled thunder, "on
designed for Mrs. Ferrier by a man named Lafargue, the owner o
the night-club? Showing her face as it looked in the days of he
beauty?"

"Paula said there *was* a mask of some sort. That's all I know
Where did you hear about the mask and the pistol?"

"Aubertin found them yesterday morning when he made a searc
of the study. Both mask and pistol belonged to Mrs. Ferrier hersel
They were identified, also yesterday morning, by her husband.
Dr. Fell groaned. "Since then, it would appear, somebody stol
them. We should have paid more attention to the Cave of th
Witches. One last point. How did you learn Miss Page had gon
to this curious night-club?"

Brian told him.

"Indentations? On the sheet of a note-pad?" Dr. Fell spoke eve
more heavily. "You put the sheet of paper in your pocket, yo

say. Have you still got that sheet of paper?"

"I imagine so. There's no reason—"

"Will you kindly look and see?"

Once more Brian put down the telephone. The jacket of the suit he had worn was hanging over the back of a chair close at hand. After groping in the side-pocket and finding nothing, he searched the other pockets with care.

"It's gone," he reported, picking up the 'phone. "I must have dropped it. I can't remember when or where."

"Oh, ah. I rather expected it would be gone. Now heark'ee!" Dr. Fell addressed the 'phone with toiling lucidity. "I am at the Villa Rosalind, as you may guess. Can you drive out here within the next hour or so, and bring Miss Page with you?"

"If it's necessary, yes."

"It may be very necessary. Aubertin means to make an arrest. This news of the attack last night will spur him on, as it should. Meanwhile, Sir Gerald Hathaway must be prevented from causing trouble, as I fear he means to do."

"Hathaway? He's not at it again?"

"Oh, yes. He is very much at it. Take good care of Miss Page, and walk very warily yourself. Before this day is ended, you may meet far more unpleasantness than you expect. Until I see you, then."

The line went dead.

Brian replaced the 'phone, and sat studying it as though it could tell him what he most wanted to know. What roused him was the noise of the doorbell, whose buzz had a rattlesnake insistence like that of the single word 'unpleasantness.'

It was Madame Duvallon, cheerful and hearty as usual: now deprived of her key, but arriving punctually at nine-thirty. Brian held the door open for her while she beamed her greeting on the threshold.

"And the young lady? She is still here? She goes well, I hope?"

"Not very well, madame. But you had better prepare a cup of tea and wake her up with it."

"And, after that, the English breakfast?"

"The very large English breakfast, madame. I am so hungry that—"

Brian paused. There was someone else in the corridor, standing

171

a dozen feet away and watching him. Conscious of nerves not at their best, he just stopped himself from snapping, "Who's there?" although he could see very well who it was.

Desmond Ferrier, in grey slacks and a chequered sports-coat, but having nothing else that was festive about his appearance, loomed up with his fists dug deeply into his pockets.

" 'Morning, old boy. And you needn't look so surprised." Ferrier showed his teeth. "You're in the telephone-book, you know."

"I'm also in the flat. If you want to see me, you've only got to ring the bell. If you want to see anyone else . . ."

"I want to see you. Mind if I come in?"

"The breakfast, Madame Duvallon."

Brian waited until Madame Duvallon, whipping off her coat and hat, had gone into the little kitchen. Then he motioned Ferrier inside, and closed the door. Ferrier, at a not very convincing swagger, strode into the living-room.

"Yes?" Brian prompted. "Have you any particular reason for being here?"

"For one thing," returned Ferrier, taking his hands out of his pockets, "I've been kicked out of my own house. Or practically kicked out. And to think I was the one who asked Dr. Fell to clear up this business!"

Brian waited.

"*I* asked him," repeated Ferrier, with a bitterness which seemed almost past bearing. "I told everyone all about him. I spread the good word. I thought his presence would be a warning. I—" Ferrier stopped. "Now he's working hand in glove with the police. Aubertin seems to have a high opinion of him, which is more than I'm beginning to have. He even defers to that little swine Hathaway; he's been doing it since Thursday night."

"Hathaway's all right; he's just a little above himself, that's all."

"Ah, yes. I forgot Hathaway's a friend of yours too."

Abruptly, bristling, they faced each other fully.

"Now what if he is?" Brian demanded. "Did you come here just to tell me all this?"

"No."

"Well, then?"

"I wanted to see you," Ferrier replied, after a pause and a faintly deprecating gesture, "because Paula asked me to."

Whereupon he dropped his guard.

"Innes, I'm serious about Paula. I'm as serious about her as you are about Audrey."

"Serious?"

"Why can't I say it straight out? Why do all of us (you too!) pretend we think honest feelings are infra dig? In the nineteen-twenties, when I was still young, a lot of people in the theatre began jeering that all the old plays were funny. If you took a part with real guts in it, if you cut loose and gave it the works, they said you were funny too. They tried to scare you with the word 'ham.' And why? Because they couldn't do a part with guts in it, so they knew they'd better not try.

"The theatre's changed now, thank God. Or at least it's changing. Even then I thought, 'To hell with this mealy-mouthed stuff. Play it in the grand manner or don't play it at all. If a line's difficult, show you know your job by getting away with it.' I mean—"

Ferrier stopped.

"Look here, Innes. Do you understand what I'm talking about, or don't you?"

"Yes. I understand."

Every time you tried to be hostile towards this man, Brian was thinking, he disarmed you with an honesty and even a naïveté that had its own appeal.

"This is real life, old boy; it's not the stage. What I'm trying to say . . ."

"What you're trying to say," Brian interrupted, "is that you really were with Paula for three hours on Thursday night. Paula doesn't cheat. She's never cheated or tried to take you away from Eve. But you think it would sound uproariously funny if you said so."

"Yes!"

"Why should it sound funny?"

"Well, it does. I'm really in love with that damn woman, though I'm a good deal older than she is. You can't understand that, Innes. . . ."

"I can't, eh?"

"But that's not the point. You guessed I was with her. Did you tell the police about it?"

"No. I promised her I wouldn't, and I've kept the promise."

173

"Then what did you tell Hathaway?"

"*Hathaway?* Not a thing. Hathaway doesn't have any concern in this."

"He oughtn't to have, maybe, but he's pulling strings. Last night, when we left you and Audrey at the Cave of the Witches, we drove straight home. Hathaway got back half an hour afterwards, with 'inspiration' written all over him. He began questioning Paula. She won't even say what she told him, but I don't like it."

"If you're worried about yourself . . ."

"For the sweet love of the sweet so-and-so," yelled Ferrier, with another of those elaborate Biblical oaths which were as much a part of his mind as of his speech, "do you think I'm worried about myself? Or ever have been? It's Paula."

That was when the telephone rang again.

The effect on their nerves was not helped by the noise of a tea-kettle, which had begun to scream in the kitchen before Madame Duvallon twitched it off the gas-burner. Nor was it helped by the voice Brian heard when he answered the 'phone.

"Forgive me for troubling you," begged that familiar voice. "But is Desmond there? He said he was going to see you. May I—?"

The sound of the voice, if not the actual words, reached Ferrier.

"That's Paula, isn't it?"

"Yes. She wants to talk to you."

Handing the 'phone to Ferrier, Brian went over and looked out of one window so as pointedly to avoid listening. Under soft sunshine Geneva wore its usual pastel colours of grey and brown and white. By craning out of the window and sideways, he could see the lake stretching deep grey-blue with the white of an occasional sail.

"But that was seventeen years ago," he heard Ferrier objecting. "It can't make any difference what you failed to tell him then! I don't see it makes any difference now."

The faint drone of the voice went on. Less than thirty seconds later Brian gave up all pretence of disinterest.

"*Cornered? What do you mean, he's got you cornered?*"

Ferrier, with a face of incredulity and collapse, listened to six more words.

"Oh, I shall be there," he said. "That's my house; they can't keep me out of it. I shall be there."

174

The 'phone went down with a bang.

"What is it?" Brian demanded. "What's the trouble?"

"Excuse me, old boy. I must take off in a hurry."

You would not have believed that a man who called himself elderly could have moved so fast. Big shoes thudded across the living-room and the entry. The front door opened and slammed.

Brian, with a sense of approaching catastrophe, had to adjust his wits so as to remember French speech when he also hurried out into the hall.

"Madame Duvallon!" he called. "You had better wake up Miss Page as quickly as possible. There may not even be time for breakfast. You had better—"

He stopped. The bedroom door was wide open. Madame Duvallon, carrying a tray with a tea-service and an enormous cup and saucer, emerged from the doorway. China skittered on the tray as it slid in her hands.

"M. Innes, I cannot wake her up. The young lady is not here."

Neither of them spoke for the next few seconds. A clamour of thickening morning traffic rose from the quais.

"M. Innes," cried Madame Duvallon, seeing his face, "the young lady has gone out. I cannot help it if she has gone out. Look for yourself!"

Brian looked.

Audrey's nightgown, a flimsy and transparent affair, had been thrown down across the foot of a tumbled bed. Her small suitcase, brought up last night from his car, again lay open on a chair. Across the mirror of the dressing-table, still unerased, mocking him, ran those words she had written in lipstick when she left the flat earlier last night instead of (presumably) early this morning.

'I love you too.' ran the words. 'Please forgive what I'm going to do.'

Whether they applied to this morning as well as last night, or whether Audrey had simply forgotten to erase them, he couldn't tell. But she was gone.

The ringing of the telephone, dinning in his ears immediately afterwards, should have brought an eagerness of hope. Instead, human nature being what it is, most comprehensively he cursed that noise because its suddenness made him jump. Madame Duvallon, a practical woman, set the perspective right.

175

"M. Innes," she proclaimed with cold dignity, "this is not good sense. The telephone: it sounds. Please to answer it."

Brian did so. The voice of Dr. Fell, hoarse and very disturbed, for the first few words was incomprehensible. Afterwards it sharpened.

"I greatly fear—" said Dr. Fell.

"Yes?"

"Matters have got out of hand. Archons of Athens! I didn't anticipate the man would carry anything so far, or lead us to so lunatic a pass. Is Mr. Desmond Ferrier still with you?"

"No; you must have guessed he isn't. Ferrier left a minute or two ago. And where's Audrey? Have you any idea what's happened to Audrey?"

"Oh, ah. I—er—have just discovered that. It would be neither quite fair nor quite accurate to say Miss Page is under arrest. . . ."

"*Arrest?*"

"Pray accept my word," roared Dr. Fell, "that you have little cause for worry. I beg you to follow Mr. Ferrier; to overtake him and stop him if you can. If not, come on to the villa by yourself. Do not argue with me; stop him!"

"Now just a minute!"

Once more the line went dead. Madame Duvallon, putting down the tea-tray, first called on her Maker and then burst into tears.

XVII

The Villa Rosalind, an unrelieved white except for its bright flower-boxes and its bull's-eye window of coloured glass, loomed up as even less pleasant a place under pale sunshine than under a dusk of approaching storm.

Its windows, shutters all closed, had a blank and empty stare. It looked deserted, despite the crowding of cars in the drive. Even its repose, like that of the woods stretching round about and the deep gully behind, gave it the appearance of a house poisoned by haunting. And perhaps from much the same cause.

Emotion rises too high. It ends in murder. With life gone and the body in decay, other forces enter and gather and whisper suggestions to the brain.

Brian couldn't help the fancy. It was true, when he barely slowed the speed of the car and plunged in towards the villa, that his heart rose up in his throat from another cause. He braked just in time to avoid smashing into the rear bumper of the Rolls.

You can't overtake a Rolls in an ancient M.G., even though traffic impedes you both and though you drive like a maniac when it doesn't.

The other car had been left there, empty amid the other empty cars. Desmond Ferrier, presumably, had gone into the villa.

And yet . . .

Even in his preoccupation about Audrey, Brian could not quite shake off that feeling of a house given over to a dead woman.

"Hullo!" he called at the front door, just as he had done the previous morning. Automatically he reached out for the bell that wouldn't work.

There was no reply.

He opened the door and walked into the lower hall.

It was nearly dark; the wooden shutters on the downstairs rooms, at both sides as well as in front, had also been closed. Only the clock, with its pendulum of a doll in a swing, stirred and ticked with endless beats. Then someone moved near the foot of the staircase.

Gustave Aubertin, Director of Police, stood with his sharp, thin face vaguely illumined by a spear of light through the crescent-pattern design in a shutter.

"Good morning, Mr. Innes. Please go upstairs. You will find some of your friends there."

The English words, though precisely spoken, were not quite as unemotional as the clock. Brian strode towards him.

"Where's Audrey Page?"

"Go upstairs, Mr. Innes."

"Where's Audrey Page?"

"She is here. But you will not see her just yet. For her own good she is being detained."

"Does that mean arrested?"

"Arrested? Nonsense!" M. Aubertin, grey of hair and even of face, made an impatient lip-movement in the beam of light. "She was detained at the airport earlier this morning."

Another realization, which should have struck Brian long before then, made him shift and rearrange memories.

"The airport. The airport! I hope you don't imagine she was trying to leave the country? Yesterday," Brian tried to speak slowly, "she sent all her luggage to the airport except a small suitcase she's got at my flat. If she rushed out and went to the airport this morning, she only wanted to get her luggage back. That's *all*."

"So she said."

"But you don't believe her?"

"Go upstairs, Mr. Innes! Have you found us so very difficult or lacking in understanding? Nevertheless, before you go—"

M. Aubertin hesitated, his sharp eyes fixed.

"There must be no more concealment by anyone," he said. "You and my friend Dr. Fell coached Miss Page in a series of lies she was to tell. No more of that, I say! Miss Page has been persuaded to confess the truth about what she saw and heard in the study yesterday morning."

"I see. Dr. Fell's being detained too? And I'm another culprit?"

"Oh, no." Sour and yet suave, angry and yet fair, the Director of Police swept out his hand. "Dr. Fell was quite right to take the course he did. So were you, though from less far-seeing motives. If we had heard Miss Page's true story at the beginning, we should have been badly misled. Miss Paula Catford has also been persuaded to confess."

"To what?"

"To every conversation with you, with Miss Page, with Mr. Desmond Ferrier, with everyone else. We have *all* the evidence. Sir Gerald Hathaway has heard it too."

"But—!"

"All is fair, I think, in setting a trap or weaving a rope. Go upstairs, Mr. Innes! I have other duties here."

"But Desmond Ferrier, I was going to say: he got here ahead of me?"

"He also is being detained, perhaps for another reason. You will not see him either. How many times," M. Aubertin cried out, "must I request you to go upstairs?"

Yes; the trap was beginning to close.

In the upstairs hall, as dark as it had been yesterday morning, the only light which penetrated was that from the open doors of the two bathrooms: each at one end of the cross-passage across the villa.

Three doors faced Brian as he reached the top of the stairs. Two of these doors, the bedroom on either side of the study, remained closed. A policeman, motionless, stood in front of each. The study door alone was unguarded, partly open, as though it invited.

Two voices spoke from inside the study. One was that of Sir Gerald Hathaway. The other was that of Dr. Gideon Fell.

"—the method," said Hathaway, "the indisputable method, which was used to commit both these murders."

179

"Which murders?" asked Dr. Fell.

"This is stupidity. Come! This is stupidity at its worst and most futile limit. Do I need to explain which murders?"

"Sir, I think you had better."

There were three persons in the study, the third being Paula Catford.

Hathaway and Dr. Fell, at least, were so engrossed that neither appeared to notice Brian as he went in. Another nasty jolt awaited him.

Though there were no shutters for the full-length windows at the rear of the villa, facing north above ravine and massed trees, the white semi-transparent curtains had been drawn on the study windows. The sun did not enter. It could not be called dark; only faintly shadowed, blurring outlines.

Against the east wall stood the big writing-table, its chromium desk-lamp not burning, but in a position to send a glow downward on the pile of manuscript underneath. Against the west wall, above the mantelpiece, ticked the white-faced clock. Round apple-green walls, covered with framed photographs where the space was not occupied by irregular bookshelves, a little filtered light slipped and swayed with the trembling of the curtains.

But there was a difference in the room's appearance.

Dr. Fell, in a big easy-chair, sat with his back to the windows. Into the middle of the study had been pushed a small circular table, and Hathaway stood beside it. Paula Catford, sick with fright, stood near the mantelpiece and looked at two articles lying on the table: a small automatic pistol and a collapsed face-and-head mask of tinted rubber, round which curled a mass of real fair hair.

"Someone wore this," said Hathaway. "Someone wore it last night. You tell me so."

"Yes," agreed Dr. Fell.

Hathaway picked up the mask, fitting it over the curved back of his right hand. Eve Ferrier's face took form above the table.

"Someone, you are further pleased to tell me, followed Audrey Page to a place called the Cave of the Witches. This mask—"

"Put it down!" said Paula. "Please, for heaven's sake, put it down!"

Hathaway whirled round.

"You must forgive me, dear lady, if I distress you. But the clear-eyed innocence of your deceit, on Thursday night, leaves me no choice. What did you say, at that time, of Mr. Desmond Ferrier? 'I don't know him well.' Now you acknowledge, to the Director of Police, you've been his fondest worshipper for years?"

"Yes. It's true. Now put down that mask!"

"Ah!" murmured Hathaway. "Someone on Friday night, then, wore it to the Cave of the Witches. And returned it, in the early hours of this morning, to that cupboard over by the fireplace. I ask Dr. Gideon Fell: is all this true?"

"No," said Dr. Fell.

"It's not true? Yet you told me. . . ."

"The mask and the pistol, it would seem, were taken and returned. Agreed."

"And the person who took them was the murderer?"

"Oh, ah. We must believe so. But what makes you so sure that the murderer was following Audrey Page?"

Hathaway's bald head jerked against the whitish glow from the windows. His moustache, his close-cut grey beard, even his face seemed to writhe in intellectual agony.

"Am I being deceived again? I was promised facts."

"True. Since you insist on making out your case, at whatever cost to the feelings of anyone present, Aubertin has allowed you to do so. He has not allowed you to draw unwarranted conclusions from the evidence."

"Someone's feelings? Tchaa! I follow truth."

"Wherever it leads us?"

"Yes!"

"Sir, Miss Page was not killed. She was not even hurt. We shall never be dazzled by your intellect if you weave dreams only from the occurrences in the Cave of the Witches." Dr. Fell sat up a little. "You have said 'murder'; you have said 'murderer.' The sole murder with which we deal is Mrs. Ferrier's. If there is an indisputable explanation for that, let us hear it."

"Am I to be dealt fairly with?"

"By thunder, you are!"

Hathaway, bristling, pointed a stubby forefinger.

"And yet, for whatever reason," he shot back, "Audrey Page is being kept from me. If I am to make a reconstruction, which I flatter myself will be better than any reconstruction you yourself have ever made, I must have someone who was on the spot and saw for himself. I must have Brian Innes, at least. Where is Innes?"

"He's here," Brian answered from the doorway.

"Ah!" murmured Hathaway with a pounce of triumph.

Still holding up the mask with his left hand inside it, turning it round so that it faced towards Paula, he bent on Brian a look at once excited and faintly derisive.

"Come in, my dear fellow! Come in!"

"But don't, I beg of you," interposed Dr. Fell, "close that door when you enter. Leave it an inch or two open. Yes; like that."

All three of them, Hathaway and Dr. Fell and Paula, looked round at him in the whitish half-gloom.

"My dear fellow," Hathaway addressed Brian with avuncular tenderness, "your sins have found you out. The authorities *know*. They know what went on in this room when Mrs. Ferrier had her quarrel with Audrey Page yesterday morning."

"Then they know more than I do."

"Oblige me," cried Hathaway, waving the mask, "by not quibbling. Are you prepared to be honest at long last?"

"If you want me to answer questions, I'm ready."

Hathaway nodded. He put down the mask on the table, beside the little gleaming metal shape of the automatic pistol. Next, with quick bustling steps, he went towards the writing-table. But he did not stop there. After what seemed to be a glance at the manuscript lying stacked tidily under the desk-lamp, he reached up and plucked down two books from a shelf above and to the right of it.

Nobody else moved. Dr. Fell, sitting back as though sleepily in the big chair, was not sleepy at all. He was watching.

Hathaway returned to the centre-table with the two books, one a small and thin one, the other large and red-bound.

"Murrell on Poisons,"* he announced, holding up the small book. "The second one," he held it up, "another of the admirable volumes by Dr. Thompson.† Both the property of the late Eve Ferrier, as we see by her name written on the fly-leaf of each. I hadn't really hoped to find them here. But I am not surprised to find them. Eh, Miss Catford?"

* Murrell's *What to Do in Cases of Poisoning*, 15th edition (London: H. K. Lewis, 1944).

† *Poisons and Poisoners*, by C. J. S. Thompson, M.B.E. (London: Harold Shaylor, 1931).

182

Paula said nothing.

Hathaway, putting both books down on the table, looked at Brian with shoulders hunched and beard out-thrust.

"Dear young man! Yesterday morning, at about nine o'clock, you ran upstairs to this room. If at any time up to this morning I had been told what you knew (only what you knew!), this affair would have been even simpler than it is. The murderer, we all agree, concocted a plot to kill Mrs. Ferrier. The design was to create a 'murder by magic,' a real impossible situation—"

"*No,*" said Dr. Fell in a voice like a pistol-shot.

Hathaway pounced round in the other direction.

"You deny that, dear doctor? You deny the murderer was trying to reproduce exactly what had happened at Berchtesgaden seventeen years before?"

"I deny it."

"Indeed, now? Explain yourself!"

"Sir, I think not." Dr. Fell raised his voice. "Some time ago you spotted the method of Mrs. Ferrier's murder, anticipating my own feebler wits—"

"Ah! You confess yourself anticipated and beaten?"

"Easily."

"That's gratifying. Come, that's very gratifying! You bungled badly at the very start, dear doctor; confession is good for the soul. Others did a little better."

Hathaway, shivering, pointed at Brian.

"Now Innes there, though ill-mannered and unobservant, is not without a gleam or two of perception when he puts his mind to it. His theory of a poisoned cigarette, as quoted by Miss Catford, was wrong and mistaken. But it was closer to truth than any effort we have heard so far.

"From Murrell," and Hathaway held up the book, "we learn a good many facts about nitrobenzene, which is also variously known as oil of bitter almonds and essence of mirbane and finally as benzaldehyde. If the fumes of its vapour are inhaled for any length of time, even in the open air, it is as deadly as when the liquid is swallowed. This occurred even to Innes. Eh, young man?"

Brian put down his wrath.

"Outside the door of this study," he said, "I could tell something was wrong with Mrs. Ferrier. That's true enough, as far as it goes!"

"Wrong? Be more explicit!"

"She was talking wildly. To me she sounded like a woman sleep-walking. To Audrey she sounded like a woman hypnotized. She ran at the rail of the balcony and grabbed at her throat just before she fell. But how could she have been poisoned at the breakfast-table?"

"She was not poisoned at the breakfast-table. Your stupidity . . ."

"Hathaway, stop this damned bragging."

"I never brag. I state truths." Again the other pointed. "You will henceforward be frank with me. I don't want your opinions; I don't want your comments. I want merely an answer, yes or no, to what I shall ask. Ready?"

"Go ahead."

"It was Mrs. Ferrier's habit, wasn't it, to work in this room every morning after breakfast?"

"Yes!"

"Nobody else used the room? It was her particular domain?"

"That's what I'm told, anyway."

"It was her habit, wasn't it, to lock and bolt that door to the hall so that nobody could disturb her? Mrs. Ferrier sat at the writing-table (there; look at it!), and wrote in longhand with a fountain-pen?"

"Well, she was there yesterday morning when Audrey looked in at the window."

"Ah! When Audrey Page looked in at the window! I don't want your comments; but I allow that one. And, when Audrey Page looked in at the window, hadn't Mrs. Ferrier been sitting at the writing-table for nearly an hour and a half?"

"Yes. But—"

"No comments, I say! What else do we know about the lady? Didn't she invariably (invariably!) wear too much perfume? Didn't we ourselves notice this from twelve feet away, on the previous night at the Hotel du Rhône? Wasn't this perfume called *Spectre de la Rose*, a heavy distillation which would blend with another rose-fragrance and blot out any fainter, alien odour? Yes or no?"

"Yes!"

"On the other hand," said Hathaway, "wasn't there a strong breeze yesterday morning? Blowing through this room? Blowing through two open windows? Dissipating all rose-odours except to one who might be leaning directly above them or beside them?"

"Leaning directly above or beside what?"

"Fool!"

"It's no answer just to—"

"Fool!" repeated Hathaway, his eyes glittering. "Recall what I told you (I myself!) of Eve Ferrier's tour through Germany in 1939. While she travelled with Hector Matthews at her side, they were constantly presenting her with a certain gift. Remember?"

"Yes. You said—"

"And, when she was presented with this gift, Mrs. Ferrier herself never carried it. She gave it to Matthews. *He* carried it for her. Now return to this room, seventeen years later. Look round for the trap that was set. Don't you see, my fatuous jester, that the secret of Mrs. Ferrier's murder may be stated in just two words?"

"What two words?"

"I will show you."

Paula Catford cried out an anguished protest. It did not stop Hathaway.

Bouncing, dedicated, he hurried over to the big writing-table. He stretched out his hand and switched on the chromium desk-lamp.

Against whitish gloom the yellow light shone out clearly. Though it left much of the surroundings in darkness, it showed with vivid effect what Brian had observed yesterday. Just to the left of the desk-blotter and the manuscript stood a glass ashtray. Just to the right of the desk-blotter and the manuscript, even more apparent, stood a bowl of roses.

"What two words, you ask?"

The breath whistled thinly through Hathaway's nostrils. Delicately, with trembling hands, he picked up the china bowl with its red roses. Still delicately, afire with triumph, he marched back to the centre table and put down the bowl there.

"Poisoned flowers," he said.

XVIII

"Those flowers?" Brian demanded.

"Oh, no. These are harmless roses, also from the rose-garden to the east of this house. The police, of course, removed the ones which were here yesterday. They were needed for chemical analysis. —Is that so, Gideon Fell?"

"Yes. It is so."

"On them, I think, had been poured enough nitrobenzene to kill? Provided the victim sat beside them, breathing the fumes for as long as she did breathe them? Is that so?"

"It is so."

"Mrs. Ferrier WAS murdered by inhaling the fumes of nitrobenzene, masked by the rose-odours and the rose-perfume she herself wore? Is *that* so?"

And Dr. Fell's voice rang back. "It is so."

"Ah!" breathed Hathaway.

Whereupon, like Prospero invoking all the spirits, he lifted a stubby arm and snapped his fingers in the air.

"Do you ask, my fine friend," he said venomously to Brian, "whether this method of killing is practical? Whether it could happen? My dear fellow, it *did* happen.

"Thompson, page 124, quotes the case of a street-hawker in Stockwell some years ago. This man, pushing his barrow of lilac, sweet lavender, whatever else he sold in the way of flowers, one day began to act as though he were mad or drunk. First he talked wildly. Then he pushed the barrow faster; next he tried to run with it; finally he staggered and collapsed.

"Nobody at first paid any attention to the barrow: it contained bunches of lavender, which smelled just like lavender if more sharply so. It was fortunate the police didn't examine that barrow for too long before they discovered the secret. When the man was taken to Lambeth Hospital, where he died, the doctor attending him found in his pocket a bottle containing nitrobenzene.

"Our street-hawker hadn't been satisfied with the fragrance given off by the lavender-bunches. He wanted to increase it, as a lure to buyers. So he had been sprinkling the blossoms with nitrobenzene, which is used in perfumery for just that purpose. But he used too much; he had been pushing the barrow too long a time, leaning over it and inhaling its contents; and the fumes killed him.

"That was accident, granted. Mrs. Ferrier's death wasn't accident. Here, in this book, is a complete blueprint for murder. Gideon Fell, can you deny this?"

Dr. Fell, who had taken out a large meerschaum pipe and a fat tobacco pouch, rolled up his head.

"Sir, I do not deny it. These legends of poisoned flowers in the Middle Ages, which the Victorians supposed to be pure fable, were not fables at all. They were most devilishly practical. —What date is written there?"

"The date of the hawker's death? How the devil should I know?"

"Sir, I did not refer to the hawker's death."

"Then what are you talking about?"

"As you say, Sir Gerald, Mrs. Ferrier wrote her name on the fly-leaf of the book. She also wrote, as so many people do, the date on which she bought it. What is the date?"

"The date is January 14, 1956. The book seems to have been bought in London. Why?"

"Go on," Dr. Fell said woodenly.

Hathaway, pale with concentration, once more pointed at Brian.

"I remind you, Innes, of my question a moment ago. When Eve

187

Ferrier, then Eve Eden, made her tour of Germany in 1939, with what were they always presenting her?"

Brian moistened his lips.

"Don't evade, young man! Answer me!"

"With a bouquet of flowers," Brian answered, "or a consecrated flag. Matthews carried it for her."

"*I* told you this when we first discussed the case? Those were the words?"

"Yes. I repeated them to Audrey on Thursday evening."

"And I myself," said Hathaway, "told Gideon Fell at the Murder Club. You, Innes, have seen the photograph album of the lady's German tour. There are half a dozen pictures of her receiving a bouquet of flowers—and giving it to Matthews. Only a fool could fail to see that the murder of Eve Ferrier in 1956, and the murder of Hector Matthews in 1939, were both done by the same method."

"Poisoned flowers at Berchtesgaden? But she wasn't carrying a bouquet of flowers there. At least, there isn't any photograph to show it."

"Ah!"

"By the Lord Harry," Brian burst out, "there'll be another murder if you don't stop saying 'Ah!' and looking like Minerva's owl."

"Oblige me," snapped Hathaway, "by refraining from this crude facetiousness. Long ago, very long ago, the notion of poisoned flowers occurred to me. But evidence was concealed. Vital evidence, I protest, was concealed from me. And from you. And from everyone. If I had known seventeen years ago what I tricked a most reluctant witness into blurting out last night, there would never have been a mystery at all."

"Last night? What did you learn?"

"Ask Miss Catford."

White curtains whispered at the windows. Paula opened her mouth, but did not speak.

"I had the solution all the time," announced Hathaway. "But it seemed impossible, it seemed out of the question. No bouquet of flowers, at least when I was watching, had been presented to Mrs. Ferrier at Berchtesgaden.

"After which . . .

"Yesterday morning, my fine friend, I went to Geneva to send a cablegram. I wasn't here when Mrs. Ferrier died by a method she herself invented. The evening newspapers, actually appearing in the afternoon, carried the shocking news of her death. I was still bewildered until, last night, Dr. Fell and M. Aubertin called to see me, questioned me, and inadvertently revealed that there had been a bowl of roses on the writing-table at which Eve Ferrier had been sitting.

"It must have been nitrobenzene on the roses. It must, it must, it must! And Hector Matthews *must* have died by the same method.

"But how? How to prove this? Miss Catford was the only survivor of that luncheon-party at Hitler's Eagle's Nest. Miss Catford, by her own admission, was looking out of a window at the terrace of the Eagle's Nest when Matthews fell. Miss Catford, as I found by questioning her, had seen something I had not seen in a crush of fourteen guests and half a dozen servants in the dining-room. Just before Eve Ferrier hurried her fiancé out on the terrace, someone handed her a bouquet of arum-lilies. No fuss, no cameras, no posing.

"Who gave it to her? Does that matter? Tchaa! You know it doesn't. But Miss Catford saw it. The bouquet was in Matthews's hands when he fell to his death. He *was* genuinely affected by the altitude before then. Poison on the flowers, held in his hands, completed the work. Miss Catford, answer me! Was there such a bouquet?"

"Yes!" replied Paula.

"Why didn't you ever mention it?"

"Why didn't anyone else? Because I never once imagined it was important. But now you're saying . . . what?"

"Eve Ferrier poisoned the bouquet. Just as I always thought."

Paula, at the fireplace, gave him a look in which incredulity had now become mixed with horror.

"Eve did that," she cried, "in the few seconds before going out on the terrace? And nobody saw her pour the poison? And it affected the poor man within another few seconds?"

"Of course."

"How could it?"

"You disappoint me, dear lady. Matthews needed only a whiff of the fumes to make him more dizzy. So the surgeon found no traces in his body. The bouquet fell with him; it was never found either. A perfect and impossible crime had been created, just as one was attempted on Mrs. Ferrier herself."

"But who killed Eve? Whom do you accuse of that?"

"Dear lady," Hathaway said in a silky voice, "I accuse *you.*"

Still the white curtains whispered at the windows, when a little breeze stirred behind them with faint running reflections of sunlight. The chromium desk-lamp lighted the writing-table. And Paula screamed.

She checked herself instantly, hands pressed against her cheeks.

"Dear lady," Hathaway almost screamed back, "Desmond Ferrier would marry you in an instant if his wife were out of the way. His wife *is* out of the way. Either you did this alone, or you did it with him as your confederate. You wore this mask last night," and he snatched up the rubber face, "because you were so bitterly jealous of Audrey Page. An affair between you and Desmond Ferrier is the secret of his wife's murder."

Fitting his hand inside the mask, so that the mimic and eyeless face looked at Paula, Hathaway stood shivering in a pallor of triumph.

"I am human, dear lady. I don't like accusing you. But truth is truth; facts are facts. You killed Mrs. Ferrier. I swore to find the answer, and I have found it. I promised to explain Matthew's death, and I have done so. I swore to accomplish a certain end of my own, and I have got away with it."

"*Oh, no, you haven't,*" said Dr. Gideon Fell.

And then, during a silence with the effect of a thunderclap, several things happened at once.

Dr. Fell, who had filled and lighted the big meerschaum pipe, abruptly took the pipe out of his mouth. Propelling himself on his crutch-headed stick, he stood up with a massiveness which seemed to fill the room. Wrath, embarrassment, apology, a deep compassion beyond words, all breathed from him as strongly as heat from a furnace.

"Don't be alarmed, Miss Catford," he said. "We shall see to it, believe me, that no harm comes to you. Whether or not Sir Gerald Hathaway believes you killed Mrs. Ferrier, nobody else does. —Aubertin!"

The study door was thrown open.

Gustave Aubertin, with a curious little smile, crossed the room to the windows. Pulling cords at the side of each window, he sent the curtains billowing open as well. Clear daylight, revealing the green-painted balcony outside and the sweep of trees below, illumined the study as well as the faces of those who stood there.

"Yes, by thunder!" said Dr. Fell. "It is time for light and air."

"It is almost time," said the Director of Police, "for more than that." He looked at Hathaway. "You have an ingenious mind, Sir Gerald. Accept my congratulations."

Hathaway's fist crashed down on the centre-table.

"I will not be treated. . . ." he began.

"Sir," interposed Dr. Fell, "you will not be treated how? As you treated Miss Catford?"

"Stop this! Mrs. Ferrier did die as I said she did!"

"For the last time," Dr. Fell informed him very clearly, "that is true. Be thankful for so much accomplishment." He looked at Aubertin. "We discussed with your police-surgeon, I think, the possibility that Hector Matthews might also have been poisoned in this way?"

"We did."

"Did the police-surgeon," Dr. Fell asked politely, "consider it possible?"

"Granting the honesty of the German surgeon, it was not possible. The inhalation of *any* fumes from nitrobenzene, or a poison like it, would have caused inflammation of the nasal passages and of the throat as well. No post-mortem could have failed to detect them."

Dr. Fell banged the ferrule of his stick on the floor.

"The death of Matthews, then, was no more than the bitter and horrifying accident Mrs. Ferrier always swore it was? The Nazi officials, though they did not know it, by ironical circumstance happened to be telling the truth? And someone, seventeen years afterwards, made use of this accident to kill Mrs. Ferrier herself?"

"So I see it," agreed the Director of Police.

Paula, who was gripping the edge of the mantelpiece, looked from Hathaway to Dr. Fell.

" 'Made use of it,' " she repeated. "Dr. Fell, who did kill Eve?"

"We are coming to that," replied Dr. Fell.

"Will you excuse me?" said Aubertin. Very formally, after looking round the room like a host who would be sure the dinner-table is ready, he went out into the hall.

("Look out," thought Brian, with a sense of dread drawing closer. "Look out!")

Paula, the pupils of her eyes dilated, glanced towards the balcony.

"Eve," she declared, "was absolutely innocent. She wasn't guilty of *anything*."

"Oh, but she was," said Dr. Fell.

"What on earth do you mean? You just said—"

"The lady," and Dr. Fell raised his voice, "was not guilty of murder. Never once in her life did she really think of murder, fond though she was of dreaming and (as I believe she told you?) of acting the part of a murderess in a film. She had lost touch with reality. If she did not commit murder, ask yourself what she did do."

"Nothing! Nothing at all!"

"What do *you* say, Sir Gerald?"

The clear light lay on Hathaway's dandified lounge-suit, on his carefully trimmed beard and moustache.

"I have had my say," he retorted, "and apparently (apparently!) I was wrong. I can do no more."

"You can do a little more, sir. For instance, you can tell us why you lied."

"Lied? About what?"

"We shall come to that too."

Hathaway's neck, bearded chin and all, seemed to rise from between his shoulders like a turtle's.

"Say what you mean! I won't have this; I resent it! My reconstruction was right in all essential points: including the fact that the murderer used Matthew's death to create a seeming miracle in the case of Mrs. Ferrier."

"Sir," Dr. Fell said gently, "don't be an ass."

"What's that?"

"Somewhat to paraphrase your own ringing battle-cry: don't be an ass. The murderer used that other death, but NOT for a seeming miracle. There has been too much loose talk about 'reproducing impossible situations,' and 'making people jump off balconies,' and so on. None of this happened or was ever meant to happen. Unless, of course, you believe the guilty person was Audrey Page."

Brian started to utter a violent protest. Dr. Fell, whose pipe had gone out, dropped it into his side pocket and turned back to Hathaway.

"Unless you believe that, there is no real parallel between the death of Hector Matthews and the murder of Eve Ferrier. Let me read you some words spoken by Dr. Boutet, the police-surgeon who performed a post-mortem yesterday afternoon and made his report early yesterday evening."

Fishing in his inside breast-pocket, Dr. Fell produced a notebook as rumpled and shabby as his old alpaca suit.

" 'Nitrobenzene,' I quote Dr. Boutet, 'is a pale oily liquid easily procured in France just over the border because it is employed for so many commercial uses. When diluted and put to a felonious purpose on flowers with a distinctive fragrance, it can be detected neither by the victim nor by anyone who does not come too near it or breathe the air too long.' "

Hathaway tugged at his collar. "But I told you all that!"

"So you did. 'When the victim breathes these fumes,' I continue with Dr. Boutet, 'he is unlikely to realize what is happening. The fumes work slowly, and in time produce an effect comparable with alcoholic excitement—' "

"I told you that too!"

"The fumes work slowly, not in a few seconds. There is no parallel, surely, in the accidental death of Hector Matthews?"

"Well . . ."

"Observe other differences. No murderer, having poisoned the bowl of roses early yesterday morning, could possibly have anticipated the entrance of Audrey Page and what ensued. Mrs. Ferrier, caught by the fumes as the street-hawker was caught at Stockwell, behaved just as the hawker did. She quarreled with Miss Page, threatened her, pursued her out on the balcony; and, in the final spasm of the poison, ran straight against a loose hand-rail which sent her tumbling to death. If none of these things had happened, no question of the balcony would have arisen at all. That is evident, I hope?"

"Of course it is," said Paula. "But what did the murderer want to do?"

"He wanted to kill, with nitrobenzene, in as obvious a way as possible, so that he of all people should not be suspected. This poison was associated with her life, not his. She would be found dead on the floor. Evidence of death by inhaling nitrobenzene fumes would be discovered within twenty-four hours: as it was. It would be assumed someone had poisoned her in the same way she *might* have poisoned Matthews. And none would ever discover—"

193

"Discover what?"

"The murderer's motive," replied Dr. Fell. "He had to kill her, and kill her very quickly, or she would have betrayed him."

"She would have—" Paula stopped. "I don't understand!"

"Do you understand, Sir Gerald?"

"No, I do not!"

Dr. Fell closed his eyes.

"My friend Aubertin," he said, "has laid on me a heavier duty than I have ever known. It must be done. But I wish I could put it off. I wish another mask need not be stripped from as unpleasant a face as you yourselves are ever likely to see. You, Miss Catford, have asked what the murderer wanted. Have you ever wondered what Mrs. Ferrier wanted?"

"No, of course not! Or, at least—"

And again Paula checked herself, as a new fear appeared in her eyes. It was Brian who answered, fighting phantoms.

"She wanted a new life. That's what she kept saying, anyway. '*I have had much trouble, you know. A new life can open for me, even a triumphant return to the stage.*' Probably none of us will ever forget how exalted she seemed, or the mood she was in at the Hotel du Rhône."

Dr. Fell, who had been standing motionless by the centre-table, opened his eyes and lifted the crutch-headed stick.

"That's it!" he said with some violence. "By thunder, you are getting warm! Never forget the Hotel du Rhône or her mood there. When you have remembered that, carry it a step further. She could have this new life, she could return triumphantly and happily to the stage (or so she wrongly thought), when what had happened?"

"When she had finished her book, she told us, and cleared herself of all suspicion in the matter of Matthews's death."

"And that was all she wanted? That was *all* which for Eve Ferrier constituted the dream and the shining illusion?"

Dr. Fell held up his hand, forestalling Brian's reply.

"Before you answer, I beg you will think of this woman as she really was: not as some have tried to picture her. I ask you to think of her at the Hotel du Rhône: her beauty gone, her nerves in rags, living only in a world of fantasies.

"Remember what has just happened to her. She has just stormed out of her own house, this house, after summoning a taxi. She has just read someone's diary; it has broken her soap-bubble universe and brought the illusions tumbling down. She has left this villa in a state of both fear and fury. Why?

"All three of you saw her, at a quarter to eleven on Thursday night, when she stormed into the hotel. Nothing, to me at least, has been more vivid than the various descriptions you reported to the police. She wears unbecoming finery, dressed for conquest. She wears even more perfume than usual. She goes straight to the dining-room. Why?"

Still Dr. Fell held up his hand.

"Again before you answer," he said in a bitter and despairing tone, "think of one more indication. Up to the time she saw Audrey Page, later that same night *after* reading the diary, she has shown no hatred towards Miss Page. Everything centres and burns round that diary, wherever it is or whoever has it now. And so, having read the diary, she goes straight to the dining-room of the Hotel du Rhône.

"All may not be lost, she thinks. She lives on illusion, even when her mind and heart both know better. 'I want to be friends with everybody!' Hear her cry that, as she said it to all of you; and remember that Eve Ferrier, like most other women amid the ruin of a dream, still hoped. Having remembered all that . . ."

Hathaway thrust out his beard.

"Having remembered it," he snapped, "are we meant to draw some deduction from it?"

"By thunder, you are!" said Dr. Fell, blowing out his cheeks. "Eve Ferrier had committed no crime, but she had committed what old-fashioned people still consider an offence. In the light of these facts, ask yourselves what offence Eve Ferrier had committed? And what was it she most wanted to do?"

"Well?"

"She had committed adultery, which had been going on for some time," said Dr. Fell. "She was mad-determined to divorce her husband, and marry the man with whom she was in love."

Hathaway's voice went up to a croak.

"What hell's nonsense is this? She was in love with her husband."

"Sir," said Dr. Fell, "are you sure?"

"She told us—"

"Oh, yes. In keeping up the pretence she and her lover had been maintaining for some time, she was obliged to say that. But you have all commented, I think, on her utter dismay when she turned away from the dining-room at the hotel—where she had been inquiring for a certain person—and saw the three of you standing there?"

"She was inquiring for her husband!"

"Oh, no," corrected Dr. Fell.

If Hathaway did not understand, it was plain that Paula Catford understood only too well. Paula, corpse-white, turned away and put her face in her hands.

"I respectfully submit," said Dr. Fell, glancing towards the partly open door, "that this could not have been so. If she had really been looking for her husband, she would never have gone straight to the Hotel du Rhône. I submit this on evidence which is certainly known to Brian Innes."

Then his voice boomed out in the quiet study.

"It is not easy to rattle Desmond Ferrier. *I* tried it, with deplorable results. Desmond Ferrier became rattled only yesterday afternoon, when Aubertin was pressing him too hard. Desmond Ferrier blurted out the fact that his favourite place to eat is the Béarn, and he prefers always to go there. He made a further slip when he added the name of the person who does prefer the Hotel du Rhône. It's bad luck, after all his frantic efforts to shield the real murderer."

Dr. Fell now spoke as though addressing someone downstairs.

"We need not go on with this. The police have the murderer's diary. Since obviously it was not Desmond Ferrier's diary, and since only one other man lives at this villa, it requires little shrewdness to see . . ."

Outside, in the hall, somebody shouted a command in French.

The door to the hall banged wide open. Somebody, running hard for the left-hand window of those two full-length windows, plunged past Dr. Fell. The centre-table, with all its exhibits, went over with a crash.

Gustave Aubertin, in the doorway, called out another command. Two policemen, each appearing on an opposite side of the balcony, caught the man who had run for the balcony in an attempt to jump to death in the way Eve herself had gone. Brian Innes does not like to remember the thrashing and screaming afterwards.

"Our strategy, it seems," observed the Director of Police, "was well pursued after all."

"Don't call it our strategy," said Dr. Fell. "For God's sake never call it *our* strategy."

And he stood for a moment breathing hard amid the débris of a rubber mask, an automatic pistol, two books, and a shattered bowl of roses.

"Oh, yes," he added to the others. "The murderer is Philip Ferrier."

XIX

Two nights later, in the restaurant called *L'Or du Rhône* in the rue du Stand, four persons had finished dinner. They sat in that back room where chicken is so admirably prepared at an open fireplace; and, if you are sufficiently favoured a guest and the night is hot enough, the management will put you close enough to the fire to make your head reel.

The night of Monday, August 13, however, had turned cool. Dr. Fell, Audrey Page, Brian Innes, and Sir Gerald Hathaway were in a mood as subdued as the evening by the time coffee and brandy were set before them.

"Do you still think, Sir Gerald," inquired Dr. Fell, "it is a pleasant pastime actually to deal with criminal cases?"

"In candour," replied Hathaway, who had lighted a cigar but did not look any too well, "in candour—no."

Brian glanced sideways, rather hesitantly, at Audrey.

"But Philip Ferrier?" He spoke incredulously. "*Philip Ferrier?*"

"You thought he could not act?" asked Dr. Fell. "He is Desmond Ferrier's son. This young man who claimed not to understand artists, believe me, is in some ways a better artist than any of you."

Audrey spoke without looking up. "What will happen to him?"

"Life imprisonment," answered Brian. "As I told his father, in the Canton of Geneva there is no death-penalty for murder at the moment."*

"Stop!" Hathaway said irascibly. "I will eat humble pie, if you insist. But I want to be clear about this. Did his father know he was guilty?"

Dr. Fell upreared above the meerschaum pipe he was lighting.

"Great Scott, no! But his father most horribly feared he might be, and feared at the start there was some relationship between his son and his wife. When he finally realized his son must be a born criminal, it was too late. Murder had been committed. The matter had been taken out of amateur hands (mine) where Desmond Ferrier could control it, and put into the hands of the police: where he could only try to smother it. In doing so, you will note, he was compelled to play a part of weirder irony than most of those he had played on the stage. And the father did not relish it.

"Indeed, it is an understatement to say he did not relish it. There were times when he was in a frame of mind near delirium. If I were to explain . . ."

Hathaway rapped on the table.

"Please do so!" he said. "Explain. From the beginning."

Reflections of firelight danced across the ceiling in the back room. Dr. Fell, a shaggy figure who looked cross-eyed and almost witless as he at last lighted the pipe to his satisfaction, blew out smoke and muttered to himself.

"Well. From the beginning," he conceded.

"A month ago, then, Desmond Ferrier paid a special visit to London to see me and beg me to come to Geneva for a visit. He said he was badly worried. He told me the story of his wife at Berchtesgaden seventeen years ago; he added (always in a joking way, so that he could retract if necessary) the hint of fears his wife would poison him."

"But Ferrier didn't honestly believe that, did he?" asked Brian. "I remember your telling him straight out he didn't believe it."

"Wait!" urged Dr. Fell. "If you allow me to continue, the sequence of events should become clear."

* There is now.—J. D. C.

Once more Dr. Fell drew reflectively at the pipe.

"Quite plainly, even to these dull eyes and ears of mine, he was on edge about *some* situation in his household. He was not telling the full truth; he was shielding someone for some reason. Several years before that, as you know, I had learned of the Berchtesgaden episode from Sir Gerald here—"

"Bah!" said Hathaway.

"At the same time Desmond Ferrier visited me, as we afterwards learned, Mrs. Ferrier began her agitation to prove her own innocence in the Berchtesgaden matter by summoning Miss Catford and Sir Gerald. (But she had invited you too, Miss Page; why?) Meanwhile, I was faced with this odd, uneasy tale from Desmond Ferrier. What situation did upset him in his own household? Whomever he was attempting to shield, it was not really his wife. On the contrary, he was making these remarks about possible poisoning. He was not even being reticent in any way about her: except on one point. He had not told me she had been twice married before. And, when I discovered certain facts about these two husbands . . ."

Dr. Fell paused, uneasily. Audrey flew out at him.

"Will you please tell me," she said, "why you attached so much importance to these two husbands? Was it because both of them died violent deaths?"

"No," said Dr. Fell. "That was important, admittedly. But it was important as showing how events had run. Beautiful women, professional charmers, and especially women of more than neurotic type, do tend to attract men of the same type. They do tend to walk in an atmosphere of disquiet and sometimes of violence.

"On the other hand, it can't be held against them as potential murderesses. It can't be held against Eve Ferrier that her first husband, an analytical chemist of unstable mind, committed suicide when she divorced him. The death of her second husband, a fighter-pilot during the Battle of Britain, was only a normal war-risk. It was another fact which made me wonder. . . ."

"What other fact?" insisted Audrey. "And what made you wonder?"

"Each of her two previous husbands," replied Dr. Fell, "had been younger than herself."

"Younger?"

"Oh, ah. And the second husband, whom I heard described as the great love of her life, had been considerably younger.

"She married this second husband in 1937. At that time, even if her age was no greater than she said it was, she must have been twenty-five or twenty-six years old. Two years later, at the outbreak of war, this man joins the R.A.F. and is presently made a fighter-pilot.

"Two years later; consider that! I might have investigated no deeper if the very dates had not been revealing. If this great love had been the same age as herself or older, was it likely he would have been accepted and trained as a fighter-pilot in a service where new-comers are old at twenty-eight?

"In point of fact, I learned he had been nineteen when they were married. If I practised a certain deception by not revealing all I knew," and he looked at Brian, "it was because I was obliged to question Desmond Ferrier discreetly while others were listening."

"Did you know about the first husband too?" Brian demanded.

"I fear I did. But then so did you." Dr. Fell ruffled his big mop of hair. "Sir Gerald, I understand, sent a cablegram to Deputy Commander Elliot in my name. It did not surprise Elliot to get an urgent request for information which he had already given me. After all, I once did send a telegram announcing I was at Market Harborough and asking where I ought to be. So Elliot replied in all good faith about the young man who had been her first husband.

"And then, when I arrived in Geneva at noon on Thursday, then I began to learn things which most of you have also learned at dif-ferent times. Desmond Ferrier, who is badly upset about something, has a son of twenty-four. This son shows by every word he speaks that *he* has much on his mind. He maintains a very curious attitude towards his father and his step-mother; certainly they maintain a curious attitude towards him. For instance!"

Though addressing Brian, Dr. Fell blinked in a distressed way be-tween Brian and Audrey.

"For instance, did Philip tell you he never dreamed Eve Ferrier had been concerned in any awkward accident at Berchtesgaden in 1939?"

"Yes," replied Brian. "He said so at the Hotel Metropole when I first met him."

"Harrumph, yes. He made the same statement to me. Now was that really possible? Archons of Athens! Since Desmond Ferrier and the former Eve Eden had been married since 1943, was it possible he had never heard a word of any kind?

"There is more than this. Desmond Ferrier swore to me they had carefully kept it from the son all those years. He said *they;* he almost insisted too much on the fact, when I asked him the direct question. The father adopted, indeed, a strange attitude towards the son's possible marriage to Audrey Page. The father lets us think, a little too obviously, that he himself could easily be smitten with Miss Page. Is he concealing something else, drawing fire on himself? Of what does he really want to warn Miss Page?

"I ask you to think over every word Desmond Ferrier said. Interpret these words in a different way from their surface or apparent meaning. Philip Ferrier—as anyone can see—really is deeply in love with Miss Page. More than this, she has money; she is suitable."

Audrey spoke in a low voice.

"Don't carry this too far," she said. "If you're talking of Phil, don't carry it too far!"

Dr. Fell regarded her gravely.

"Of myself I need carry it little further," he said. "But I must draw your attention to certain incidents which took place under the eyes of one or the other of you. And I must mention a possibility which occurred to me soon after I arrived here.

"Desmond Ferrier's affairs with women, in the past, have been many and notorious. Even now he is half-ready to accuse himself of designs on a young lady, Audrey Page, very much younger than himself. It would be a comment on human nature, I thought, if the real designs were the other way round: that is, the designs of his once-beautiful wife on a step-son very much younger than *herself*

"And, as we now know from so many details of the confession made by Philip Ferrier, that is precisely what had happened. With a character like that of the woman, and a character like that of the boy, it led to disaster.

"Their affair began nearly two years ago. It demoralized Eve Ferrier. In this handsome youngster, with a surface charm but an inner hardness which perhaps only his father suspected, she believed she had found the reincarnation of her 'great love,' the young fighter-pilot killed in the Battle of Britain.

"Philip played up to her. It flattered his vanity, as it so often does Whereupon he grew bored just as she grew more intense. In January of this year, '56, Desmond Ferrier and his wife visited London; their son was with them, and he met Audrey Page. I regret that this part must be told," and Dr. Fell looked at Audrey, "because it will be told in court.

"Now Philip is a very vain young man. If you had ever seen that—"

"I did see it," Brian interrupted curtly. "But I didn't let the impression register strongly enough."

Dr. Fell blinked at him.

"You did see it? When?"

"The same Thursday night, at the Hotel Metropole, when Philip called to take Audrey out to dinner. That young fellow's manner when he spoke just four words, '*Who's that with you?*' should have suggested more than it did. He saw me standing beside a window with Audrey; he didn't even know who I was. But a good deal was expressed at that moment. Anyway, go on about—about the confession."

"Shall I go on, Miss Page?"

"Yes! Yes! I'm sorry I said that." Audrey stared at the table. "Because I shall have to make a confession too."

"Oh, ah. In London, last January," Dr. Fell resumed, "Philip Ferrier met this young lady here. He wanted her, very much, and he thought she wanted him. He was in no enviable position, with the elder woman at his side and doting on him. Momentarily he got out of the difficulty, he has told the Director of Police, with an inspiration which could have come only to a potentially first-rate criminal.

"Eve, now living in her world of dreams, has been speculating further. 'Is it possible we can ever acknowledge our great love?' she has been saying to an impatient and desperate young man. 'If we were to admit it and marry, what would the world think? Could we ever do that?'

"Hence the inspiration. Of course they could, Philip suggests. He is not really interested in Miss Page, he tells Eve Ferrier, *but it must be plain that his father is*. If the son lets the father cut him out with Audrey Page, then the way will be clear. The father marries a younger woman, and the son in turn will be happy to seek consolation with Eve herself.

"It was the very basis of all stage-intrigue, by which some of these people lived and one of them died. Eve Ferrier, not a criminal but a born intriguer, saw nothing strange in it. She was dazzled. She was overjoyed. Philip would 'pretend' to be interested in the girl, and she would 'encourage' it. At the proper time, when they can discard all masks, Philip will reveal that his real love is for Eve.

"Of course Philip never meant to do that. To get what *he* really wanted, he knew he would have to kill his step-mother.

"And the father, no fool, partly guessed what might be going on. He could not guess all of it, or what form its explosion would take. He could only stand by in horror, wondering what he ought to do.

"If you have ever felt less than charitable towards Desmond Ferrier, I ask you to be charitable now. His many, his notorious affairs are boomeranging back in the worst possible way. If he is wrong, and it is only his own evil mind which makes him suspect all this, there will be hell to pay in the event he accuses his wife or his son. If he stays silent, and he happens to be right, what sort of catastrophe may overtake them?"

Dr. Fell paused. His pipe had gone out; his red face was heavy and lowering.

"Well—!" he added reflectively.

"Events, in the first months of this year, began to march towards a predestined end. But here I am indulging in a deplorable practice of anticipating the evidence. Let us forget this. Let us consider the situation only as it presented itself to me when Ferrier came to me in London, and I arrived here to learn what I could learn.

"Mrs. Ferrier was talking ecstatically of a 'new life.' She had decided, or someone had persuaded her, on a triumphant return to the stage. She had decided, or someone had persuaded her, that first she must celebrate this by writing her memoirs: working always in a room, the study, which nobody else used. Meanwhile someone had been whispering rumours about her, rumours about the alleged poisoning of Hector Matthews. She had decided, or someone had persuaded her, to demonstrate her lily-serene innocence by summoning an assorted little group to the Villa Rosalind.

"Wow! I repeat: wow!

"It was not reasonable to suppose she had been whispering rumours about herself, nor did any of her acts look like a prelude to murdering somebody. If any dirty work had been planned in that household, Mrs. Ferrier would appear to figure not as a possible murderess but as the probable victim.

"By the same token, at first glance, the potential murderer would have seemed to be Desmond Ferrier himself. He had been throwing out hints about poison. And yet, in my dunderheaded fashion, I could not accept this either.

"Even apart from the fact that I knew him as essentially an honest and easy-going human being, often weak as we all are weak, *he* could not be opening a new life for Eve. Despite her words, the evidence showed she really cared as little for him as he cared for her. He would never have suggested a return to the stage, nor would she have behaved so joyously if he had. Furthermore, if he talks too much about poison and his wife dies of it, suspicion will rebound heavily on him. That's not the plan of a murderer. It looks rather as though his talk were a warning to somebody other than Mrs. Ferrier. 'Don't do this; keep off; change your mind; don't be a fool!'

"If I eliminated both those two as potential murderers, only one other person (in the household, at least) was left. Still bearing in mind that this was only a possibility, I watched the events of Thursday afternoon and Thursday night.

"Upstairs, at the villa, Mrs. Ferrier discovered something which upset her universe and sent her straight to the Hotel du Rhône. Since she knew her husband's reputation, would she have been so *shocked* to hear of any affair with another woman?

"Well, you know what happened at the hotel. Somebody had slipped into her handbag a bottle of the perfume she always wore. She would not discover anything wrong until she found the bottle, and held it up, and discovered its contents were the wrong colour. It was at least possible she would make this discovery in public. But why sulphuric acid? And where had it come from? And, above all, why a perfume-bottle?

"Desmond Ferrier, who had left me at a night-club off the Place Neuve, hurried back there to give me the news. In doing so, upset, he revealed his state of mind at every word. The name of Audrey Page was commented on with a vengeance. He was worried about his son, as he showed. But he now pretended to think Miss Page was in danger: which in a sense she was, but not from a poisoning-attempt by Eve Ferrier.

205

"I let him know the direction of my suspicions, and told him plainly I believed it was his wife who might be in danger. He didn't like this, as two of you saw. Having got as far as that, I now proceeded to make one of the great blunders of my life."

Hathaway, not without satisfaction, drew the air through a hollow tooth.

"Yes," he said. "I am unrepentant enough to think you did."

"How?" Brian asked.

Hathaway simmered, but decided against calling anyone a fool or an idiot.

"Years ago at the Murder Club, as I have kept repeating," he announced, "I outlined the Berchtesgaden case. I gave broad indications that Matthews might have been killed with a poisoned bouquet of flowers."

"But Matthews wasn't poisoned! It was an accident. You yourself couldn't prove anything, because nobody said a word about any flowers at Berchtesgaden, and nobody said a word about the roses in the study at the villa until we actually saw them there!"

Dr. Fell quieted an incipient uproar.

"The possibility," he said, "should have been considered. If Philip Ferrier did plan any attempt on the life of Mrs. Ferrier, I was expecting something crude—as crude as the sulphuric acid—against which I could guard.

"The sulphuric acid, true, was meant as a threat and a warning. But its real purpose was to call attention to the perfume-bottle. When the lady was found dead, we were meant to think immediately of roses and rose-perfume. The notion did cross my mind, but I rejected it. Since Matthews had not been poisoned, I firmly rejected the vision of poisoned flowers.

"Do you remember? On Friday morning you drove out to the villa in a panic. I told you you need fear nothing. I said I had a glimmering of what Hathaway suspected; but, since I could see no evidence of it, I all but jeered at the idea.

"And then?

"Mrs. Ferrier pitched off the balcony. Audrey Page had walked by accident into the middle of it; she would surely be involved, as I agreed, unless we told a story to protect her. We went along the balcony. One look into that study told me that a bowl of roses stood beside the place where Mrs. Ferrier had been sitting. Every bit of evidence—Hathaway has since outlined it—showed poisoning had been done with flowers. And so, in protecting Miss Page, we had to take a different line."

Here, as though remarking on the devilishness of all human circumstances, it was Audrey he addressed.

"You follow that, don't you? Innes wanted to deny you were with Mrs. Ferrier when she fell to her death. He wanted to say you were far away. If they suspected you of throwing her from that balcony, it would have been an admirable idea. On the other hand, since a poison-trap had been set, such a course might have been fatal.

"If you *and* Desmond Ferrier were suspected of setting the poison-trap, you yourself wouldn't have been there to watch it work. You would have been far away. Hence I could not let Innes give such testimony, or let you give it either.

"My best plan was to insist on the truth; the presence of poison —to be exact, nitrobenzene—should be discovered within twenty-four hours. One question, incidentally: when Mrs. Ferrier was raving at you, did it occur to you she might not have been talking about her husband at all?"

Audrey shivered.

"It occurred to me afterwards," she said, "and I told Brian it did. But at the time: no! We were talking at cross-purposes. She was talking about Philip, and I thought she meant her husband; I said I'd never even looked at him. But she never mentioned the man's name."

"Did you suspect afterwards it might have been Philip?"

"No! Not even when I knew it must have been somebody else, and tried to get information from Mr. Ferrier at the Cave of the Witches. But before then . . ."

"Before then," grunted Dr. Fell, "we may say mildly that cross-purposes had involved everybody in a muddle I despaired of setting right.

"This was inevitable. Each person, from the beginning, behaved in accordance with his or her particular temperament; and there are some tolerably flighty temperaments among the lot of you. It would be unjust to say Eve Ferrier had a pathological passion for men, as Innes has told me somebody did say; it would be unjust to

207

call Philip Ferrier a willing murderer. Both these two were too innately respectable to the verge of stuffed-shirtdom: too conscious of the world's opinion.

"Mrs. Ferrier did have a passion for men younger than herself. She tried to conquer this years ago: first by becoming engaged to a man much older than herself (Hector Matthews), and later by marrying one (Desmond Ferrier). If the one had money, and the other a famous name, that was sound practicality. But it wouldn't have worked with the one; it did not work with the other.

"Philip Ferrier would have protested, and still protests with tears in his eyes, he never wanted to kill the old girl. But his own practicality wouldn't endure the situation; his life, his future, his sleep were all threatened; he feared her too much; she should not live, and he got his opportunity.

"In London, last winter, Mrs. Ferrier bought a book called *Poisons and Poisoners*. Aubertin and I found this book in the study on Friday afternoon; it helped me in persuading Aubertin. Hathaway found it later. As you said, Sir Gerald, it provided a blueprint for murder.

"Eve Ferrier saw, with genuine horror, how she *could* have killed Matthews at Berchtesgaden. She had done nothing of the kind; men of Matthews's age are susceptible to high altitudes as well as high passions. But she could have done this, since the German police-surgeon had mentioned poison at the time. It made her frantic to prove she hadn't. Especially since Philip, inspired by the same book, had been circulating rumours—and meant to use the device—against *her*."

Hathaway, glowering, called for attention with a rap on the table like an insistent ghost.

"You tell us," he inquired, "she herself could have been caught and killed by a device she was aware of?"

"Of course. See Dr. Boutet's medical evidence."

"In what way?"

"The victim, we learn, is overcome by a poison that destroys the judgment like alcoholic intoxication. The damage is done before the victim understands. Surely, Sir Gerald, considering the thumping lie *you* told on Friday evening, you can accept this?"

Audrey, who stood in some awe of Hathaway, regarded him with astonishment.

208

"Sir Gerald wasn't telling the truth either?"

"With dire results as regards my sanity," retorted Dr. Fell, "nobody was telling the truth. Including your obedient servant. On Friday night, wishing to question you, Aubertin and I called at Innes's block of flats in the Quai Turrettini; Sir Gerald and Philip Ferrier were with us. (Remember that; it becomes important later.)"

"But what . . . ?"

"By this time Sir Gerald, from the conversation of Aubertin and myself, was utterly convinced the person who used the poison was Mrs. Ferrier herself. He did not know how the lady had been caught in her own trap. He only knew the poison had been added to roses from the garden. So he tried to strengthen his case by swearing Mrs. Ferrier had gone into the garden before breakfast.

"She hadn't. Other witnesses, including myself, could testify she hadn't. He was trying to make his case too good; and it nearly landed him in trouble. Later, with a whoop and shout, he pried certain admissions from Paula Catford, and pitched on Miss Catford as the guilty person. If he agrees with Emerson that a foolish consistency is the hobgoblin of small minds, he could not have shown it better."

"I believed—" Hathaway began with some passion.

"You believed it was for the best? Oh, ah. So did everybody else. Actually, nobody went into the garden on Friday morning. The bowl of roses had been in the study from the previous day. Philip Ferrier, the last person who came downstairs to breakfast, added poison before he joined us at the breakfast table."

Here Dr. Fell, trying without success to light his pipe again, made fussed gestures.

"Tut! Aroint ye, now! Once more I anticipate events. Let us return to Friday morning just following the discovery of the murder, when I questioned Desmond Ferrier in the drawing-room at the Villa Rosalind. This was in the presence of Paula Catford and Brian Innes, before the arrival of the police.

"Never have I had such little success. All I discovered was the answer to a question no longer of any importance: that is, where had the murderer got the sulphuric acid?

"Paradoxically, as Dr. Boutet wrote, to buy nitrobenzene is fairly simple. Under its various names as essence of mirbane or benzeldahyde or artificial oil of bitter almonds, it has many commercial uses.

But we may not, without provoking some curiosity, stride into a chemist's and demand sixpennyworth of oil of vitriol. Indeed, I had been wandering about the villa looking for some bottle or container which might have held the stuff: until, in the drawing-room, I recalled Innes's remark. . . ."

"My remark?" interposed Brian. "About what?"

"About the motor-cars," answered Dr. Fell.

"You mean Philip got it—?"

"He got it out of the battery of a carefully preserved old-time motor-car from the nineteen-twenties: a car, by the way, which only Philip used. The sulphuric acid in modern batteries is better protected. However, when I owned one such car in the dimmer days of my slimness, I can recall tipping over the battery by accident and seeing sulphuric acid run out of it like beer out of a bottle.

"But what good was this information? None!

"In the drawing-room, then, I tried to make Desmond Ferrier speak out and tell what he knew. I let him see how much *I* knew. Because of some remarks made by Paula Catford, he saw his own awkward position (and Audrey Page's) with most uncomfortable clearness.

"And yet he refused to speak out."

Dr. Fell heaved a gusty sigh.

"I could scarcely have expected him to denounce his own son, you inquire? Well, but there was even more in it than this. Temperament had begun to dance again. He has found (I hope and I also believe), he has found his own great love in Paula Catford. Too much frankness on his part might have thrown suspicion on Miss Catford—as, later, Sir Gerald did throw suspicion on her. Nor could he resist playing the noble role of the hero wrongly accused.

"Paula Catford knew he had not been in the Cave of the Witches the night before, as he swore he had. She knew he had been with her in her hotel-room between shortly past seven and shortly past ten. She begged him to stop acting.

"And still he refused.

"By thunder, that did it! There was no choice but to throw in my lot with the police.

"I could still protect Audrey Page, who had been innocently embroiled. But I could no longer protect Desmond Ferrier. Even I, notorious for circumventing and flum-diddling the law when my personal feelings are involved—as Ferrier well knew, when he hurried to consult me at the beginning—could not be expected to shield Philip. Certainly I could not risk another tragedy."

"That's not the first time you've mentioned another tragedy," Brian said. "What other tragedy? And to whom?"

"Either to you," replied Dr. Fell, "or to Audrey Page. In actual fact, you escaped it only by one whistle and the grace of God."

Heavily apologetic, the man who could tolerate all things and never preached sermons, Gideon Fell nevertheless shook his head when he blinked at Audrey.

"Come!" he urged. "The possibility of another move on the murderer's part had existed since Thursday night. After promising Innes you would never go near the Villa Rosalind, young lady, you allowed yourself to be taken there in the hope Innes would follow you. To anyone who saw you on that Thursday night it was plain you cared not one scrap either for Philip Ferrier or for Philip's father. It was Innes you cared for, I think?"

"Well, I don't deny it," declared Audrey, meeting his eyes. "He —he wants me to marry him."

"My dear young lady, there is no need to apologize. But I saw this at the Villa Rosalind on Thursday night. Paula Catford saw it, and commented on it next day. The question was: had Philip seen it? If so, there might be all kinds of trouble."

"*Had* Philip seen it?"

"Harrumph. Well. Whether he saw it or not, he had very good reason to know it on Friday night. Oh, Bacchus, he had!"

"How? And, if you'll please tell me, how much did Paula Catford know or guess?"

Dr. Fell looked down over his several chins and sighed again.

"In answering both those questions at once, we can wind up the whole case."

For a few seconds he concentrated, gathering together the filaments of his scatterbrain.

"From what Innes told me yesterday, Sunday," he continued, "Paula Catford's behaviour may be indicated without difficulty. She was upstairs at the villa on Friday morning, listening outside Sir Gerald Hathaway's bedroom, when Innes and I were discussing the best way of shielding *you*. She could not really believe you and Desmond Ferrier were engaged in a hectic love-affair; she knew

211

too well she was the favoured one. On the other hand, such knowledge has never entirely convinced any woman when doubts worm in.

"Following this, during the celebrated interview in the drawing-room, Ferrier built up such a case against himself and you—both as lovers and murderers—that her wonder increased. Finally, that night, you 'phoned Desmond Ferrier at the Villa Rosalind; and Miss Catford picked up an extension-receiver to listen. Immediately afterwards Ferrier left the house.

"She knew you two were meeting, but she had no idea where it would be. So she begged permission to accompany Aubertin and myself (together with Philip Ferrier) when we drove to Geneva for the purpose of questioning first Hathaway and then you. Since she could guess where you were hiding out, as she informed Innes, she nipped ahead of us to Innes's flat and discovered there would be a meeting at the Cave of the Witches.

"Mark one thing! In her heart, or so I firmly believe, Paula Catford could still not credit either an intrigue or a murder planned between you and Desmond Ferrier. No: as I have learned since then, she overheard Aubertin and your obedient servant putting their heads together at the villa. Either from something Ferrier had let slip, or from what she could deduce by her own nimble wits, Miss Catford had begun to suspect Philip.

"She couldn't reveal that, of course; she was too loyal to Desmond Ferrier. It was simply that she wondered about you and Ferrier; she had to have her doubts settled. And this could be done, she felt, if Ferrier openly admitted his love for her by saying frankly he had been with her on Thursday evening. That, and that alone, must have been her purpose in going with Innes to the Cave of the Witches."

Now it was Brian who sat up, shushing Audrey's questions and drawing Dr. Fell's attention.

"Just a minute! You and Aubertin had put your heads together as soon as that? You had decided . . . ?"

"We had decided on the murderer; we had decided on the method. All I did, in the way of making myself suspect, was to provide Miss Page with an alibi for the crucial time before breakfast when the flowers were poisoned. Aubertin overlooked that."

"And afterwards?"

"Well! Desmond Ferrier's admission that his son always preferred to have dinner at the Globe Restaurant or the Hotel du Rhône was confirmed by a 'phone-call to the dining-room at the latter place. Eve Ferrier *had* asked for Philip there: though Philip, on Thursday night, actually took Miss Page to the Richemond. The discovery of Philip's diary was a clincher.

"Consequently, when Aubertin and I drove to Geneva with Paula Catford, we encouraged Philip to accompany us. Aubertin wanted to have him followed from that time."

"Followed?"

"Of course. If we could prevent it, there must be no more murder-attempts."

Again memory opened its vistas to Brian.

"You had Philip followed from the time you and Aubertin entered the block of flats where I live? Isn't that so? When the policeman reported, 'Mr. Director, the signal has been given,' did that mean the shadow was ready to take over from there?"

"It did. Philip, already in none too pleasant a mood either towards you or towards the young lady who was frankly staying at your flat, went with us when we took the lift to the flat. Neither you nor Miss Page was there, admittedly. But the front door was wide open, as you know. Our party separated afterwards; and Philip, who had walked smack into some revelations that upset him still worse . . ."

"Revelations? What revelations?"

"Have you forgotten the sheet torn from the note-pad? The paper you lost?"

Brian said nothing.

"The address of the night-club," Dr. Fell explained patiently, "brought out from pencil-tracings in Audrey Page's handwriting, was inscribed on that paper. You couldn't find it next day; Philip had picked it up in your flat. Also in her handwriting, scrawled blatantly in lipstick across a mirror in your bedroom, was a message beginning, 'I love you too—'"

Dr. Fell paused, blinking over his eyeglasses.

"And that," Brian asked, "was what sent him to the Cave of the Witches?"

"Oh, ah. After he had first taken a taxi back to the villa, to procure a convenient automatic pistol and a convenient mask he could slip on in the dark. This over-reserved young man had gone berserk; his fine plan was in ruins; a brilliant and brutal murder had been committed for nothing; and somebody must pay for it. He had quite literally a shot at making you both pay. Unfortunately, the police-tail spotted nothing wrong at the Cave of the Witches; as you yourself said, nobody spotted anything wrong. And, when Aubertin and I heard of this murder-attempt next day, Aubertin was already prepared to close in. He dared not wait.

"Thus we come to the last scene of the last act.

"I was ordered to (harrumph) discuss the evidence in the study, while Aubertin kept Philip outside in a position to listen. But, by thunder, I insisted the boy's father shouldn't be there to watch his son's arrest! With cross-purposes still working—"

"Desmond Ferrier returned to the villa?"

"He did. Amid many oaths he was detained in another room, where he could neither see nor hear. Oaths continued to shower from Aubertin when another unexpected guest turned up. Philip's arrest could not have been exactly welcome to Miss Page either. Unfortunately, when she went to the airport for the not-very-sinister purpose of picking up her luggage, one of Aubertin's men thought she was trying to escape. He detained her and in triumph sent *her* to the villa, where she must be kept out of the way until the curtain was down.

There was a long silence.

"As a last word, my dear sir," and Dr. Fell blinked at Hathaway, "as a last word, I will give you a piece of advice against the time you are next tempted to try your hand at solving a problem in murder."

"Indeed?"

"Desmond Ferrier, by getting me to the villa before anything had happened, hoped my presence would stop any games his son might have in mind. He shouted to the world I was there, as he told Innes. It had no effect at all. Philip, though not officially an actor, had more stage-blood in his veins than his step-mother and fully as much as his father. Take warning, Sir Gerald: as Philip said himself, it is not easy to cope with stage-people."

Hathaway, putting down his cigar, put all irascibility into a few words.

"I am no longer interested in crime," he said.

"Oh, ah! But if you should be—?"

"Why do you limit it, Dr. Fell? Why do you confine it to a noble profession like the stage? It is not easy to cope with people: full stop. By God, I have learned my lesson in that! It is not easy to cope with *people*."

>>> If you've enjoyed this book and would like to discover more great vintage crime and thriller titles, as well as the most exciting crime and thriller authors writing today, visit: >>>

The Murder Room
Where Criminal Minds Meet

themurderroom.com

www.ingramcontent.com/pod-product-compliance
Ingram Content Group UK Ltd.
Pitfield, Milton Keynes, MK11 3LW, UK
UKHW040435280225
455666UK00003B/78